# Hidden Talents

♥

*very hot paranormal romance*

## EMMA HOLLY

cover photo: phillyphotog, phildate

# CHAPTER ONE

Dusk settled over the city of Resurrection like a blanket of bad news.

*That's me*, Ari thought, flexing her right fist beside her hip. *Bad news with a capital B.*

This wasn't just whistling in the dark. Ari had been bad news to some people in her life. To her parents. To every teacher she'd had in high school. *You'll come to no good*, they'd threatened, and she couldn't swear they'd been wrong. Certainly, she hadn't turned out to be a blessing to Maxwell or Sarah. Because of her, Max was in the hospital with too many broken bones in his arms to count, and Sarah was God knew where. But at least Ari was trying to change that. At least she was trying to be bad news to people who deserved it.

To her dismay, Resurrection, NY wasn't what she'd been led to believe when she'd looked it up on the internet.

She stood on the crest of a weedy hill outside the metropolis, her presence hidden by the deeper shadow of a highway overpass. She'd been expecting a down-on-its-luck backwater. Storefronts stuck in the seventies. Maybe a real town square and a civil war battlefield. Instead, she found an actual cityscape. The skyline wasn't Manhattan tall, more like Kansas City. Few buildings looked brand new, but many were substantial. They formed a grid of streets and parkland whose core had to encompass at least five miles. This was definitely more than a backwater. Resurrection reminded her of city photos from the early decades of the last century, when *skyscraper* meant something exciting. What could have been a twin to the Chrysler Building stuck up from the center of downtown, reigning over its brethren.

Finding the Eunuch among all that was going to take some doing.

*You have to find him*, she told her sinking stomach. If she didn't, she and her very small gang of peeps would be looking over their shoulders for the rest of their lives. At twenty-six and thankfully still counting, Ari had endured more than enough hiding. She was stronger now. She'd been *practicing*. Henry Blackwater, aka, the Eunuch, wouldn't know what hit him.

"Right," she said sarcastically to herself. She'd be lucky if she got out of here alive.

But faint heart never vanquished fair villain. Ari knew she'd been born the way she was for a reason. Maybe here, maybe soon, she'd find out what that reason was.

# CHAPTER TWO

No one messed with people who belonged to Adam Santini. Unless, of course, the person messing with the person was also Adam's relative.

"You. Ate. My. Beignets." To emphasize his point, Adam's irate cousin, Tony Lupone, was bashing his brother's head against the squad room floor.

Since Rick's skull was made of sterner stuff than the linoleum, he laughed between winces. "What sort of cop—*ow*—eats beignets anyway?"

"Your faggot brother cop, that's who. Your pink-shirted faggot brother cop who's whupping your butt right now."

Amused by their exchange, Adam leaned back against Tony's cluttered desk. The precinct's squad room was a semi-bunker in the basement. A mix of ancient file cabinets and desks were balanced by some very revved-up technology. Grimy electrum grates on the windows protected them, more or less, from things that went bump in the night outside. The hodgepodge suited the men who manned it better than most workplaces could. Rough-edged but smart was the werewolf way. At the moment, Tony was so rough-edged his eyes glowed amber in his flushed face. His big brother could have defended himself better than he was, if it weren't for his rule against hitting his siblings.

"Ow! Lou!" he complained to Adam. "You're supposed to be my best friend. Aren't you going to call off this squirt?"

"You're the one who ate his fancy donuts."

"All dozen of them!" Tony snarled, his grievance renewed. "I brought them in to share."

"Shit," said long-haired Nate Rivera, Adam's other cousin, once removed. "Now *I* want to whup you."

Considering even-tempered Nate was growling, Adam judged it time to end the wrestling match. "All right, you two. Enough. Rick, I'm docking your next paycheck for the price of his beignets. Dana, if you'd be so kind, raid the coffee fund and pick up another batch for tomorrow night."

"None of which you're going to enjoy, Mister Pig!" Panting from the exertion of trying to give his brother a concussion, Tony rose and pointed angrily down at him. "You can choke on your damned donuts."

Wisely, Rick remained where he was while his little brother stalked back to the break room, where his heinous crime had been discovered. The dress code for the detectives was casual. Rick's gray RPD T-shirt was rucked way up his six-pack abs. His concave stomach didn't betray his gluttony. His fast werewolf metabolism saw to that.

"My head," Rick moaned, still laughing. "Come on, cuz. Give your beta a hand up."

Adam sighed and obliged. None of his wolves were small, but Rick was six four and all muscle. Even with supe strength, Adam grunted to haul him up. "Some second you are. You had to know this would cause trouble."

"I couldn't help myself. The box smelled so good. Plus, he was totally obnoxious about bringing them in for everyone."

"So you knew you were stealing food from my mouth?" Nate interjected, not looking up from his paperwork. "Not cool."

"He's sucking up. Ever since he came out, he's been—" Rick snapped his muzzle shut, but it was too late.

"Uh-huh," Nate said in his dry laid back way. He'd spun around in his squeaky rolling chair to face Rick. "Ever since he came out, your brother stopped being a butch-ass prick. In fact, ever since he came out, he's been the nicest wolf around here. You don't like that 'cause you're used to being everyone's favorite."

"Crap." The way Rick rubbed the back of his neck said he knew he was in the wrong. Being Rick, he couldn't stay dejected long. A grin flashed across his handsome olive-skinned face. "Can't I still be everyone's favorite? Do I have to turn gay too?"

"I don't know," Nate said, returning to his work. "So far only gay boys bring us good breakfasts."

Seeing Rick's private wince, Adam patted his back and rubbed. Touchy-feely creatures that werewolves were, the contact calmed both of them. He knew Rick was still working on accepting his little brother's big announcement. Werewolves were some of the most macho supes in Resurrection, a city that had plenty to choose from. Adam knew Rick loved his brother just as much as before. He suspected Rick was mostly worried Tony would end up hurt. Being responsible for policing America's only supernatural-friendly town made the wolves enough of a target. Turning out to be gay on top of that was as good as taping a target onto your back.

"Tony will be all right," Adam assured his friend. "Everyone here is adjusting to the new him."

Rick rubbed his neck once more and let his hand drop. Worry pinched his dark gold eyes when they met Adam's. "They're pack. They have to love him."

Adam didn't believe this but wasn't in the mood to argue. Plenty of folks endowed being pack with mystical benefits. Some were real of course, but as alpha, Adam wasn't comfortable relying on magic to cement his authority. He thought it best to actually *be* a competent leader.

"Boss," Dana their dispatcher said. The young woman had her own corner of the squad room. Apart from its cubby walls, it was open. Banks of sleek computers surrounded her, each one monitoring different sectors of the city. The sole member of the squad who wasn't a relative, Dana was the most superstitious wolf Adam had ever met. Anti-hex graffiti scrawled across her work surfaces, the warding so thick he couldn't tell one symbol from another. How they worked like that was beyond him. Despite the quirk, Adam took her instincts seriously. Right then, she didn't look happy. Her silver dreamcatcher earrings were trembling.

"Boss, we've got a suspected M without L in the abandoned tire store on Twenty-Fourth."

*M without L* referred to the use of magic without a license. Adam's hackles rose. Jesus, he hated those. "Who's reporting the incident?"

"Gargoyle on the Hampton House Hotel." She touched her headset and listened. "He says it's a Level Four."

Adrenaline surged inside him, making his palms tingle. Gargoyles were rarely wrong about magical infractions. While the strength levels went up to eight, four was nothing to sneeze at.

Thumb and finger to his mouth, Adam blew a piercing whistle to get his men's attention.

"Suit up," he said. "We've got a probable ML on Twenty-Fourth."

"Don't forget your earpieces," Dana added. "I'll help coordinate from here."

Adam's men were already loping to the weapons room. "Load for bear," he said as he followed them. "We don't know what we're in for."

∞

Resurrection, New York couldn't have existed without the fae. For nearly two hundred years, it had sat on an outfolded pocket of the fae's other-dimensional homeland, *in* the human world but only visible to a special few.

Those who wandered in from Outside found it less alien than might be expected. The founding faeries had used the Manhattan of the 1800s as their architectural crib sheet. Since then, the bigger apple had continued to provide inspiration. Immigrants especially liked to recreate pieces of their native land. Resurrection had its own Fifth Avenue and Macy's, its own subway and museums. Little Italy still flourished here, though—sadly—its theater district was as moribund as its role model. Adam was familiar with the theories that Resurrection was an experiment, created to see if human and fae could live peaceably as in days of old. Whether this was the reason for its existence, he couldn't say.

The only fae he knew were exceptionally tight-lipped.

Whatever their motives, Resurrection had become a haven for humans with a trait or two extra. Shapechangers of every ilk thrived here. Vamps were tolerated as long as they behaved themselves. The same was true of demons and other Dims: visitors from alternate dimensions who entered through the portals. If a being could get along, it could stay. If it couldn't, it had to go. And if the visitors didn't want to go, Adam and the rest of the RPD were just the folks to make sure they went anyway.

The job fit Adam better than his combat boots, and those boots fit him pretty good. He loved keeping order, protecting the vulnerable, kicking butt and cracking skulls as required. The only duty he didn't like was apprehending rogue Talents. Sorcerers were trained at least, and demons who went dark side were generally predictable. Talents were the wild cards in an already dangerous deck. Their power was raw, depending not on spells but on how much energy they could channel. That amount could be a trickle or a mother-effing hell of a lot.

The previous year, a Level Seven Talent who'd gotten stoned on faerie-laced angel dust had taken down the six-lane Washington Street Bridge. Just popped it off its piers and let it drop in the North River. If the bridge's gargoyles hadn't swooped in to save what cars they could, the loss of life would have been astronomical. Adam still had nightmares about talking the tripping Talent into surrendering. If tonight's incident ran along similar lines, he might need a vacation.

Along with the rest of his team, Adam clutched the leather sway-strap above his head. Nate was driving the black response van because no one else dared claim the wheel from the ponytailed Latino. They all wore body armor and helmets, plus an assortment of protective charms. Their rifles leaned against the long side benches between their knees. The guns could fire a range of ammo, both conventional and spelled. Rick, who had a knack for effective prayer, was quietly calling on the precinct's personal guardian angel. Sometimes this worked and sometimes it didn't, but even the atheists among them figured better safe than sorry.

"God," Tony said, tapping the back of his head against the van's rattling wall. "I hope this isn't another thing like the bridge."

"Amen," Carmine agreed. The stocky were was the oldest member of their squad, the only one who was married, and—yes—another of Adam's cousins.

Before he could smile, Adam's earpiece beeped.

"You're four blocks out," Dana said. "The gargoyle is reporting another series of power flares. Still nothing higher than a Four."

That was good news. Unless, of course, the Talent was warming up.

"Okay, people," Adam said. "Watch your tempers once we get inside. Be safe but no killing unless you have no choice."

He didn't warn them against hesitating. Given their inbred hair-trigger werewolf nature, hesitating wasn't an issue.

∞

The defunct tire store sat on a small parking lot between a very well locked print shop and a transient hotel. Apart from the hotel, which wasn't exactly bustling, the area wasn't residential. A cheap liquor outlet on the corner drew a few customers, but the main business done here after dark was drugs. Most of the product filtered in from the human world. Since this was Resurrection, some was also exotic. If you knew who to ask, you could score adulterated vamp blood or coke cut with faerie dust. Demon manufactured Get-Hard was popular, though it tended to cause more harmful side effects than Viagra. Every EMT Adam knew had asked why they couldn't get GH off the street. All Adam could answer was that they were doing the best they could.

Policing Resurrection couldn't be about stamping out Evil. It had to be about making sure Good didn't get swallowed.

The reminder braced him as he and his team ran soundlessly from the van onto the buckled and trash-strewn asphalt of the parking lot. His scalp prickled half a second before a soft gold light flared around the edges of the boarded-up back windows.

Adam had answered previous calls to this location. The rear section of the tire store was where vehicles had been cranked up on lifts for servicing. Fortunately, there was plenty of cover for slipping in. Unfortunately, lots of flammables were inside. Adam took the anti-burn charm that hung around his neck and whispered a word to it. That precaution seen to, he hand-signaled Rick and Tony to split off and block escape from the front exit.

This left Adam, Carmine and Nate to ghost in the back.

The flimsy combination lock on the door to the service bay had been snapped—probably magically. Adam and his two detectives ducked under the low opening. Inside, the scent and feel of magic was much stronger, the air thicker and hotter than it should have been in autumn. A male voice moaned in pain farther in, standing Adam's hair on end. Without needing to be told, Nate peeled off to the right. Adam and Carmine took the left.

Scattered heaps of tires allowed them to creep up on their goal without being seen. One bare bulb dangled from a wire, lighting the far end of the garage. In the dim circle beneath it, the Talent had her moaning victim tied to a plastic chair. The sight of her stopped Adam in his tracks. Christ, she was little. Five foot nothing and probably a hundred and small change. She looked to be in her twenties and wore the kind of clothes street kids did. Ripped up black jeans. Ancient T-shirts that didn't fit. Her oversized Yankees jacket had its sleeves torn out and was decorated with unidentifiable small objects. Her hair was a shade of platinum not found in nature, standing in white spikes around her head. A swirling red pattern was dyed it, as if her coiffure were her personal art project. What really got him though, what had his breath catching in his throat, was the clean-cut innocence of her face. Outfit and hair aside, she looked like a tiny Iowa farm girl.

It made his chest hurt to look at her. The part of him that needed to protect others wanted to protect her.

Knowing better than to trust in appearances, Adam shook the inclination off. He tapped the speaker fixed into his vest with the signal for everyone to hold. The victim was still alive. They could afford to take a minute to discover what they were up against.

As they watched, the girl lifted her right hand. Pale blue fire outlined her curled fingers. Her already bloodied victim shrank back within his ropes. He was some kind of elf-human mixblood with long gray hair. He was a lot bigger than the Talent, but that didn't mean their fight had been fair. Despite the elfblood, he didn't give off much of a magic vibe. A near-null was Adam's guess. His run-in with the Talent had left damage. He looked bad: both eyes swollen, bruises, shallow cuts bleeding all over. Though he seemed familiar, as injured as he was, he was hard to identify. Even his smell was distorted by blood and fear.

"I can do this all night," the Talent said in a voice that was way too sweet for a torturer. "Or you can tell me where to find the Eunuch."

Carmine and Adam came alert at that. This was a name they knew too damn well.

"Lady," said her bloodied victim. "I have no idea who you mean."

The girl closed her glowing hand gently. The man she was interrogating arched so violently he and the plastic chair fell over. He screamed as blood sprayed from a brand new cut on his chest. Carmine started forward, but Adam gripped his shoulder.

"Wait," he murmured. "That cut was shallow. He's not in immediate danger."

Carmine shook his head but obeyed. When the man stopped writhing, the girl drew a deep slow breath. With no more effort than gesturing upward with one finger, she set man and chair upright. Despite the situation's danger, something inside Adam let out an admiring *whoa*.

"Clearly," she said, "you think you ought to be more afraid of your boss than me."

"Lady," panted the injured man, "*everyone's* more afraid of him."

The girl's lips curved in a smile that had Carmine shivering beside him. Admittedly, the expression was a little scary. For no good reason Adam could think of, it made his cock twitch in his jockstrap.

The Talent spoke silkily. "I'm glad we've established you know who I'm looking for."

Adam expected her to cut him again. Instead, discovering her victim did know the Eunuch inspired her to up the ante on her torture. The blue fire she'd called to her hand now began gleaming around her feet. She was drawing energy from the earth—and no piddling amount either. Her glowing hand contracted into a fist, and her victim's face went chalky. Adam was pretty sure she was telekinetically squeezing his beating heart. Unless she was really good at medical manipulation, she was going to kill him.

"*Go*," he said sharply into his vest microphone.

Even in human form, werewolves weren't slowpokes. What went down next was textbook perfect. Adam and his men were on the Talent so fast she didn't have a chance to shift her attack to them. Nate got her nose squashed down on the oil-stained floor, then snapped electrum plated cuffs snug around her wrists. The cuffs were charmed so she couldn't break them, no matter how powerful she was. The Talent struggled, then cried out as Nate yanked her roughly onto her feet.

He dropped a depowering charm around her neck for good measure. Immediately, the energy-charged air settled back to normal. The girl gaped at the enchanted medal, then straight up at Adam. Adam's heart stuttered in his chest. Her eyes were a breathtaking corn-fed blue, her lashes a thick dark brown. The twitch she'd sent through his cock morphed into a throb. Carmine shot him a look of surprise. Adam fought an embarrassed flush. The smell of his arousal must have gotten strong enough to seep through his clothes.

"'bout time you showed up," the girl's victim huffed. "This bitch needs to be locked up."

Carmine flipped up his face shield and turned to consider him. The man flinched back, obviously wishing he'd refrained from complaining.

"Aren't you Donnie West?" Carmine asked. "'Cause I know we've got a handful of outstandings on your drug dealing ass."

"Uh," said Donnie, abruptly recognizable under his bruises.

"That's what I thought," said Carmine, and let out his belly laugh.

Through all of this, the Talent's eyes moved from one of them to the other, taking in their gear and their guns and getting wider by the second. When Rick and Tony caught up to them from the front, Tony's upper canines had run out and his amber eyes were glowing. The girl sucked in a breath like this shocked her, though a partial change when younger wolves got excited wasn't uncommon.

"What the—" she said before having to swallow. "What the hell kind of cops are you?"

Still holding her from behind, Nate's slash of a mouth slanted up in a devilish grin. "Well, what do you know," he drawled. "Looks like we've got ourselves an Accidental Tourist."

# CHAPTER THREE

Nothing Ari had encountered since arriving in Resurrection had been normal. First, the air smelled funny, like a light flowery perfume, even near the sewer grates. It felt funny too, as if Ari had thrown back one too many shots of espresso. The hair on her arms was prickling and the sidewalks—despite having the usual cracks and stains—were strangely buzzy underfoot. She caught herself tiptoeing and had to force herself to stop.

No one stared at her, luckily. The last thing she wanted was to draw attention.

She'd managed to find Resurrection's Chinatown, the general location of which the MapQuest maps hadn't lied about. Though the Eunuch wasn't Asian, he was addicted to Chinese food. If he wasn't holding court over a plate of Peking duck somewhere, his goons were getting him take-out. Ari figured if she lurked here long enough, she'd have a chance to spot one.

What she spotted instead was seriously weird. Lots of Chinese restaurants in Manhattan hung ducks in their windows. It was an assurance that they roasted good birds in there. What hung in these windows wasn't birds. To be absolutely truthful, they looked like miniature skinned people.

At first, she'd thought the streetlights must have confused her eyes, but the creepy things were displayed everywhere. One restaurant had taped an English translation to the glass under the bold swish of its Chinese sign.

*Gnomes*, it declared. *Freshly caught.*

Surely, this was the locals' idea of an inside joke.

Ari had shuddered and tried to avoid looking . . . which was when she noticed the placard inside the entrance doors: *No Flaring Beyond This Threshold.*

What did that even mean? Were people trying to do gymnastics on the tables?

She just could not figure this place out. Deciding to take a break and get her bearings, she left the five-block stretch of Chinatown to slip as unobtrusively as she could into a packed coffee house. From experience, she knew crowded places were good for hiding in. This one's *No Flaring* sign was compensated for by the one that said *Free Hot Spot.* Sadly, Ari's tablet didn't work when she pulled it out, though the other customers' seemed to.

They were a motley bunch. Young. Middle aged. A lot of older guys with long hair. She found a spot the next table over from two high school girls in prissy plaid uniforms. They were chattering a mile a minute in a language she couldn't for the life of her recognize. They were also texting at the same time—normal enough, she guessed, given what she'd observed of her more popular peers when she was their age. What wasn't normal was that beneath their long shiny hair, their ears were pointy.

*O-kay*, she thought. Interesting fashion trends around here.

"Coffee?" inquired a kind looking older waitress who'd snuck up on her from nowhere.

"What?" Ari asked, taken by surprise.

The woman gestured with a well seasoned stovetop espresso pot. "You have to order if you want to use the hot spot."

"The hot spot doesn't work for me," Ari said, though no doubt she still had to buy something.

"It should work," said the waitress. "Our magician refreshed it just this morning."

Ari blinked. Maybe this was their pet name for their IT expert. She was trying to come up with a sensible response when she spotted one of the Eunuch's occasional go-to guys on his way out the door. Even in this crowd, his long shining gray hair stood out.

"Excuse me," she said, sliding out from her seat. "I see someone I need to say *hello* to."

Once outside, she followed Donnie West until he stepped into an alley to light one of his sickening clove cigarettes. Oddly enough, it smelled like nirvana here. It must have tasted like nirvana too. He took a drag so deep he might have been trying to pull it into his toes.

With his eyes closed in bliss, he wasn't hard to sneak up on.

"Hey," she said, judging a brash approach was best. "Got one of those for me?"

"Shit." He jerked straight with shock, his cigarette falling to the ground. "Don't you know better than to take people by surprise?"

She suspected he recognized her. They'd never spoken or been this close before, but she'd seen him talking to the Eunuch lots of times from across a room. In addition to which, she wasn't easy to forget, what with her hair and her special gift. She sighed at the realization that he wouldn't even admit that much.

She'd need more than a bluff to get what she needed out of him.

She only meant to give him a telekinetic nudge, to remind him she was a scary chick whose questions ought to be answered. Somehow, the energy that rushed into her when she pulled was a heck of a lot more than she was used to. The power swooshed out of her into him, slamming him into the brick wall and nearly coshing him senseless.

*Whoa*, Ari thought, even as she tried to pretend she'd meant to do exactly that. Talk about chugging too much caffeine. Her heart pounded like an old-fashioned locomotive behind her ribs.

"Shit," Donnie cursed, on his knees with one hand checking for bumps behind his head. "You can't be here like this."

"Obviously I can. And you are going to tell me where I can find your boss."

"You're crazy," Donnie said. "Plus, I don't know what you're talking about. I don't have a boss. I'm an independent entrepreneur."

Like a Yugo driver who was suddenly behind the wheel of a Porsche, Ari used the lightest touch she could to open a cut across his forehead.

Never the bravest soul, Donnie tried to crawl away. She stopped him by floating his still lit cigarette an inch away from his eye. How easy this was shocked her.

"I might be crazy," she said, her voice gone a bit breathless. "Why don't we go somewhere quiet to discuss it?"

She'd spotted the empty tire shop on her way in, filing it away as somewhere she might crash without depleting her cash supply.

The garage bay seemed the ideal spot for questioning Donnie—at least until the SWAT team or whatever they were showed up.

Having her face shoved into cement while being handcuffed was no party, no more than her power being shut off without warning. She didn't like her glimpse of the latecomer's teeth or the others' weird big-ass guns. The rifles looked like weapons from the *Alien* movies, just too many parts for comfort. That two of the cops still had them trained on her didn't ease her nerves. What really pissed her off, though, was that they'd interrupted just as she was getting somewhere. Given how little she'd enjoyed torturing Donnie, she didn't think it should go to waste.

The hot Latino guy said something cryptic about accidental tourists, which she didn't try to understand.

"I want a lawyer," she said, though she really didn't. Lawyers were as bad as cops—and how would she explain what she'd been doing? She'd learned young that she couldn't afford to let people see her doing her thing.

Which brought up another squirmy point. None of the members of this SWAT team seemed surprised by she'd done.

The other hot guy— Okay, be honest, the really, *really* hot guy with the incredibly soft green eyes and the mouth built for wickedness, put up his gun and stepped closer. Ari shouldn't have been surprised that her body went haywire. She'd been pulling more juice than she ever had in her life, and that was bound to create fallout. Still, it didn't feel appropriate that her pussy melted like hot candy at his approach. His green eyes darkened, tiny sparks seeming to glow in the irises. He wet his fallen angel lips as if they'd gone dry. Ari could have sworn this made her dizzy.

"I'm sorry," he said in a voice as rich and deep as French roast. "You're not entitled to a lawyer. Public defenders are only for citizens."

"I'm a citizen," she retorted, trying to stiffen up her spine while he was staring at her that way. God, he smelled good. Like spice and man and how the hell did he find shirts to fit shoulders that fucking broad? She cleared her throat, sorry she'd thought the word for what she wanted to do to him. "I was born in Kansas."

It had been Iowa, but to a New Yorker—as his accent proclaimed him—what was the difference?

Really Hot Cop smiled at her.

Logically, his smile couldn't have been what pushed her over the edge, but her circuitry did choose that precise moment to blow its fuse. The warning tremor ran up her right arm, giving her a second to gasp before she dropped to the floor convulsing.

Or almost dropped. Really Hot Cop and Handsome Latino Guy caught her as she fell, saving her from splitting her skull. This was the only luck she had. The coppery taste of blood told her she'd bitten her tongue.

"Get a bite stick," Really Hot Cop barked out.

She was making the grunting noises she did when she had a fit, though why she bothered being embarrassed she didn't know. Really Hot Cop stroked her cheek like he didn't mind.

"You're okay," he said, his voice the most soothing she'd ever heard, the kind any girl would wanted crooning her to sleep after sex. "You're okay, sweetheart. This will pass. You just channeled too much power."

Ari would have gaped if her facial muscles hadn't been clenching. He'd called her sweetheart. Even though he'd watched her nearly kill a man, even though he seemed to know about her freaky gift. The cop who'd sported the long incisors—thankfully normal now—helped Hot Cop wedge a bite stick gently between her teeth. Though she knew it would help, Ari hated being vulnerable. For some reason, she hated it ten times as much right now. She wasn't weak, not anymore. She was a survivor.

Survivor or not, tears started trickling out from her eyes. Sometimes they came when she overloaded and sometimes they didn't, but tonight they wouldn't stop.

"Shh," Really Hot Cop said, pulling her to his chest. His hold was strong enough to keep her from flailing. "You're all right, honey. I've got you safe with me."

∞

Adam cradled the girl in his lap in the back of the response van. Her muscle spasms had lasted about five minutes, after which she'd conked out in exhaustion. Adam had seen worse magical ODs—fatal ones even. He just hadn't seen any that hit *him* quite so hard.

He couldn't seem to let go of her. He was strapped in the safety harness on the long side bench but he felt off balance, his usually solid-as-a-rock inner gyroscope suddenly wobbling. He had an erection, for Pete's sake, the thing seriously straining the elastic of his black jock strap.

He tried to distract himself by examining the collection of miscellany she'd pinned or otherwise adhered to her sleeveless Yankees jacket. The portion he could see included what was probably other peoples' lost buttons, a small white feather, two miniature silver spoons of the sort espresso drinkers stirred sugar with, six pennies, one euro, a subway token, and a laminated ticket stub from a band he'd never heard of. Thanks to his grandmother, Adam had a touch of Sight. When he fingered the stub, his brain caught a flash of the girl he held standing in a crowd, so excited as music bombarded her that she squeezed the hands of the people to either side of her. The joy in her astounded him, the love she felt for her companions . . .

He shifted his eyes, trying to See the memory clearer, but letting even a little more of his barriers down sent a fresh wave of lust up his erection. He squirmed in his seat and winced, a muffled grunt breaking in his throat. It occurred to him that this reaction wasn't professional.

From the looks his packmates were sliding him, they thought he was off his rocker.

"So," Nate threw over his shoulder from his spot up front at the wheel. "Tell me again why we aren't taking this perp straight to headquarters."

"She crossed the city border," Rick said from the opposite bench. "Without an invitation. If we take her to HQ, we'll have to hand her over to Magical Mentoring."

Magical Mentoring's reputation was about as good as the outside world's foster care system. It meant well, but too often it simply screwed people up.

Adam's arms tightened protectively around his burden.

"Well, I'm no fan," Nate admitted, "but this *chica* nearly killed a man. She needs some kind of training. I mean, she was one determined girly, slicing Donnie West up like that."

"She was trying to find the Eunuch," Carmine explained patiently. "We need to question her. See if she knows more about that slippery bastard than we do."

"I get that," Nate said, "but—"

Adam's anger rolled out of him as a growl. Without meaning to, he'd put his alpha power behind it, pushing at the others' natural inclination to submit to his will. He did this so seldom the other men's eyes widened.

Up front, Nate swerved the van slightly in the lane before pulling himself together. "All right then. End of discussion."

Because Rick was his second and a power in his own right, he held Adam's eyes longer than the others. "You okay, cuz?"

"He's getting around that age," Carmine said helpfully. "Baby hunger hits some males hard."

"I am not *that age*," Adam snapped, maybe more sharply than he should have if he wanted to be believed. "I'm only thirty-nine. And anyway, that one true mate crap is bullshit."

"How can you think it's bullshit?" Nate asked from up front. "Weren't your parents twin flames?"

They had been, he guessed, but that didn't mean Adam had to believe in that hearts and flowers stuff for him. His parents had been really sweet, kind of eccentric people. Adam was down to earth. Falling in love as hard as they'd fallen just wasn't practical.

"She is kind of hot," Tony observed thoughtfully. He frowned as the others' eyes cut to him. "What? Just because I'm gay, I can't have an opinion?"

"It's pheromones." Carmine's gaze remained averted, but his subtle smile said he was enjoying ragging on his boss. "There's only so hard you can fight when they kick in."

"He's just being protective," Rick said firmly. "Adam's alpha. If anything's kicking in, it's those instincts."

Rick sounded suspiciously like he was trying to convince himself.

Adam sighed, realizing he'd cupped the back of the girl's head, coaxing her cheek to rest more securely on his shoulder. Her spiky platinum hair was surprisingly soft between his fingers. He couldn't deny she smelled incredible to him, which was supposed to be a sign that you'd found a mate. *A* mate, though. Not your sparkly-warkly gift from the universe. Biology he believed in. Romantic mumbo-jumbo not so much. Whatever this girl was to him, the scent of her perspiration was making him break into a sweat. His canines itched in their sockets, threatening to run out each time he caught a whiff.

An image of her naked on her hands and knees popped into his mind. Him pumping into her from behind, sinking his canines into her nape and gripping to hold her still. The fantasy was vivid enough to make his cock start leaking. She was so damned little. He hadn't known he liked little women. He'd never gone for them

18

before. Now he couldn't think of anything but finding out how much foreplay it would take to squeeze his throbbing dick inside her.

A lot would be fine with him. He'd be delighted to lick her all over. To grab that spiky hair in both hands and attach himself to her breasts. To nuzzle into her cunt and lap up her juice. She'd probably taste as good as she smelled. Her body felt tight in her thrift store clothes. Little breasts. Little waist. He bet her round little butt was as firm as a new apple . . .

His eyes went hot. He closed them half a second before his men would have seen them glow. His body shuddered as he tried to get it under control. He hadn't known an erection could hurt this bad.

If he wasn't careful, he was going to make a genuine ass of himself.

"Almost there," Nate said, turning onto Saltpeter Street.

Saltpeter was their neighborhood's main drag, where the businesses clustered. All of them lived off it on Alchemist's Way, within a stone's throw of each other in the four-story brick rowhouses that dated back to the 1910s. The streets were shady, the shopkeepers knew their names, and the instinctive comfort of having pack close by was something none of them had ever rebelled against.

They might not have the privacy other folks enjoyed, but they sure as hell had each other's backs.

Rick, Tony, and Adam all lived in the same building, with Adam taking the two top floors. They shared the roof deck, from which they could wave at Rick and Tony's parents on their slightly smaller deck next door. Mr. and Mrs. Lupone were both amazing in the kitchen, so living cheek by jowl like this was no hardship. Nate, who lived in the lofts two doors down and across the street, let them out in the dimmer stretch between two street lights and drove off to park the van.

Dimmer stretch notwithstanding, they were kind of conspicuous in their black response gear with their unconscious charge.

"Get the door," Adam said to Rick, because his beta always remembered which pocket held his keys.

There was no elevator, but the girl wasn't much of a load for his wolfish strength to get up three flights of stairs.

"You smell different," Tony said when they reached his door. "Maybe Carmine is right about you hitting your mating age. Maybe this girl is your perfect match."

Unlike his brother, Tony sounded hopeful this was the case. That was all their pack needed. Former butch-ass prick Tony turning into a pansy-ass romantic.

# CHAPTER FOUR

A ri was having the best dream of her life. Someone wonderful was holding her in his arms, someone big and warm who nuzzled her ear and murmured that everything was all right. The dream was also kind of sexy. She wriggled under the covers, enjoying her arousal. The only thing that bugged her was how her wrists were stuck together.

Her eyes snapped open as she shocked awake. She was lying in a strange bed under a bunch of blankets with her hands cuffed in front of her. She did a quick inventory. The coin on a chain the Latino had used to shut off her power still hung around her neck. Someone hadn't hesitated to make her comfortable, because her shoes, jacket, and baggy outer T-shirt had been removed, leaving her in jeans and a tank top with a shelf bra. It was night, and a small table lamp was on. Three big men were in the room with her, one of them sitting in a grannyish looking armchair he'd pulled up beside her.

He was looking straight at her.

*Really Hot Cop*, she remembered, staring into his soft green eyes. She couldn't seem to look away from them, though locking gazes with someone she didn't know was a weird thing to do. He'd changed out of his assault gear into a snug white T-shirt and black sweatpants. Man, he had some muscles, like slabs packed one on top of another. His shoulders were as broad as she'd expected.

She lifted her cuffed hands under the blankets, aware they must have been removed at some point; they'd been secured behind her before. "Do I really have to keep wearing these?"

For some reason, her question made Hot Cop blush. "You do," he said seriously. "You're a dangerous felon."

Okay, so Hot Cop had a sense of humor. That didn't mean she had to like or—God forbid—trust him.

"If I'm so dangerous, why haven't you arrested me?"

"We'll get to that," Hot Cop said. "Why don't you tell us your name?"

"Why don't you tell me yours?"

Hot Cop's sexy mouth curved up. His lower lip was slightly fuller than the upper, with a dent in its soft middle. "I'm Adam Santini, and these are Tony and Rick Lupone."

"And you are cops, for real?"

"They're detectives. I'm their lieutenant."

Hot Cop's eyes weren't budging from hers any more than hers were from him. His hair had been hidden by his helmet. Now she saw it was shiny black—a little long, a little shaggy, with a hint of a wave. Gold winked beneath the base of his strong tanned throat, possibly a St. Michael medal. Ari should have been more unnerved by how good it felt just to stare at him. It was like the sight of him was food and she'd been starving. Usually she felt awful after one of her fits, but every cell in her body hummed with pleasure. Between her legs she was embarrassingly achy. Her nipples were so tight the stretchy bra in her tank top stung. Was the rest of him as impressive as his shoulders? He looked older than she was, thirty or thereabouts. Did that mean he'd be experienced in bed?

"I'm Ari," she said before her overheated imagination could wander down that road.

"Ari," he repeated. He didn't ask for her last name. Maybe he suspected she wouldn't say. Her head gave a funny swoop as he continued to stare at her.

"How did you get into Resurrection?" the one called Rick asked her.

Reluctantly, Ari shifted her gaze to him. Though his tone was slightly belligerent, this seemed a harmless enough question. "I took the suburban train, then walked from the last station."

"You walked."

Ari's eyebrows shot up. "I couldn't spare cab fare. Was I supposed to fly?"

Rick's brother Tony snickered as if he knew a joke she wasn't in on.

"Look," she said, losing patience. "What's with this town anyway? Why is everything so wonky?"

Adam opened his mouth just as a flash of motion behind the window next to the bed drew her attention. Ari turned to see what had caused it and let out a bloodcurdling scream. A giant gray face stared at her through the glass. It wasn't a mask or a statue, because its features were moving. Not only that, its lion-like body was held in the air by flapping leathery batwings.

"Hey there," it said in a low rumble, waving one clawed front paw. "Level Five, okay!"

Then the creature stuck up its opposable furry thumb.

Ari couldn't help it. She screamed twice as loud as before.

"Jesus." Adam kneeled up on the bed to slap his hand across her mouth. "I thought you were a badass. You're going to have the neighbors calling the cops on us."

The giant gray thing's face twisted in what she swore was apology. Then it flapped its wings harder and flew away. Adam released her mouth.

"Wh—" Ari panted. "What the fuck was that?"

"Gargoyle," Tony answered, sounding completely entertained by her reaction. "They're our self-appointed National Guard. Lots of them like to hang out near where cops live."

"A gargoyle," she repeated.

Seeing she wasn't screaming anymore, Adam sat back in his granny chair. Maybe she shouldn't have, but Ari couldn't resist looking at him again. "Really? A *gargoyle?*"

The smile she was getting to like way too much stretched his gorgeous face. "I don't know how to break this to you, Ari, but you're not in Kansas anymore."

∞

Ari's head hurt too much to think, though probably she should have been glad the cops had stopped asking her questions so they could explain the situation she'd tripped into.

They'd moved the conversation from Adam's guest room to his nicked-up round kitchen table. Tony ordered two extra large pizzas, which the men ate almost entirely by themselves. Not only was eating pizza in handcuffs a challenge, but after the first slice Ari's appetite had stalled.

She was in the land of Faerie, a place whose borders she could cross because of her freaky gift. The cops who'd taken her hostage

Emma Holly

were werewolves. Gargoyles were real. Ditto for vamps and sorcerers. Probably more stuff too, but she hadn't been able to force herself to ask.

*And gnomes*, she realized with a shudder. Her stomach dropped. She hoped the meat on the pizza had been regular sausage.

"Gnomes?" she asked raspily. "I, uh, saw some hanging in a restaurant window in Chinatown."

"Pests," Adam said. "Like squirrels."

"They're not intelligent," Tony reassured her. "Not like dogs or cats. Or gargoyles. Now those are some smart cookies. Their language is just so different people assume they're slow. One saying *hi* to you is a compliment."

"But—" She swallowed. "Gnomes weren't in that pizza, were they?"

Rick choked on his soda. "No," he said as Adam slapped his back. "Most non-Asians don't like the way they taste."

She gave thanks for small favors. "What about the girls with the pointy ears I saw in the coffee shop?"

"Elves," Adam said.

This made her smile at last. Elves were real? That was kind of awesome.

"Don't get too excited," Tony warned. "They're mostly just people. It's not like *Lord of the Rings*."

"You watch our movies?"

"And your TV. There's a special channel for imported programs. We like to know what's going on out there, in case it affects us."

Or in case someone like her stumbled into their pocket of Faerie. She sat back in her slatted chair, trying to wrap her head around what she'd learned. She smoothed her fingers back and forth on the rim of Adam's kitchen table. It looked so real with its chipped paint and old scratches.

"It is real," Adam said.

Ari blinked and looked up at him. She knew she hadn't spoken aloud. "Why is my gift stronger here? Back home, I have to concentrate pretty hard to move anything."

"This is Faerie. There's more magic for you to tap into."

Adam's steady green gaze was making her head do that swoopy thing. She caught the table's edge as she began to sway.

"You're tired," Tony said, startling her by scraping back his chair and rising. "We'll catch up with you tomorrow."

"You want us to clean up?" Rick said, giving his brother a scolding slap on the back of his head.

"I'll take care of it," Adam said.

He didn't show them out. Ari guessed their relationship was too casual for that. *Cousins*, he'd explained. They seemed close, like they knew each other well. Except for being werewolves, they could have been any three guy buddies from Brooklyn.

Adam didn't rise until they were gone. "Stay," he said when she would have gotten up to help. "You look ready to fall over."

She wasn't. His sheer sexiness was making her weak-kneed. "It is kind of hard to dry glasses in handcuffs."

He ignored the hint, though he might have suppressed a smile. It felt strangely good to be alone with him in his apartment, right and wrong at the same time. She watched him toss the pizza boxes, scrape the plates, and stack the dirty dishes inside the sink. He turned on the water and squirted out dish liquid. The sounds were so domestic they were surreal.

"So," he said as they lulled her. "Why are you looking for the Eunuch?"

As interrogation methods went, she had to admire it.

Ari let out a sigh. "He hurt some friends of mine. I wanted to see if I could get him off their back."

"How do you know him?"

Adam wasn't looking at her, just soaping and rinsing plates with those slablike muscles shifting sexily in his back. Ari tried to calculate the angles. Answer. Don't answer. Trust a little and see what she got in return. Adam didn't seem like someone who'd be on Henry Blackwater's payroll. Then again, if he was, he'd already know what she was going to say. She drew a breath and made up her mind.

"In my world," she said, "Henry Blackwater . . . collects people like me."

Adam shut off the water and turned, his narrow hips leaning back against the edge of the sink. How tall was he anyway? Six one? Six two? His legs looked ten feet long in the black sweatpants. Because they seemed dangerous to stare at, she dragged her eyes back up to his face. His brows were drawn together in a furrow above his nose.

"You didn't know that," she realized.

"No." He dried his hands on a checkered towel. "We know what we think he does here in Resurrection, but it's been very hard to prove. He makes a lot of money dealing drugs, and it buys him too many obfuscation spells."

Ari supposed he meant this literally. "He deals drugs in my world too. He also runs a gambling racket. That's what he wanted me for. With my gift, I could make things happen that no one else could predict. A odds-on favorite horse would flag in the final stretch, or a roulette ball would drop in a certain slot. More and more, the things he wanted me to do weren't so harmless. I told him I was quitting, and for that he hurt my friends. None of us are anybody special, but they're everything to me."

He nodded like he understood, then sat opposite her again. The chair creaked under his muscled weight. "How did he find you?"

"That's his thing. He has a knack for spotting people with special talents. Psychics who aren't fakes. Healers who really do. He gets something on them so they have to work for him. In my case, I was on the street when he found me. All he had on me was that I was hungry."

She heard the bitterness in her confession. He did too. He stretched his big hand across the table and covered both of her handcuffed ones. Ari's jaw tightened even as pleasure rushed through her at the heat of his palm.

"If you're underage or don't want to use your name, you can still get jobs in New York, but at the least you have to be clean and fed. My friends and I couldn't pull that off until Blackwater threw me the occasional assignment. Until then, we were living under bridges and begging. Sarah busked in the subway with her guitar, but that was only safe if one of us could stay with her. She was pretty and guys would—" She cut herself off before her mouth ran away with her.

"The rest isn't your business," she said stiffly.

His thumb stroked her knuckles. "Ari . . ."

His voice was gentle and deep, stroking nerves only sound could reach. Chances were, he was being nice to soften her up, but she wanted to tear off his clothes and forget every trouble she had with him. She didn't even know if she could have sex with him. Would it turn her into a wolf if she did?

"He comes here every couple months," she said, ignoring how husky the words came out. "Nobody knows what he does, only that he disappears. Some of his goons go with him, but they don't share details. I only found out where he went because he jotted it in his dateminder. I used my gift to break it out of his locked desk drawer."

"And you followed him here?" Adam shook his head like he couldn't believe anyone would be that stupid.

"I told you. Maxwell and Sarah mean everything to me."

They were all she had. No other souls in the world would care or even notice if she ceased to exist.

She thought about the last place she and her friends had lived. The apartment hadn't been as nice as Adam's, but it was good. No roaches. No leaks. An actual bedroom for the girls to share. A big bright window with light for Max to do his artwork by. He paid his share of the bills as a wall painter, but art was his calling. Of course, the stratospheric New York rent was a struggle once Henry Blackwater made sure Ari lost her hostess job. Max kept his until Henry's goons broke his fingers. God, he'd cried that night. Only the second time she'd seen him do it, the first being when he'd confessed he was in love with Sarah. *Things were finally getting better for all of us*, he'd choked out with his beautiful hands lying immobilized by splints and bandages in his lap. *What's wrong with us? Why can't our dreams come true?*

Ari's throat closed with emotion. She turned away from Adam, unwilling to let him see the personal things in her eyes.

"You're close to this Maxwell?" Adam asked.

The discernible growl in his voice yanked her attention back to him. Color was rising faintly in his lean face.

"Sorry," he mumbled. "That's not my business either."

In spite of everything, Ari smiled. He was jealous. He thought Maxwell was her boyfriend.

"He kissed me once," she said, unable to resist teasing him. "But it was a mistake. He's been in love with Sarah forever."

Sarah was the fragile one in their little trio, a sweet-faced beauty with light brown shampoo-commercial hair and a heart so tender she'd give her last penny to someone worse off than she was. Max and Ari were tougher, but they loved her.

"I see." Adam cleared his throat and stared at the table. His cheeks were bright red now.

Ari laughed. "Jeesh. For such a sexy dangerous guy, you're adorable."

Maybe she shouldn't have called him sexy. When his head came up, his eyes were fiery. His irises glowed like a gas stove's flame, the green edging into blue. Ari's breath caught and she jerked back against her chair. Her breasts might have been small, but they were sensitive. Her nipples felt like someone was pinching them. Warm sleek fluid gushed from her pussy, dampening her panties. Adam's nostrils got wider. He flattened his hands on the table top until their knuckles paled from pressure. His gaze dropped to her mouth and stayed there.

"I want to kiss you," he rumbled like hot gravel.

His canines were sliding out like his cousin Tony's had earlier. This shouldn't have aroused her, but more cream trickled out of her. His lengthening teeth made her think of erections.

"I don't think I'd stop you," she said faintly.

He licked his gorgeous lips, his tongue leaving a wet trail. "I want to do more than kiss you."

A blaze of heat swept through her. Ari stretched her handcuffed hands toward him. "You could take these off first."

He shook his head, a tight side-to-side motion.

"You can trust me," she said in her most persuasive voice. "I didn't run away when you let me pee earlier."

Again, he wagged his head. "You're in my custody."

"Not officially. Unless you've got a thing for bondage."

Adam began breathing more quickly. Ari must have hit an accidental bull's-eye. She couldn't remember making a man pant *before* they were in bed.

"I don't," he said defensively. "At least, I never thought I did."

He looked at her helplessly. God, she wanted him—all flushed and horny and embarrassed. She wanted him to pant harder. Wanted him to thrust into her and feel so good he cried out. She licked her own lips, and he let out a groan. Ari decided.

"To hell with it," she said huskily. "You like these cuffs so much they can damn well stay on."

He came out of his chair so fast he shocked her. He stopped when he saw she'd tensed. His lungs went in and out like bellows. "I'll be careful," he said.

She didn't know what that meant, but right that second it didn't matter. She stood and he was so much taller she felt silly. He didn't, apparently. He bent, one hand behind her head, the other resting light as air on her waist. He caressed the strip of skin above the waist of her low-slung jeans.

"Ari," he murmured, the way he said her name making her shiver. "Don't cut yourself on the points of my incisors."

Oh man, that just did it for her. She stretched up and kissed him. The tip of his tongue slid like wet silk between her lips, instantly enchanting her. His mouth was the perfect cross between cushy and masculine.

"Mmm," was all she could say at how good he tasted. His tongue was courting hers, gentle, slick, the damp huffing of his breath on her cheek almost too much of a turn on. She turned her head and invited him deeper. As he RSVP'd, another sexy growl rumbled in his chest.

To her delight, her encouragement turned him a bit less gentlemanly. One broad hand wrapped around her bottom, pulling her off her feet. He hiked up her weight like it was nothing, and maybe to him it was.

He turned, and her back bumped what she assumed was the refrigerator. Pressing her into it, he kissed her harder, deeper, those long canine teeth threatening to cut her lower lip. She opened wider and wrapped her legs around his trim waist.

"Ari," he whispered, breaking free for a breath.

She used the opening to drop her cuffed hands behind his neck.

"I like your teeth," she said.

He closed his eyes like hearing that hurt him. This time when he slanted his mouth over hers, the deep kiss didn't end for long minutes. If this had been a movie, the violins would have been swooning. They both were breathing raggedly when he withdrew at last.

"Move me lower," she said as his glazed eyes stared into hers.

"Lower?" His voice was thick with arousal.

"You're too tall. I want to feel your erection between my legs."

His body jerked, his fingers clamping tight on her butt. "All right. Just . . . don't be afraid if it feels too big."

Ari smirked. She'd heard that once or twice before. Then he moved her, and she realized maybe his warning was justified.

"Wow," she said, gaping up at him.

He grimaced, not rocking into her yet, just rubbing her jean-clad crotch lightly up and down the middle of the stone hard ridge. It was hard to judge, but his cock felt like ten inches. Ari turned the teensiest bit leery.

"You know how to operate your power tool, right?"

This time, his smile was the smug one. "I do."

"Girlfriend?"

He shook his head. "Not in a couple years. Not serious, anyway."

She wondered at that. He seemed like a man women would snap up and hang onto. Not that this was her business.

"Can we actually— I mean, would it turn me into a wolf if you and I did the deed?"

His breath caught flatteringly. "No. There has to be a blood exchange and a ritual. And your Talent might make you immune. But—" He hesitated, that cute little furrow creasing between his brows. "Werewolves can impregnate Talents, even using birth control."

She didn't think she imagined that his hard-on got harder. Evidently, kissing women in cuffs wasn't his only kink.

"I would never force you," he said. "Not to do anything."

The weirdest thing was, she believed him. Ari didn't trust anyone lightly and she wasn't sure she ever trusted completely. This cop radiated sincerity like he did heat. Her chest went tight at the idea that he wasn't lying.

Since she couldn't speak, she kissed him again.

∞

Maybe Adam should have fought what was happening, but he couldn't make himself. However good Ari's reasons for her actions, she was a criminal. She was also younger than he was, a newcomer to Faerie, and a member of a different race.

Actually, that caused his instincts to prod him harder. Talents made good werewolf mothers. Sometimes women of their own race couldn't control their need to shift and miscarried. Maybe Carmine was right about him having baby hunger. He wanted to spill inside this girl so bad he was practically whimpering.

Then again, maybe he just plain wanted inside her.

He groaned as she rocked against him, the denim seam that clasped her pussy compressing his zipper. She started sucking his tongue and a hot chill sluiced down his spine. He hurt from wanting her, and he had a sneaking suspicion she felt the same. He shoved her harder into the fridge, driving the hand that had been cradling her head under her soft tank top. He reminded himself he didn't jump into sex with women he'd just met. Unfortunately, the warm silk of her breast felt like heaven under his palm. He caressed a delicious circle over the curve.

She moaned, arching into his massage. Holding her was like trying to control an eel without hurting it. She had a lot of strength for such a little thing. Her nipple was a hard tight pebble, and twice as hot as the rest of her. Since the rest of her was plenty hot, that was saying something.

He wrenched free of her mouth. "Gotta suck this."

He shoved up her shirt and ducked.

"Unh," she said as he latched on, her hips bucking hard against his aching dick.

She was moving like she was going to come. Hungry for that, he suckled harder, pulling the nipple and areola between his canines, curling his tongue around the tightness it was rubbing.

"Adam," she gasped. "God."

Her scent rose, her cream saturating her panties to wet her jeans. Adam backed off before he gave in to the urge to bite her.

That was the sort of thing he didn't do without discussion.

"Why are you stopping?" Her voice was rough, her Iowa blue eyes glassy with desire.

Long explanations were beyond him. Feeling more than a little crazed, he laid her back on the kitchen table and undid the front of her ripped up jeans. She hadn't come yet, but he knew how to make her.

"Can I?" he asked, fingers splayed across her warm little belly. "Can I pull these off and go down on you?"

Her eyes got big, her sharp tipped breasts going up and down with her hard breathing. Even in human form, his ears were sharp enough to hear her heart thundering. His lust cranked higher inside his veins.

"Yes," she said, cuffed hands curling into fists. "Please."

The *please* did it for him. Most male werewolves had a dominant switch or two. He yanked the worn black denim to her ankles, fell to his knees, and sank in. She tasted even better than he'd thought she would, rewarding every lick and suck with fresh cream. It was humbling, really, to be desired this much. Growling out his approval, he buried his face in her, using his fingers to rub what he couldn't tongue, not letting up for a second until she came with a throttled scream.

He didn't let up then either, not until she stopped twitching.

"Oh God," she panted, her body sagging on the old wood.

He rose over her, his weight held off her by his elbows. His Saint Michael medal dangled down on its chain, and he hoped the policemen's guardian wasn't taking offense at this. Ari blinked a couple times before her eyes would focus.

"I felt your teeth," she said in a shaky voice. "I felt them nudging to either side of my clit."

His canines were still run out. He was too wound up for them not to be, nor were her words likely to change that. He licked the sweet taste of her from them.

She watched his tongue as if it fascinated her. "Do women always come that hard for you?"

"Sometimes," he said honestly.

He felt her hands turn within the cuffs. They were directly beneath his groin, and her fingertips half petted, half scratched the pounding hump of his erection. The pleasure this stirred was so insane he gasped.

"Don't stop," he said when she paused. "That feels incredible."

"Would you—" Resuming her tantalizing scratching motions, she wet lips as pink and plump as rosebuds. "Would you like me to suck you off?"

Lightning streaked through his cock. Those lips on him . . . That tongue . . . "I would like it," he said, his throat almost too tight to push out the words. "But that isn't what I want most right now."

"What do you want most now?"

"I want to fuck my cock between your cuffed hands and come on your bare belly."

He wanted it so badly he sounded angry. The blush left over from her orgasm deepened, setting her cheeks aflame. Her grin broke out a second before her chuckle. "Oh, you *so* have a fetish for bondage."

"Maybe," he conceded, enjoying her amusement. "But so far you're the only woman to bring it out in me."

She liked his answer. She smiled slyly from under her dark lashes. Her cuffed hands wrestled with the drawstring that kept his sweatpants secure on his hips. As the waistband gapped, she dug into the opening. Adam's stomach jerked with anticipation.

"Hm," she mused, catching her lower lip under small white teeth. "Not boxers and not briefs."

His breath sucked in as she freed his heavy length from the tight jockstrap.

"Boy," was all she had to say, her palms and fingers stroking him warmly from base to crown. He sensed she was measuring him. "Boy, oh boy, you are some handful."

He tried to speak, but only got out a moan. Her touch was fearless: not too hard, not too soft, and wonderfully thorough.

"You're wet," she whispered, both thumbs finding his pre-ejaculate and swirling it around.

His head dropped down beside her neck. He couldn't stop it. He had to rub his aching eyeteeth against her skin. Ari squirmed on the old table.

"Do you want to drink my blood?" Still whispering, she sounded more curious than horrified.

He shook his head, swallowed. "It's a wolf thing. We like to . . . bite the neck of our partners to hold them in place when we come. It's an instinct from our animal halves. We don't need to break skin."

He didn't mention that sometimes they liked that as well.

"Ah," she said. Her hands had just gotten hotter, perspiration dampening her palms as she cupped his balls and squeezed gently. "Are you going to come soon then?"

He groaned and kissed her, his tongue reaching deep to taste and claim. She kissed him back a little shyly. She was eager, but he could tell she wasn't used to letting go completely. He wanted to make her let go, more than he'd have thought possible.

"Man, you can kiss," she panted when he released her mouth again.

He smiled down into her dazzled expression. *This is the girl for me,* he thought.

He waited for the rational part of him to dismiss this as mystical mumbo-jumbo, but it wasn't obliging him. *Yes,* his mind said firmly instead. *That was a true thing you thought.*

He didn't know whether to believe this, but he could deal with it later. Right then, he had other priorities. He moved his hips, nudging his length through her hands. Her eyes got dreamy at the feel of him sliding.

Most likely, his did too.

He sighed as her fingers curled around him.

"You could do that tighter," he said hoarsely. She did it tighter, and he began to thrust. Lord, it felt good. Her hot little hands. The slight rattle of the cuffs. The electrum plating smoothed their edges where his penis glanced over them. The charm that powered them gave off a slight tingle. Adam didn't want to rush these assorted pleasures, but his increasing urge to come had him rolling his hips faster.

Ari turned her head and nipped his earlobe.

He cursed. This was something wolf lovers did. Her doing it turned up the current that ran through his sweet zones. Sensation rose sharply inside his groin.

"Fuck my hands," she whispered, fingers tightening rhythmically on his shaft. "Fuck the hands you trapped in these pretty cuffs."

He hadn't known he liked dirty talk any more than he liked petite females. Her comment sent him into a spin. He was growling, sweating, his mouth open on her neck with both sets of canines run out so far they hurt. He hoped she couldn't feel the lower ones. Some non-weres thought two pairs looked too animal. Then again, Ari might not mind. How fast she was breathing was amazingly sexy. Pleasure coiled to the point of pain . . .

"Fuck," he gasped. "I want in you so bad."

He pushed downward with his hips, angling his cockhead to jab her belly when his shaft shoved beyond her wrists. The crazy amount of precome he was leaking smoothed his way really well. She made a sound, low and excited. He went faster.

"Yes," she urged. "*Go.*"

His balls seemed to jump upward. The climax was a knot inside them—tighter, stronger—and then the feelings swelled so big they simply had to burst.

He came with a foghorn moan, hot spurts shooting over her hands and abdomen. He almost bit her but managed to hold off. The orgasm wrung him out harder than usual, like riding the crest of a long rough wave. She petted him all the way through it, seeming to know when his nerves turned raw and he needed her to gentle.

He wanted to collapse, but on top of her was the only place, and he was heavy. Groaning, he pulled free of her hold, tugged up his sweats, and sat shakily in one of the kitchen chairs.

"Whew," she said after a few seconds. She sat up, panted, and hopped off the table to pull up her cotton panties and black jeans. Her mouthwatering little breasts were no longer situated where they belonged in her tank top's bra. She rearranged both with a lack of self-consciousness that startled him. Werewolves weren't known for their modesty, but that was mostly the males. Only long-time lovers had acted this way with him. She stepped between his sprawled knees as if they were old friends.

"That was good," she said, giving his shoulders a comradely pat. "You're hot stuff for a guy who lives in Faerie."

Adam's jaw was hanging, so he closed it. Was this sort of hook-up usual for her, and if it were, why did that bother him?

His expression must have betrayed his thoughts. She gave one of his biceps a joshing punch. "Don't look so serious. Even cops must be allowed to have fun."

Fun. His stupid subconscious was trying to tell him she was The One, and she thought this was fun. He shook himself, throwing off the annoying twinge of hurt. Probably he'd just imagined the voice in his head. *Biology*, he reminded himself. His hormones were playing tricks on him. Any second, he'd snap out of it.

"You think I could use your shower?" she asked. "I'm kind of—" She gestured toward her front with her still cuffed hands.

Adam couldn't keep from swallowing. He'd really cut loose on her, the pearly stain of his semen starting to soak into her thin T-shirt. He liked how big the mark was. Liked the way their strongest scents had mingled. Cream that hadn't dried darkened the crotch of her jeans.

"Adam?"

"Sure," he said, his brain stuttering back from its side trip. "Just let me get clean towels and . . . and the key to those things."

She smiled brilliantly.

"You shouldn't use that as an excuse to run," he warned her, not convinced she'd given up the idea. "I know you're worried about your friends, but my team and I want to help you. It's in our interest, as well as being our job. You don't know what sort of trouble you could get into here alone."

Her smile sobered. She considered him for a moment with big blue eyes he wouldn't have guessed could look that sharp. "Okay," she said. "No more running until you give me a reason to."

Her choice of words gave him pause. *Until* she'd said. Not even *unless*. Clearly, their accidental tourist had a few trust issues.

∞

He knew he'd smell her in the shower when he used it after her. Even though he'd waited an hour. Even though he ran the hot water first.

Her scent was in every moist molecule of air.

A growl rumbled in his belly as his cock increased in weight and lifted. He tried ignoring it, but by the time he'd finished soaping the rest of him, the thing was sticking up like a red flagpole.

He didn't think he'd been this hard since his mid twenties.

Giving in, he soaped his ball sac, using a slow firm pressure. Stretching his testicles felt good enough to rest the back of his head against the tile enclosure. He'd rub one off. Maybe two. Then he'd be relaxed enough to sleep. He wouldn't think about how Ari had halfway screamed when she came, how her clit had felt and tasted against his tongue . . .

When he moved one hand to his shaft, when he tightened the grip and pulled, his canines ran out full length. Unable to restrain the urge, he rubbed his spine against the wall like it was itching. Fuck, this was what he needed. He fought a groan as his pleasure rose. The wall to this shared bathroom adjoined his guest room. He didn't need Ari hearing him jerk off. For all he knew, she'd offer to join him.

He didn't think he was ready to take whatever this was further. Even thinking about rushing into it with her excited him. He moved his right hand faster, slick and snug on his throbbing shaft. Werewolf body temps could get sultry. His dick was hot enough to burn, but—holy hell—jerking off tonight was intense. He tugged faster, giving the sensitive inch underneath the flare a more emphatic share of friction. His knob wanted in on the action, but he was saving that for later. He planted his feet wider on the tile, thigh muscles bunching, hot needles of spray hitting his chest and balls.

Gasping, he turned his back to the water and re-soaped as fast as he could. He liked his masturbation slippery. Liked it hot and wet and as tight as a woman's cunt. He saw Ari's breasts in his imagination, half-bared by her disarranged T-shirt, nipples peaked and red from her orgasm. A moan backed up in his throat. He couldn't wait. He switched hands: the left now fisting the shaft, the right thumb and fingers circling quick and hard on the glans.

*Would you like me to suck you off?* came her sweet sinner's voice in his mind.

His spunk exploded, shooting out and splattering the tile. Eyes squeezed shut with bliss, he worked both hands at top speed and let the giant orgasm roll. Jesus, it wouldn't stop. It was like before with her on the kitchen table and the handcuffs. The long hot wave of pleasure gripped every nerve and twisted.

"Fuck," he breathed, the curse having to come out.

He was panting—shaking, to be truthful—his locked knees and the wall of the shower holding him upright. His shoulders blocked the water. The results of his lengthy ejaculation hadn't washed away yet. He saw he'd sprayed the width of the enclosure, from waist level to the floor. Did he always come this much? Were Ari and his alleged baby hunger doing something new to him?

His keen were hearing picked up a muffled sound. His dick recognized it before his brain. The noise was Ari's orgasmic cry, likely stifled in her pillow. Ari's quick little fingers were moving rhythmically on wet flesh. Shit. She was masturbating. His dick shot up and got rigid in two heartbeats.

You'd have thought it hadn't just shot its insides out.

For a couple seconds, all Adam could do was watch it stick out and shudder in front of him. When that got old, he gripped himself to stroke off again.

The sounds in the guest room had stopped, which was probably for the best. If he heard the Talent do that again, he might not make it out of this shower with his dick still attached to him.

# CHAPTER FIVE

Ari wasn't a huge fan of masturbation. She did it, of course. Everybody did. There had simply been too many instances in her life when it was inconvenient to need to. She'd been happy to let her hormones sleep for weeks at a time. On the rare occasions when she'd had sex, it was more of a friendly thing than a production.

Meeting Adam Santini seemed to be changing that.

The need to get off had seized her last night. He'd given her a superior climax on the kitchen table, better than she was comfortable admitting. She should have slept like a baby, but then she'd heard the shower go on. She'd been lying in the nice clean bed, idly picturing Adam naked under the spray. Any woman would have done the same, but her clit had suddenly gone crazy and she'd absolutely had to shove her hand into her panties.

She was glad the shower had been so noisy. The climax had been intense. She hadn't been able to hold in a cry as it broke.

But no reason Really Hot Cop had to know what he'd done to her.

After that, she'd lain awake for awhile, staring out the window beside her bed. Adam's snug little guest room overlooked a small fenced yard and faced the back of another line of rowhomes. Brimming pots of mums decorated the fire escapes, lights glowing here and there behind window shades. The neighborhood looked normal. Blue collar. Clean but not spotless. A shadow swept across the three-quarter moon, making her shiver.

Maybe the gargoyle had flown over.

She wondered if Maxwell was okay in the hospital. She'd been able to heal his hands after Henry's goons broke them that first time. It had taken her a couple days, and she'd had two fall-down fits from pulling so much power. The second time they'd come after him, the damage was too extensive. Max had refused to even let her try, claiming he was afraid she'd stroke out. It occurred to her that if he'd been here in Resurrection, she might have had sufficient juice to succeed. Or someone else would be able to. Adam had implied lots of people had gifts here.

She wriggled lower in the covers, wondering why Henry Blackwater had bothered to collect her. If Resurrection had so many Talents, why didn't he recruit them? It was a puzzle she wasn't going to solve snuggled up warm and safe in Hot Cop's soft guest bed. She also wasn't going to figure out where Sarah had disappeared to. Her female BFF had her issues, but she adored Maxwell. If she'd known Maxwell was laid up in that hospital, she have chained herself to his bed.

"Keep them safe," she whispered to the deity her parents had tried to claim as their personal bully boy. "You know they rely on You more than most people."

Maybe it was because the air in Resurrection held more magic. Warmth washed through Ari's limbs after she said the prayer, relaxing some of her tension. She slid into sleep with a rare sense of personal safety.

"I can wiggle my teef," piped a voice behind her.

Ari's eyes flew open. It was morning. Sun flooded through the dry rain spots on the window, practically blinding her. Something tugged the blanket that covered her.

"Wanna see?"

Ari turned warily. A boy about three years old stood beside her bed. His hair was black and shiny, his happy eyes the same soft green as Adam's. When he saw he had her attention, he used his fingers to pull back his upper lip. Sure enough, his little canines went up and down.

"Wow," Ari said, because some response seemed to be expected. "That's awesome."

The boy giggled. "You have a fwog in your fwoat."

"That's because you woke me up." Facing the boy on her side, she pulled the blanket higher on her neck. Were little boys supposed to see grown up women in tank tops and panties?

"Are you naked under there?" he asked, wide-eyed.

"No," Ari said. "I'm just shy."

The boy absorbed this, obviously feeling no obligation to leave on that account. "My Unca Tony is gay," he announced. "My mommy is his sister. She cwied, but Daddy said at weast she wouldn't have to worry about him chasing squirrels all the time."

"Skirts," Ari corrected without thinking.

"What?" said the boy, his rosy mouth open.

"Your dad probably meant— Oh never mind. Chasing squirrels all the time would be bad."

"They're fast," the boy agreed. "But it's fun when you get 'em up a tree."

The door to her room opened, allowing a dark male head to poke in. "Shit," said Unca Tony. "Sorry. Babysitting duty this morning. The pup got away from me."

"Not apposed to say the 'S' word," his nephew scolded as Tony scooped him up by the waist. "The lady didn't mind, Unca Tony. She was talking to me."

Tony rolled his eyes over the boy's head. "Sorry," he said again. "We've got breakfast going if you're hungry."

The boy squirmed in his arms and started barking as Tony carried him out. The yipping sounds were so convincing they made her laugh. Of course, considering the boy *might* turn into a puppy, the realism wasn't surprising. Out in the hall, Tony let out a growl, at which his nephew whined and fell silent.

Ari's eyes went round. She realized she'd just eavesdropped on an actual wolfish discussion.

Pretty sure the door would stay closed, she tugged down the window shade, then swung out of bed and dressed. Someone— Adam, she imagined—had stacked a clean sweatshirt and jeans on the granny chair. They were women's garments, slightly big for her but wearable. He must have slipped in while she was sleeping. That made her feel both unnerved and touched.

Some men wouldn't have cared if she had fresh stuff to wear.

With very little concentration and the help of the bathroom mirror, she got her hair to stick up the way she liked, so Maxwell's custom red design was displayed just right. That done, she was ready to go out.

She felt as shy as she'd claimed to the boy when she stepped into the crowded kitchen. Rick and Tony were there, plus an older couple she suspected were their parents. Both the couple were cooking, with the boy plunked nearby on the counter, swinging his feet and gnawing on a strip of jerky. Adam sat at the kitchen table, stirring pancake batter inside a bowl.

He looked straight up at her.

God, she wished she weren't remembering what they'd done on that table mere hours before. Her face went hot, his turned pink, and then, "Hey, lady!" squealed the boy.

She should have looked away from Adam, but it seemed she *had* to hold his gaze a few seconds more.

"Her name is Ari," Tony murmured.

"Hey, Awi!" the boy called just as loud as before. "I'm Efan!"

Ari laughed, and the spell was broken, her eyes freed from the enticement of Adam's gorgeous green orbs. Mr. and Mrs. Lupone introduced themselves, and they ate a noisy chaotic breakfast together. There didn't seem to be a special occasion. Apart from Ethan, no one made a fuss about her being there. Ari sat and watched them, struck dumb by their camaraderie. At its best, her family hadn't been anything like this. At its worst, eating with her parents had been like trying to walk on ice barefoot—a series of "godly" pronouncements interspersed with prim silence. When Ethan finished eating, he crawled around barking on the floor butting people's calves. None of his relatives objected. Indeed, his grandfather leaned over periodically to scratch him behind his ears.

"Can Ethan change?" she leaned close to Adam to ask.

"He won't until he's five or six," he said, leaning in as well. "Until then, he likes to pretend."

"He showed me he can wiggle his teeth."

Adam grinned. "That's the werewolf version of flirting. He probably thought you were pretty."

His soft green eyes gleamed mere inches away from hers. As she stared back at them, mesmerized, their green began shading into blue. The faintest, most delicious scent rose from him, like a cedar grove warming in the sun. She wanted to roll in the smell until it was all over her. Under the table, one of Adam's knees pressed harder against hers. His lips parted a second before he jerked back from her, blinking.

"Well," he said, his voice a little throaty. "Maybe I should start clearing."

"Oh you can leave that to us," Mrs. Lupone demurred. "We invited ourselves this morning. And it's your day off. Why don't you and your nice young lady take an after breakfast stroll?"

"I'm not his—" Ari stopped when Adam gave his head a small shake. Maybe he didn't want his aunt hearing about cop stuff. "Um, sure. A stroll sounds great. Thanks for the awesome grub."

"You're welcome," Mrs. Lupone responded with her eyes sparkling.

Ari hadn't realized she'd been tense, but she took her first truly easy breath of the morning when she and Adam exited the rowhouse's front street door.

Adam was as quiet as she was. The day was a picture perfect autumn creation: crisp, sunny, the trees that grew from the railed-in planters in the sidewalk starting to turn scarlet. The borrowed sweatshirt she wore was the ideal weight for the weather. As they walked, Adam plunged his hands into his cargo pants pockets. Ari couldn't decide what to do with hers.

He stopped beneath the maple at the next corner. "You okay?" he asked. "You've had a lot of shocks in a short span of time."

Ari snorted. "Not the least being woken up by a three year old."

Adam's shoulders hunched as he dug his hands deeper. "Werewolves don't exactly stand on ceremony."

"I didn't mind. I just haven't hung with a lot of kids."

"You were fine with him. Good, actually." Apparently, Really Hot Cop blushed at the drop of a hat. He looked away from her to the Italian grocery on the corner. Bins of fresh apples glowed in the dappled sun, so bright Snow White would have been tempted to bite one. Ari restrained an urge to pinch herself. For all she knew Snow White was a real person here.

When Adam turned back, he'd pulled his cop side into his face again. "I need to debrief you. Get everything you know or even think you know about the Eunuch."

"O-kay," she said slowly.

"Also—" He reached out to lightly touch the base of her neck. "You should wear the depowering charm Nate . . . gave you if you go out. It doesn't just damp your magic, it inhibits other people from reading how much you have. Level Five is high enough to draw attention. You wouldn't want Blackwater putting it together that you've come here gunning for him."

Ari stuck her hands in her pockets, then realized she was echoing his posture. "How many levels are there?" she asked, refusing to pull them out and make herself more conspicuous.

"Eight," he said. "It's called the Bunscombe Scale. The gargoyles invented it. One to three is nothing you'd notice if the person were in your world. The ability to change shape gets you ranked a five, but the demarcations aren't black and white. Most weres don't *do* magic, they just *are*."

"That gargoyle called me a Level Five."

"You probably are. Magical Mentoring would have to test you to be sure."

"Magical Mentoring?"

Adam grimaced. "It's like foster care for Talents who wander into the Pocket, which happens more often than you might guess. Their counselors train you to control your gift. Spell out the rules for what's allowed and what's not. Plus, you get officially registered, which you have to do before you can take the certification test. Some things citizens can't do without a license."

*Like torture people*, she thought.

"Strictly speaking, there's no license for that. A couple government departments do it anyway, but they're not supposed to."

Ari pulled her hands from her pockets and crossed her arms. "You read my mind."

"I only can do it sometimes. I have a touch of the Sight. My grandmother was an elf."

She couldn't help it. Even though she was irritated, she had to laugh. "Lemme see your ears."

He smiled as she brushed his silky locks behind one, then stood on tiptoe to see. Their shape was perfectly normal.

"Pointy ears are recessive," he informed her.

Because touching even his ear felt a bit too good, she dropped her hand. "This place is so freaking weird."

"Bad weird?"

His expression seemed serious. "No," she said, caught by his gaze again. "Not bad . . ."

Why was he looking at her like that? Like her answer was important? The air in her lungs thickened. His hands had taken her upper arms, and his thumbs were sweeping over the soft sweatshirt.

"Ari," he said huskily. "I can't seem to stop touching you."

She couldn't either. Her hands were on his waist. He bent to kiss her, and she could have sworn it had been eons since she last tasted him. The kiss was harder than the night before, nearly fierce. She stretched into it, kissing him back with more abandon than she'd known she had in her. She drove her hands under the thin T-shirt that seemed to be all the warmth he needed. His skin was silk laid over hot muscles. When she scratched lightly up and down his spine, he groaned and stabbed at her tongue with his. Ari sucked it as hard as she could, delighting when this made his canines extend.

"Jeez," he gasped, wrenching free. "I could fuck you right out here in the street." His groin was mashed against her belly, the giant hump at his crotch making his point for him. Between her legs, her clit felt like it had swollen to the size of a strawberry. It pulsed like a mariachi band throwing a party.

His full lower lip, the one with the dent in it, was reddened from kissing.

Ari took two tries before she could speak. "I guess people don't have sex in the street here."

"No." He dragged his slightly open lips up her cheek, inhaling as he went. His teeth found her earlobe and took a delicate nip. "Fuck, Ari, you smell good."

It killed her to hear him say this. As a werewolf, his nose was better than hers. If she wanted to roll around in his scent, what must he want to do with her? Shivering, Ari pushed away. She had a mission. She needed to focus. This thing with Really Hot Cop was getting out of control. Adam didn't help when he took both her hands in his and squeezed. The pressure of his fingers was unaccountably erotic.

"Debriefing," she reminded him shakily.

"Right." He released her hands to run one of his back through his thick black hair. "I'll call the team. We can go over it together."

∞

The Lupones were still at Adam's place watching Ethan. Evidently, Adam's apartment contained fewer breakables. Rather than request they leave, Adam collared Rick and Tony and headed across the street to Nate Rivera's.

Hot Latino guy lived in a big loft space, no walls except for his fancy bathroom and some storage. He was a clothes horse, for sure. In his bedroom corner hung more nice suits than Ari had seen outside a department store. They were organized by color on long rolling racks like you'd see burly guys pushing along the Garment District's streets. Nate's ceiling went up forever to exposed pipes, and cool little paintings Max would have loved hung on the rough brick walls. The place was so slick Ari wasn't sure where the others found the nerve to prop their feet on his ottomans.

The only absent team member was Carmine. He was spending his day off with his wife and kids.

Nate served everyone coffee in matching miniature off-white cups.

"You sure Nate's not the gay one?" Ari heard popping from her mouth.

From a mile away in his open kitchen, Nate shot her the fish-eye.

"Wolf ears," Tony said, touching his own. "They can hear pins drop."

Adam suddenly found Nate's copy of *Urban Style* deeply interesting.

*Shoot*, Ari thought. He must have heard her getting off last night. She struggled against her blush, but it wasn't easy when Tony's mouth curved up. Unlike his brother, he appeared to like the idea that Adam was hot for her.

Nate set a second French press of coffee wrapped in a quilted cozy on his low glass table. "Now that we've got our caffeine supply, maybe our tourist would like to spill her info on the Eunuch."

"Maybe you'd start by asking what you want to know."

"Names," Rick said, leaning forward from the sculptural white couch he was sharing with his brother. His manner held the same edge of challenge it had last night. "Associates. Enemies. Other Talents who work with him."

"You don't have names?"

"We have some names from here, but we've never succeeded in getting a spy in his inner circle. Our understanding of his operation is sketchy."

Ari wasn't as comfortable answering him as she was Adam, but she'd agreed to this. "Well," she said, propping her forearms on her thighs, "he doesn't seem to travel without his entourage. He's got six or seven goons he favors, who stay with him in whatever place he's leasing. He moves maybe twice a year, and always goes high end. Like, penthouses with park views. Some of his pet Talents live with him. Others like me have outside jobs. We only come to him when he calls. Every so often, one of his pets disappear. The junkies especially don't last long."

"They disappear," Adam repeated. Like her, he sat on his own chair. She noticed he'd angled it more toward her.

"Most of us assume they die. Whatever he has them doing seems to burn them out. Or maybe they OD the old-fashioned way."

"But you don't know for sure what happens to them." Nate's manner was intense but in a different way from Rick's. He seemed to have no beef with her, just a naturally skeptical nature. His chair was red with black cow spots and shaped like an egg. He would have looked silly in it, if he weren't giving off such a danger vibe.

"No," she agreed. "We don't know for sure what happens. One day they're there, and the next they're not."

"Do you remember names?" Nate pressed.

"I put the ones I know in my tablet. Blackwater hates computers. It seemed a reasonably safe way to keep track."

Ari shifted her gaze to Adam, who exhaled resignedly. He understood what her raised eyebrows were asking. "Yes, I confiscated your tablet." He pulled it out of the army green rucksack he'd brought with him. He held the device between his knees for a moment and looked at her. "Nate has a converter that can make your tablet run on local power. It would be helpful if you gave him permission to look at it."

"And if I don't?" Ari asked, curious to hear the answer.

"If you don't, we have to get a warrant, or what we find won't be admissible in court. If we need a warrant, we'll have to turn you over to Magical Mentoring."

"And that you truly won't enjoy," Tony said helpfully. "You're a rogue Level Five. If you're lucky, Mentoring will only keep you in protective custody for a couple months."

A couple months were more than Ari could afford to delay. As long as Blackwater stayed in Resurrection, Maxwell and Sarah were safe. If he headed back to New York and was still in a rage over Ari's rebellion, she didn't want to guess how he'd take revenge.

"Give Nate the tablet," she surrendered.

Nate rose and took it to a sleek office area that was set up along one wall. The others followed, so she did too. The plug Nate stuck in the tablet's port looked ordinary, but when it powered up her scalp prickled. She pointed out the file she'd been keeping her records in.

"Password?" Nate said over his lean shoulder.

Ari's face heated. "Godlovesme2. With a numeral at the end."

Behind her, Adam's hand settled on her back. His palm didn't rub her, but it was warm. He kept it there while Nate cross-searched the police database with the names in her file. Metrosexual werewolves could be techno-geeks, she guessed, because his long fingers seemed at home on both machines. Less than ten minutes passed before he straightened.

"None of these Talents are in our system," he said. "If the Eunuch brought them here, they're not registered."

Tony's side brushed hers as he leaned in to see the screen, his big body warming hers unself-consciously. "We could ask the gargoyles. They usually notice new magic folks."

"Eh," Rick said dubiously. "Gargoyles are notoriously bad with names."

"I have pictures," Ari offered, causing all four men to look at her. "My camera phone never seemed to work around Blackwater, but my friend Maxwell managed to sketch a few."

For the first time, Nate regarded her with respect. "*Chica*, you are not as blonde as you look. Maybe those hair spikes haven't punctured your brain."

Ari didn't know whether to laugh or be offended. Her style was her style, the same as Nate's was his. Deciding to ignore the dig, she showed Nate where she'd hidden the scans of Maxwell's sketches. He sent the file to his printer.

"These accurate?" he asked, showing them to her.

His printer must have had a charm on it. Maxwell excelled at capturing faces, but his sketches had printed out like photographs.

Ari gulped and nodded. Seeing those missing faces just as they'd been in life was eerie.

∞

Ari was getting to Adam, not just her smell or her looks but who she was. Her password was the latest chip in his defenses. Someone must have told her God didn't watch over freaks like her. If he'd known who it was, he'd have given them a piece of his mind. And good for her, for knowing better. This *chica*, as Nate called her, had spirit.

They returned to Nate's sitting area, where they could pass around her friend's pictures. Adam knew his men were searching their sharper than normal memories for faces they might have come across in the past. Rick was the last to go through the stack.

When he finished, the beta flapped the pages on his thigh. "What do you used unregistered Talents for?"

"Illegal stuff," Tony answered.

"Right," Rick said, his gaze unfocused, "but here in Resurrection, they'd be limited to small tricks. Any use of power above a three, and they'd be too likely to set off the gargoyles' alarms."

"Maybe the Eunuch has better shields than we know about," Nate said.

"Maybe. But Talents aren't so good at precision work. The bigger the job, the more unpredictable their results. Everything we know about the Eunuch tells us he's an anal guy." He looked at Ari, his expression hardened by the guardedness in it. "From what she says, the Talents who disappeared were burned out. If that's true, how much would they be able to do even here?"

"Huh," Tony said, flopping back on the modern couch.

Nate leaned forward as he dropped back, his graceful brown thumb and finger pinching his lower lip. "There are a couple of demon species who don't mind being paid in people. He could be using his discards as bribes."

"Oh!" Ari exclaimed, popping straight in her chair. Adam wasn't happy to discover his hackles tightened when the other men looked at her. His possessive tendencies shouldn't be rearing their heads like this.

Nervous at the attention she'd drawn, Ari rubbed her thighs through the jeans he'd borrowed from Tony and Rick's sister. "Okay," she said. "First, demons are real too?"

"'fraid so," Tony confirmed.

Ari's throat worked, but she nodded, inspiring a flare of pride in him. "All right, maybe some of the stories people whispered about Blackwater weren't as crazy as I thought."

"What stories?" Adam asked gently.

God, he loved the way her eyes locked on his. The connection felt like pure warm gold being poured down his spinal cord, comforting and sexy at the same time. He was only distantly aware of Nate quietly snorting. He doubted Ari heard it at all.

"People said he'd made a deal with the devil. They said that's how he could find gifted folks like me. One girl claimed . . ." She hesitated.

"Claimed what?"

"She claimed that instead of trading his soul, he'd given Satan his dick. It's true he never had sex with anybody. Not girls, not boys. I assumed he was impotent, and put out that story himself to make it seem scary instead of lame. But maybe it's true. A demon is like a devil, isn't it?"

"Some are," Adam admitted. "The hell dimension residents who come to Resurrection have to have enough control over their dark sides to keep from being deported."

Ari shivered, obliging Adam to suppress an urge to hug her. "So offering up your manhood could be a good way to seal a pact? To get yourself more juice if maybe you'd been born a Level One?"

"A damn good way," Adam said. "And turning over burned out Talents who'd never be reported missing might be the cost of continuing to do business."

She shivered again, and Adam reached over to squeeze her knee. He hoped it comforted her. On his side, the contact sent heat zinging up his tailbone.

"This is speculation," Rick pointed out. "We need evidence if we're going to bring him down."

Reluctantly, Adam released Ari's knee. "I'm open to suggestions."

Rick pulled a face to say he didn't have any.

"Come on," Nate broke in impatiently. "Am I the only one who thinks Ari here would make ideal bait?"

Adam's canines slid down as his lip curled back, a snarl rising in his throat before he could stop it. Nate had *not* just suggested that.

"Whoa," Nate said, hands lifted, palms exposed. "Just consider it before you go ballistic. Blackwater wants her on his leash again. If we let him find her, he'll think it was his idea to yank her back to heel. It'll never occur to him she's a plant."

"She's a civilian," Adam growled. "A human. We aren't throwing her to that bastard like she's a fucking steak."

"If you'd stop thinking with your dick for two seconds—"

As alpha, Adam had more speed than any of his pack. He had Nate and his stupid egg chair flat on their backs before the lower ranked wolf could defend himself. Adam dearly wanted to tear him apart, but settled for yanking him up and slamming him into the raw brick wall between his front windows.

"Shit," Nate gasped once enough of his breath came back.

He was no weakling and didn't immediately submit. Right that second, this wasn't the smart option.

"Bare your neck," Adam barked, shaking him so hard his head snapped back. His eyes were hot and glowing, his voice supernaturally low and thick.

"Sheesh," Nate muttered, but he lifted his chin out of the way for him.

Claiming his due, Adam pressed his extended canines around the other man's wildly racing pulse. Werewolves healed wounds fast. He wouldn't kill Nate if he bit down and tore, but it might be a near thing. His more primitive side really wanted to test that.

"I'm sorry," Nate said, his hands coming to Adam's ribs to rub them soothingly. "I didn't realize how serious you'd gotten about her."

He meant it. He wasn't just offering empty submission. Adam shoved his inner wolf back into its cage and stepped back. He hadn't realized how serious he'd gotten either. He couldn't apologize, but he did nod to Nate in acceptance. Both of them were shaking just a little as Nate rubbed his reddened neck. They hadn't come this close to a knock-down drag-out since the pack had been formed. Once a cop passed his courses at the Academy, leadership was decided by combat in wolf form. Back then, Nate had thought he'd be squad alpha. When he also hadn't won the fight for beta, the loss had been hard on him. He was as strong as Rick or Adam, and certainly as smart. For whatever reason, his genes didn't send the same signals. Rick and Adam's wolves had been able to control his.

"You two done?" Tony asked from the living room. "Not that watching you two go at it wasn't ree-diculously hot."

Nate snorted and they returned to their chairs, Tony having set Nate's fallen egg upright. As Adam hitched up his cargo pants and sat, Ari followed his movements with rounded eyes. The part of him that was trying to watch its back with her wished he didn't feel so satisfied that her pulse was thudding.

"Here's the thing," Nate ventured cautiously. "We need to get close to Blackwater's operation somehow."

The back of Adam's neck started prickling again. Before he could speak, Rick did.

"We can't use Ari," he said, the first time he'd used her name that Adam could recall. "We don't know what the Eunuch is doing to the Talents who disappear. Even if we wired her some way he wouldn't spot, we couldn't move in fast enough if she was in trouble."

Tony cleared his throat with a humorous flourish, and Adam felt a gratitude for his presence that was becoming familiar. Ever since he'd given up on proving how tough he was, Tony had turned peacemaker. Werewolf aggression being what it was, they could always use more of those.

"I have an idea," the squad's youngest member said. "One our fearless leader might actually go for. We ask the gargoyles to do an enhancement spell on Adam. He's already got a gift. If he could pass for another Talent from Outside, the Eunuch might not be able to resist scooping them up as a pair."

"That could work," Rick said, "except gargoyles don't usually do spells for members of other races."

"They might this time. I'm not sure how the Eunuch twisted their tails, but they hate the bastard as much as we do. Plus, the one outside Adam's window seemed to take a shine to Ari. Maybe he'd do it as a favor to her."

"We'd have to get the undercover work approved," Nate put in.

"The Mayor could green-light it," Tony said. "Outside normal channels so it won't get back to Blackwater. Hell, considering Ari's a Level Five, he'll probably want to meet her regardless."

"Hold on," Adam said before everyone got too excited. "If the gargoyles agree to concoct a disguise for me, we don't have to involve Ari."

Ari made a sound of protest, then shut her mouth when he looked at her.

"You could stay *safe*," he said emphatically.

Nate must not have learned his lesson as well as Adam thought, because he began to laugh. "Boss, have you forgotten what this girl was doing when we found her? She's going *mano a mano* with the Eunuch whether you tag along or not."

"Is that true?" Adam asked her.

"Uh," she said, squinching up her face. "Yes?"

"Well, fuck," he said, pretty much astounded. "How exactly are you hoping to get him to lay off your friends? No matter what you concede to a man like that, he'll just ask for more. He'll own you, Ari. And that still won't guarantee your friends' safety."

Ari looked extremely uncomfortable.

"Boss," Nate said almost gently. "Ari might not want to tell you this, on account of us being cops, but I'm pretty sure she intends to fry Henry Blackwater from the inside out. She is a freaking Level Five, after all."

"That kind of was the plan," she confessed. "At least once I saw what I could do with my power here."

"Well, fuck," Adam said again. Ari was either extremely crazy or extremely brave. If she wasn't killed by Blackwater's cohorts, she'd spend the next forty years in jail.

"You can't," he said shakily. "We have to respect the law."

"*You* have to respect it. If your way doesn't work, I have to take him out any way I can. My friends are only in danger because of me. They saved my life when I first landed on the street."

Her big blue eyes shone with earnest tears, pleading with him to understand or maybe not to stand in her way. Compared to him, she was a kid, and she was ready to do this thing. It was his job to lay his life down for other people—his nature, if it came to that. He knew then he'd have laid it down for her twenty times over.

"I guess we'll have to make sure my way doesn't fail," he said grimly.

∞

Apparently, Adam knew Resurrection's mayor. He didn't have any trouble getting an appointment for that evening, after official office hours.

"We're set for seven," he said, shutting the phone that looked pretty much like hers, the only difference being that its logo said *Elfnet*.

They stood on the shady pavement outside Nate's loft. The others had gone their separate ways. Ari's body felt very aware of Adam's, too aware really. She wondered if Ethan and his grandparents were still at Adam's house.

Adam rubbed the back of his neck. "You want to walk a bit?"

She nodded and he set off without a word, seeming as tongue-tied as she was. Ari took in the neighborhood: the convenience stores and cafes, the dry cleaner with the blue-skinned man in the turban behind its high counter. The subway entrance resembled the ones at home, down to the chewed gum squashed in the cement steps. Ari made a mental note to return on her own if she got a chance, so she could study the subway map. That made her feel untrusting and ungrateful, which maybe was what pried her mouth open.

They'd reached a little Greek restaurant with an old striped awning and a collection of chairs and tables roped off on the broad sidewalk. It reminded her so much of Mikos that she stopped in her tracks.

Adam stopped as well and put his warm hand on her shoulder. Ari didn't pull away. She liked the way it felt.

"Are you hungry?" he asked. "Do you want to go in?"

"I was a hostess in a restaurant like that one."

"Were you?"

She felt him watching her face but didn't turn to him. At the nearest table, a paper napkin fluttered in a metal holder. If she answered, would it count as sharing? "I worked my way up from busgirl. I liked it. It was peaceful."

"I can't imagine working in a restaurant as peaceful."

"Mikos had its dramas, but they were never very important. Two months ago, Blackwater told the owner he'd beat him senseless unless he fired me."

Adam's hand stroked her spiky hair, though he said nothing. Ari fought the tears that wanted to rise in her eyes. "Mr. Mikos was a nice man. He'd save things from the kitchen for me to take home to my roommates. Little treats he knew we couldn't afford. Max was addicted to their baklava."

"Did something happen to your boss?"

"No," she said, grateful for it. "I just can't see him anymore. He wanted to go to the police, but I knew they couldn't protect him from someone like Blackwater."

"Ari." He turned her to him, making her look at him. "I'm not the sort of police you're used to. My men and I are going to make sure this turns out all right."

Maybe he would. He certainly seemed to believe it.

"I've never met anyone like you," she confessed.

He smiled, a hint of wistfulness in it. "That makes two of us."

He was beautiful to her then. Ari was pretty, she supposed. She did what she could to make her looks interesting. Adam seemed interested at least. When his fingers slid around her face, his eyes turned heavy and followed them.

"Ready to go home?" he asked.

His voice was husky and—God—the lust that tightened inside her was powerful. It heated and clenched not just her pussy but every muscle from head to toe.

Ari had thought she was a normal woman when it came to sex, but clearly more than half of her had been asleep until now. She nodded, unable to answer. Adam must have sensed why. His eyes flared at their backs, and he caught her hand in his before turning back toward his house. The part of her that had never had a romantic boyfriend loved how sweet and unthinking the gesture was. Adam liked her, and therefore he held her hand. Of course, the way he squeezed her fingers made her worry she'd combust.

"Where do your parents live?" she asked, fumbling for a distraction.

"They're dead," he said. "They worked together in Portal Management. Something went wrong and they were caught in an explosion."

"I'm sorry," she said, surprised how much she meant it. "Were you close?"

"Yes." His fingers tightened on hers again. "I feel lucky for that. They've been gone for a couple years."

His profile was sad but calm. He grieved, but it hadn't destroyed him. Awareness tugged at her mind. Maybe the loss hadn't destroyed him, but it had done something.

"You said it's been a couple years since you had a girlfriend," she blurted. He turned to her in surprise. "Sorry, I shouldn't have—"

"No," he interrupted. "I guess that probably is the reason I haven't dated anyone seriously. My parents . . . my parents had the kind of relationship people write love stories about. They defied their folks to marry each other, and to go into the work they did. Portal Management is too close to *doing* magic for most weres. They consider it contrary to our heritage. But my folks felt it was their calling, the way they were meant to serve."

"Were they good parents?"

"They were wonderful." Adam wagged his head and laughed. "Sometimes they joked that a cuckoo had snuck me into their nest. We could be pretty different in our attitudes, but as much as they loved each other, they loved me more. They added their love together for me. It was an awesome way to grow up. When they died, it made me think about what I . . . wanted out of life."

Ari knew he'd meant to say what he wanted out of *marriage*. She gnawed her lip and looked at the sidewalk, hard pressed to imagine a more different model for the wedded state than the one she'd had. Her parents had been in agreement but not in love—not that she could tell, anyway.

The gulf between her and Adam felt impossibly awkward. They reached the steps of his building and went up them in silence.

"Keys," he said, letting go of her hand to dig them from his pocket.

Why was watching him work a lock intimate? Despite the confidences they'd just exchanged, this hadn't been a date. Ari wasn't heading up these stairs for a good night kiss.

When he opened the door to his apartment, the stillness inside informed her they were alone.

"My aunt and uncle must have taken Ethan home," he said.

He rubbed the front of his pants legs like he was nervous. The motion drew her attention to his zipper. Adam had an erection. Not a small one either. The pressure of its fullness outlined it clearly against the cloth.

"Sorry," he said, noting where her slack-mouthed stare had landed. "That fight with Nate got to me. It's a werewolf thing. Testosterone and all." He swung the door closed behind them. "I'll just shut up now."

She caught his arm to stop him. "That boner isn't just for Nate. Your fight was a while ago."

He smiled wryly down at her. "True. Also Nate wouldn't know what to do with it."

"I do," she said, and cupped it in both hands.

He let out a sound surprisingly like a purr. His palms slapped the paneled door to either side of her head. Braced then, his hips rolled into her rubbing, causing her pussy to turn molten. "You sure you want to do this?"

Ari dug in harder and sank down to her knees. "You have *no* idea," she assured him.

His desire for her must have been stronger than his desire to argue. He helped her with his tab and zipper, then pulled out his cock for her. She hadn't gotten a good look at him last night. He was big and dark and his swollen veins made her lick her lips. Ten inches might not have been an exaggeration. From her current perspective, he had quite the monolith.

"Your hands are in my way," she observed.

He made a sound like she was going to kill him. A small clear bead seeped from the opening in his tip. "I don't want to shove too far in."

"Don't worry, honey. I'll tell you when to hold yourself again."

She hadn't meant to call him *honey*. Hoping he hadn't noticed was probably futile. Since he didn't comment, she could pretend it was no big deal. In any case, the picture he presented was too yummy to turn from. Once he let go, she steadied his shaft herself. She didn't suck him immediately. Instead, she lapped him, lollipop style, from his pulsing base to his quivering satin tip. His groans were her inspiration, his clenching thigh muscles her best praise. "Do you like your balls played with?"

He grunted in answer and planted his feet wider.

She licked his ball sac and tugged it, then massaged the smoothness behind it with firm fingers. His musky smell flew up her nose, the hint of cedar dilating all her veins. If that weren't enough of a turn-on, his prick stood more vertical, the freaking Empire State Building of erect penises.

"Please," he groaned. "Take me in your mouth."

She didn't have to remind him to hold himself. He pulled his shaft down from his belly and steered it between her lips. The head was smooth as it breached her, and so hot that if she hadn't been drooling for him already, she would have then.

"Oh God," he moaned, pushing carefully. "Ari."

What was it about grateful guys that flipped her switches so thoroughly? Since he was taking care of the non-deep-throating, she dragged his pants to his knees and worked her fingers into the muscles that were bunching admirably. She sucked him deeper, licking at his grip on the lower part of his shaft.

"Shit," he gasped, clearly liking that.

His legs were spread too far to pull his cargo pants to his ankles, but she could still drive her hands inside them over his calves. His body rolled as she squeezed them, his sweaty palms squeaking on the door.

"I don't—" he said, then had to stop when another sensual undulation took hold of him. "I don't want you to finish me this way."

He dropped before she could argue, on his knees with her. Their gazes locked, heating her even more. "Lift your arms," he said gutturally.

She lifted, and he pulled the borrowed sweatshirt over her head. She was bare beneath it, going braless usually not a big thing for her.

It was a big thing for him. He palmed her and groaned, plucking her nipples with his fingers until she thought she might come from that. He didn't give her a chance.

"On the floor," he said, already pushing her down.

Her jeans were halfway down her legs before her brain remembered she ought to be stopping him. "Wait."

He pulled off her socks and bent to kiss her hipbone. "I know," he said. "I won't. Condoms are only about seventy percent effective for weres, and maybe sixty for alphas."

Only sixty for alphas? Did that mean he was even more manly than his detectives?

"You're not—" She started panting as her cotton panties went the way of her socks. His big hot hand slid deliciously up her thigh. Boy, it was hard to think. "If we start this, you're not going to want to stop."

"I will anyway."

He kissed her into silence, which she discovered she didn't mind at all. As he lowered his weight to her, she realized he was naked too. *Oh shit*, she thought, because he felt so good. He was big and hard and her hands wanted to play all over him. His chest was hairy, his butt amazingly tight and small. She moaned like she didn't think she ever had in her life. His cock dug into her thigh like a hot baton, leaking excitement. She was going to be the one who had to be told to stop.

She had a sneaking suspicion he pulled the thought from her head. He flashed a grin and rolled her on top of him. His entryway had a plush dark rug, cushioning for her knees. She pushed up and her hands found his heavy pecs, unable to resist kneading into them like a cat. He was as sensual as a cat himself. His eyes glowed up at her, his incisors jutting lower than his other teeth.

"This is nuts," she said, her voice more breath than sound. "There are so many reasons we shouldn't be doing this."

He seemed perfectly happy to ignore good sense. His hold settled on her hips tightly enough to stir an extra thrill. "Rub you labia up my dick," he growled. "Your hands as well. I want all the pressure you can give me."

Ari's arousal ran out in a big hot gush. She fell to him and kissed him, writhing against him crazily. That made him moan, and then they both went a little nuts. He got one hand between them, causing a little rubbing war with hers. When his thumb found her clit and mashed firmly over it, she stopped struggling and let him take precedence. She was so wet they had to work really hard against each other to get enough friction.

"Oh God," he groaned, his fangy mouth stretching wide on her neck.

"Do it," Ari said. "Bite me. You're not going to freak me out."

"Can't," he gasped, and groaned louder.

She got his big blunt tip right against her clit, then curled two fingers under his rim on the other side. He stiffened and shoved at her.

"Shit," he said. "Too close."

She didn't want to move. She wanted to come with him pressing there, like a fucking plum that was going to burst.

"Okay," he panted, seeing she was determined. "I'll hold off until you go. Just try to do it fast."

The idea that he was struggling did her in. She went with a wailing keen, but coming wasn't enough. Her body wanted to feel him shoot, no matter how risky the closeness was. She ground down so wildly she might have hurt him. He grunted in reaction but didn't ejaculate—not even when she came for, like, three minutes.

He was trembling as she finished, eyes screwed shut with erotic agony, blood trickling from his lip where he'd bitten it. Knowing she damn well owed him, she didn't wait until her muscles recovered. She crawled down his heaving body, combed through his pubic curls with her fingers, and took his throbbing prick in her mouth. This must have felt good to him. His hips came all the way off the rug.

The sound he made wasn't a word or a growl. She grasped his root and suckled, giving him everything she had, her tongue, her lips, until she could taste how close he was. The fearlessness of her methods broke him. His hands forked into her hair like claws, his cock shoving into her and thrusting between her tongue and palate. He didn't go too far, but, man, he went fast and furious. She cradled him as well as she could. Maybe ten groaning seconds later, he started shooting straight down her throat.

He came like she had. Like the world was ending, and this was his last chance. Wild noises tore from his throat, her name jumbled among them. She sucked him until he stopped pumping, then gently licked the last drop from him. She didn't think she'd ever done that, or enjoyed it so much. He tasted good to her, her own special sex dessert.

"God," he said as she crawled back up beside him.

She couldn't do anything but hold him while they both tried to catch their breath.

"Mm," he finally said, recovered enough to stroke his hand down his spine.

The petting felt really nice. Ari wanted to fall asleep, just let down her guards and sink. Knowing that wasn't a good idea, she rubbed her face across his chest hair instead. Maybe in a while they could do that again.

"Why didn't you bite me?" she asked. "Would it have hurt me too much?"

"Not exactly." He trailed out a lengthy breath. "It hurts some, but most weres who do it think the pain's a turn on."

"Then why hold back?"

His hand caressed a path to her butt. "Biting to draw blood links lovers together, until one of them changes form again. It makes . . . their attraction to each other contagious. If I were aroused, you'd be too."

Ari smiled against his pec. "That's already happening."

His amazing body shifted under her. "It would happen more intensely. It's not usually a good idea unless a couple is . . . comfortable with each other."

By *comfortable* she was pretty sure he meant *serious*, like his parents had been. Which why would he be about her? Or vice versa? She wasn't here to find Mr. Right. Even if she had been, she didn't believe in that. Lovers came and went. Friends were for keeping, if you were lucky. Just because Adam got her hotter than any man ever had didn't make him her forever pal. Men like him didn't stick by women like her that long. Nobody stuck by women like her. To think they would was like a dog asking to be kicked.

Despite her thoughts, when Adam groaned and sat up, she wished he'd kept on holding her.

"We need to shower," he said.

She didn't think he meant together.

# CHAPTER SIX

D on't be nervous," Adam said.
    This was interesting advice, considering how jittery he was. The yellow cab had dropped them in front of a Greek temple sort of building. Three tiers of marble steps ascended to a grand facade, which resembled the Metropolitan Museum, thanks to its towering columns. The white stone that clad it appeared to glow— and possibly did—in the rosily setting sun.

"This is City Hall?"

"Central Library," Adam said, pointing out the chiseled letters that stretched across the triangular pediment.

A large shape glided toward the roof and landed, probably a gargoyle. When Ari squinted, she thought she saw more dark heads and wings roosting there.

"The Mayor is also our Librarian," Adam said.

The way he said "Librarian" made it sound important. Even uttering the title had rattled him. He tugged his nice sport coat straighter and buttoned it, after which he resettled his shoulders and started up the steps. Ari's shorter legs had to work to keep up.

"Will he have you fired if he doesn't like your request?"

"No," Adam said, his expression going even more uptight.

Ari decided to shut up. Adam had borrowed a dress for her from Ethan's mother, Maria. Fortunately, it was lightweight. She didn't sweat it up too much climbing all those steps.

She was used to public buildings having security, but no guards were posted behind the revolving entrance door. Maybe nobody dared intrude here without permission, or maybe the library was protected magically. Ari's skin *was* tingling as they went in.

"This way." Adam directed her up yet another flight of white steps.

The Central Library seemed abandoned. They passed no one but a few giant old paintings—classical scenes of nymphs and gods who were up to no good. The Mayor's office was on the second floor. A figure eight lying on its side was the only identification on the frosted glass in its door. The faint flowery smell Ari had noticed everywhere in Resurrection was stronger here. It wasn't cleaning fluid or perfume. Here, outside the office, a whiff of woods and grass joined the flowers.

Adam filled his lungs for courage and knocked lightly on the door.

It swung open without anyone touching it.

"Come," said a low male voice.

Ari's knees threatened to buckle. She didn't know why. The voice was pleasant but ordinary, as was the man who sat behind the battered schoolteacher's desk inside. He shut the file he'd been reading and smiled at them. He seemed young for a mayor. Thirties maybe, with short brown hair and crinkling eyes. His jaw was strong, his nose slightly crooked. He gestured them toward guest chairs that hadn't been in front of his desk a moment before.

When Adam caught Ari's elbow, she found she could walk after all.

The room they entered was on the smallish side, with pale blue walls, no carpet on the floorboards, and one tall uncurtained window behind the desk. Its glass was frosted too, the light that glimmered through it milky. Low bookshelves lined the side walls, their contents sparse and dusty. The space was very plain, hardly decorated at all.

"So nice to see you again," the Mayor said to Adam, rising to shake his hand.

"Sir," Adam responded. When the Mayor let go, Adam rubbed his palm against his pants leg like maybe he'd got a shock.

"Would you like to?" the Mayor asked her, his arm extended in offering.

Ari didn't look at Adam. She was an independent agent. She didn't need his permission or guidance. If she secretly wanted it, that was her problem. She let the man they'd come to meet clasp her hand.

The instant his skin touched hers, she knew damn well there were more than eight levels on the magical measuring scale. Power thrummed against her at the contact, so immense and yet so gentle she might have doubted it was there. Planets would rotate backwards for power like that, and maybe whole galaxies. She rocked back on her heels after he let go.

"I guess I know how you won the election," she burst out.

Adam inhaled sharply beside her, but the Mayor laughed and sat. "I *try* not to cheat. Sometimes it's difficult."

She sat herself, and Adam did as well.

"Ari," said the Mayor, though she was relatively certain her name hadn't been mentioned. "I like visitors. New blood is interesting."

"I'm glad you think so." This was honest, but probably impolite. At least Adam didn't gasp this time.

The Librarian's eyes were a strange color, not quite gray and not quite silver. They seemed to shift as she looked into them, like an optical illusion to make you think you were falling. What the hell sort of creature was he? One of the fae who'd built the city? A demon? Something even more peculiar?

He met her regard patiently, as if he were accustomed to being stared at. Belatedly, Ari realized that whatever she was sensing behind his gaze, he'd be reading much more in hers.

With a decided effort, she wrenched her attention to her hands, which she'd clenched in her lap. Her fingers were slippery from sweating.

"I have your warrant," the city official said, though thankfully not to her. He slid the manila folder he'd been perusing across his desk to Adam. "I also took the liberty of calling the Gargoyle Council. They're waiting to talk to you on the roof."

Adam took the folder and rose stiffly. "Thank you, sir."

Since their interview seemed to be over, Ari pushed up too. Some impulse made her bow to the Mayor before she left, though neither mayors nor librarians were royalty. His eyes met hers one more time.

"Good luck," he said softly.

She had to be imagining what she saw in his expression. Totally scary dude though he was, he seemed sorry to see them go.

Adam wasn't sorry to leave.

"Jesus," he said, settling his coat again once the door swung shut. "God help me if I ever get used to that."

With strides so brisk she had to run to keep up, he led her to the next set of stairs. To her relief, he slowed as he went up them.

"What is he?" she asked in an undertone.

Adam shook his head tightly. "Better not to ask, I suspect."

Ari couldn't help agreeing any more than she could help being curious.

∞

Adam's occasional meetings with the Mayor tended to leave his bones shaking in their sockets. He couldn't put his finger on why the man terrified him. The Mayor had never harmed Adam or his pack. His many terms leading the city were unsullied by scandal. Benevolence and fairness seemed to be his bywords. No one Adam knew hated him, regardless of their species.

Nonetheless, before he could push the roof access door open, Adam had to wipe a sheen of sweat from his face.

A flock of silent gargoyles awaited them outside. He'd never had a formal meeting with their Council. The Police Commissioner was the person who handled that. Adam held the metal door for Ari, whose steps out onto the roof were a bit unsure. She walked close enough to his side to reach out and touch but not so close she'd appear to be cowering. Adam gave her props for nerve. Everything she'd experienced this evening was new to her.

When they were a car's length distant from the front gargoyle, Adam touched Ari's arm to let her know she should stop.

Gargoyles were unnerving to be close to. The youngest could be two or three times human size. The oldest only looked small from street level. The huge gargoyles who'd saved the cars from the Washington Street Bridge disaster had probably hit the five century mark. Though they were flesh, their uniform gray coloration caused them to look like stone. Only their irises were different hues. If they were motionless or sleeping, they were difficult to distinguish from statues. From what Adam knew of their culture, amongst themselves they communicated telepathically. When using spoken language they were less adept, though—as a rule—they were highly intelligent.

The particular gargoyle who faced him—the Council's leader, he presumed—had a bovine head attached to a lioness's torso. Her wings were feathered and folded gracefully on her back. Some sort of tail swished behind her as she inclined her great stony head to him. Limned by the fading light, her outline was as big as a city bus.

"Greetings, werewolf," she said in a voice like millstones turning.

"Greetings, ma'am," Adam responded respectfully, knowing gargoyles weren't big on titles—or names, for that matter. "I appreciate you agreeing to speak to me."

Beside him, Ari bobbed an awkward curtsey.

The Council leader's head swung around to face her. "My son talk you."

A smaller gargoyle shambled out from behind her bulk. He was only as large as a minivan. He lifted his lion's paw in a friendly wave, his broad goblin's mouth grinning. The gargoyles who flew might have any sort of animal wings. His were those of a bat, but no less graceful than his mother's.

"He sorry scream," said she, sounding disapproving of her son's behavior.

"That's okay," Ari assured her. "I was only startled. I feel honored he said *hello*."

"Hmph," said the matriarch.

Her son ducked his head to hide what Adam suspected was a mischievous smile.

"Ma'am," Adam said. "Before we start, might I ask you to look at a few pictures? They're Talents from Outside who have disappeared. We're wondering if any of the gargoyles noticed them doing magic here."

Unsure how to hand the sketches over to a being with paws so large, Adam pulled them from his pocket and spread them across the roof in front of her. Only the gargoyle leader looked at them, but only she needed to.

"We sorry," she said after a few moments. "No see these."

Though he knew the people in the pictures might have family or friends, Adam didn't ask if she was sure, just gathered up the printouts and shoved them away again. An instinct he couldn't have traced beyond knowing it was wolfish told him his introduction of an unexpected topic was a faux pas. He shut his mouth and waited.

After a pause to consider him, the Council leader folded her lion's forelegs one over the other. "Mayor say you disguise."

"Yes," Adam confirmed, relieved he hadn't thrown a permanent wrench in their negotiations. "I need to be mistaken for a Talent from the world outside our borders. If you'd consent to enhance my small gift temporarily, that would be helpful."

The giant gargoyle blinked at him. "What trade you?"

This Adam was prepared for. "I and two of my friends own a building on Alchemist's Way. Would your people be interested in landing rights?"

A stir rustled through the flock. Gargoyles might land anywhere casually, but how long they were allowed to stay depended on the property owner's tolerance for their race. Landing rights gave them access for the term of an agreement.

"It's a good strong building," Adam added. "Depending on the size of the gargoyle, the roof could easily support three or four."

"Your friends law also?"

Adam repressed his smile at the leader's question. Policemen fascinated gargoyles, perhaps because of their own affinity for protecting and serving. "They are police detectives," he said gravely.

The Council leader twisted back toward her son. Their matching tails twitched as they stared at each other, engaged in a communication Adam hoped would come out in his favor. When the lead gargoyle's attention returned to him, he was unable to decipher her alien expression.

"Would like nest rights," she said. "One gargoyle only. One hundred years."

Adam's eyebrows shot up. Nesting rights were a big commitment. Essentially, the gargoyle would take up residence on his roof. It wasn't permitted to make itself a nuisance, but it also couldn't be shooed away without taking the case to court.

"Your son would be the nester?" he asked, wanting to be clear.

The smaller lion-bodied gargoyle nodded, his yellow eyes bright with interest. His goblin face wasn't as hard to read as his mother's. Adam thought he perceived a hint of shy eagerness, like a high school freshman who longed to hang out with a quarterback. That could end up being annoying but, considering what he was asking, the request was reasonable.

"Agreed," Adam said.

The lion-bodied gargoyle let out a little crow.

His mother's slapping tail silenced it.

∞

Ari hoped the night wouldn't get much weirder, but she wasn't holding her breath. As odd as the Mayor had been, standing on a roof with a dozen gargoyles took the prize for not-normal. Not only wasn't she in Kansas, she was barely in the real world. Hard as she tried, she couldn't keep her hands from shaking. It didn't help that with the sun gone down, she was freezing in her short-sleeved dress.

Adam and the gargoyle's matriarch were debating what sort of Talent he ought to impersonate.

"Sight no good," she said. "You need flash."

"That would be better," Adam said politely as if he talked to giant stone people every day. "But don't you need to build on a gift that's already there?"

The lady gargoyle spread her feathered wings proudly. "Twelve here. Much magic. Pick any gift."

"Wait," interrupted the boy gargoyle, the one who'd gotten permission to live on Adam's roof. "Girl cold."

"Oh," Adam said, spinning around to her. "Sorry, I didn't think."

Before Ari could decide if she was embarrassed, Adam had his dark sport coat whipped around her shoulders. Once she was in it, no way would she let it go. The silk-lined cloth was warm from his body. And it smelled just like him.

Adam bent to look into her eyes. "You hanging in, sweetheart?"

"F-firebug," she said through her chattering teeth. "Henry Blackwater loved the one he used to have. He was always having him burn up things. After he disappeared, he never could find another one."

"Hm," mused the head gargoyle. "Fire-starting big flash gift."

"And a hard gift to control," Adam said.

"Hah!" barked the lady gargoyle. "You hot practice much!"

Apparently, the telepathic version of this joke was hilarious. The formerly silent gargoyles burst into thunderous laughter. Ari grinned herself. Unless she misunderstood, Hot Cop's sex appeal was apparent across species.

The sight of Adam blushing like a schoolboy didn't lessen her amusement. That he didn't know how to respond was obvious. Seeing his dilemma, the lady gargoyle's cow face appeared to smile.

"No worry, werewolf," she said, her crunching voice actually sounding kind. "We give just-right power. First, though, you bite girl."

"Uh." Adam glanced at Ari and back to the gargoyle. "Me bite girl?"

The lady gargoyle made shooing motions with her front paws. "You bite girl. Two for one."

"My mother wants you two to entwine your energy," her son interjected in perfectly intelligible English. "If you form a moon bond, the Eunuch will be more likely to take you both. He won't even realize why he wants to."

His mother stomped the roof so hard with one back paw that a crack formed in the concrete.

"Sorry," said her son, though he didn't seem very. "I'm just trying to move this along."

She glowered at him, which—considering her size—would have made Ari quail. Her son held firm. After a few more heartbeats, she turned her great brown eyes to Adam. "You bite girl," she said stubbornly.

Adam looked helplessly at Ari. A pulse beat in his neck, visible in the rooftop security lights. The quickened rhythm told her he was only part reluctant. Another part of him longed to do exactly what the head gargoyle demanded.

Feeling very much the same, Ari shrugged under his jacket. "Who am I to argue? If that's what we need to do, you bite girl."

∞

Ari's eyes were nervous, though—like his—her respiration was coming more shallowly. Adam dragged one hand down his mouth, where the throbbing length of his fangs reminded him how intensely he wanted to go along with this.

Hoping he was thinking clearly, he reached for Ari's wrist.

"We need to speak alone," he said over his shoulder to the head gargoyle. "I promise we won't be long."

"We wait," she said. A second later, she and her compadres had settled into such stillness they could have been statues.

Aware that this was as private as they were going to get, Adam tugged Ari a bit too fast into the stairwell. She stumbled as the heavy door clanged shut. Adam caught her, then slid his hands under his jacket to frame her waist. This wasn't likely to help either of them make a rational decision, but at that moment he couldn't not touch her.

Her hands came to his chest and stayed there.

"I'm not sure we have a choice about this," she said.

The stairwell's landing was lit by a single bulb, which illuminated her upturned face. With the rose-pink flush in her cheeks, Ari looked more innocent than ever.

"I want this too much," he said, using all his self control not to pant.

"Are you afraid you're going to hurt me?"

"I'm afraid I'll shove up your dress and fuck you into this cinderblock. From behind," he added. "With my fangs sunk into your nape like a dog."

Her baby blue eyes widened. "O-kay," she said slowly.

"Don't fucking say *okay*. My dick is so hard it's about to burst. I want this too much to do it nice."

Her hands slid to his shoulders and back to his chest muscles. His yellow button-down business shirt was no barrier to pleasure. Waves of hot sensation rolled directly from her caresses into his groin.

"Who says you have to do it nice?" she asked, just about slaying him.

"Ari, I don't have protection. I think—" He didn't want to get into this, but he kind of had to. It wasn't like he could keep denying it. "You may have noticed you and I have out of the ordinary chemistry. I think you might be my mate."

"Like your soul mate?" Her nose wrinkled unsurely.

Yes, said the irrational corner of his mind. "Like my genetic mate," his mouth corrected. "The . . . a woman who'd have healthy babies if I got her pregnant. If I take you in this stairwell, feeling the way I do, I'm not letting you leave until you've got a womb full of my puppies."

Her touch fell from him. "Oh," she said.

God, it shouldn't have hurt him. They'd just met. No matter what his hormones were clamoring for him to do, he shouldn't be thinking about her having his children. To his dismay, she must have seen what he felt in his expression. She pressed her hands to her mouth.

"Don't," she said. "Please. This is not an insult to you. I don't think any man has ever thought of me as . . ." She trailed off and shook her head. "You have to understand. Taking care of myself is more than I can manage sometimes."

Her worried eyes eased the blow to his pride somewhat. He stroked his finger around the shell of her ear.

"Just do it quick," she suggested. "Don't give yourself a chance to lose control."

Adam groaned. She so didn't understand what this would be like. "If you think it's hard for us to resist each other now . . ."

"We can do it. We'll just focus on our priorities. And it's not like there aren't other ways to fool around besides intercourse."

He knew there were. They just wouldn't be what their instincts would be screaming for them to do. He looked into her big hopeful eyes and sighed. She was right about one thing. They really didn't have a choice.

"Turn around," he said gruffly, though he wasn't certain if the change in position would make his inevitable struggle better or worse. "I want you facing the wall for this. And take off my jacket first. Trust me, I'll keep you warm."

She removed the garment, folding it carefully before setting it on the floor. His dick hardened even more at her actions, the tip leaking through his jock. When she flattened her hands on the dull white paint of the cinderblock, her palms level with her shoulders, arousal stabbed up his shaft.

"Like this?" she asked breathlessly.

Her little killer body was a shadow inside the thin flowered dress. He licked his upper lip between his lengthened canines, his lust for her savage. She'd arched her buttocks out just a bit. He wondered if she knew what that did to him.

"That's perfect," he said hoarsely.

He stepped right up behind her, then growled, then shoved his throbbing front up and down her in one long rub.

"Oh God," he gasped, because it felt so good. Her spiky platinum hairstyle left her nape bare and vulnerable. Adam pressed his nose to it and groaned. "I'm going to come in my pants the second I bite down."

"Unzip," she said, one hand slapping back onto his insane hard-on. His spine rolled when she squeezed it. "Unzip and come in my hand."

Cursing, he wrenched the casual trousers open, tore his dick from his jock, and trapped her hand around him. He *made* her rub him, though clearly she wasn't inclined to resist. The dominant in him needed to exert force.

Grunting at the pleasure that wasn't quite enough, he thrust both their bodies toward the wall. "I want in you, Ari. I want to fuck your pussy."

"Bite me instead," she panted, her body writhing under his.

He yanked up her dress and shoved his second hand down the front of her panties. Her curls were soft, her labia hot and wet. Finding her so ready drew another terrible groan from him.

"Bite me," she repeated throatily.

"I want to fuck you. I want to be in you."

He worked her hand along his cock with the same heightened speed that he rubbed her wet plump clit. Maybe he could save them if he pumped hard enough. Maybe he could save the world. He felt Ari racing toward release as fast as he was, her pelvis working jerkily in his hold.

"Adam," she moaned, tipping her neck forward, exposing it more for him. "Please, Adam. Please bite me."

He drew his tongue up the silken perspiring skin. The hormones in her sweat slammed him, locking little keys into his. He'd never felt anything like it, not with any of his lovers. His testicles tightened even as they got heavier. He wanted her enough to lose his mind.

Biting her had been an even worse idea than he'd realized.

Naturally, every cell in his body demanded he go ahead.

"Christ," he cursed as his fangs slid a fraction longer. Both sets were out, lower and upper. Ari was too gone to notice, straining on the cusp of her orgasm. The knowledge shoved him right to the edge with her.

His jaw seemed to widen by itself. Unable to stop, he turned his head to clamp it around her nape. The scent of her excitement rose. She shuddered, he licked . . .

Then he let all four teeth break skin.

They came in a simultaneous firing of instantly conjoined nerves. Her blood hit his tastebuds and he shot harder. Werewolves had a vestige of the *bulbus glandis*, a sphere of extra erectile tissue at the base of their penises. It wouldn't tie them to their partners like real canines, but it did activate when males were near a female with whom they'd be fertile. Adam's gave an agonizing throb of pleasure as what felt like a gallon of seed pumped from him, ejecting fast

71

enough to burn him from the inside. A second later, Ari's cream spurted over his fingers, as if praising what he'd done. Praise was hardly necessary. The climax was quick and hot and so intense it almost drove him to his knees.

Unbelievable though it was, the orgasm ended about a year too soon. Adam could have gone with her like that forever. He was limp when he pulled himself from her hold, but somehow that didn't quell his yearning.

Ari sagged to the wall with both palms braced on it again.

He had a hard time forcing his jaw to unclamp.

"You okay?" he asked, afraid to touch her again.

She nodded, then sighed and turned around. She pressed one hand to the back of her neck where he'd bitten her. "I think I'm still bleeding."

"If I lick it, it will heal faster."

Her gaze held his. "I could do it myself. My gift can heal simple injuries."

"Please let me," he said softly.

She hesitated, then dropped her hand and presented her nape to him.

The mark was unsettlingly beautiful to him, a reddened ring of teeth with four slight punctures. The cuts only bled a little. His saliva had already healed them partially. Standing close behind her, he traced the circle he'd left on her with gentle thumbs. It gave him great satisfaction that her shoulders relaxed.

"Would you mind if I left the bruises?" he asked. "They'll tell people you're . . . with me until next moon."

"I'd like that," she said softly.

Her caressing voice sent goosebumps across his skin. He kissed her before he licked her, and when he licked her, he felt as if his tongue were saying *I love you.* He couldn't fight the emotion, even if the words stayed inside. Perhaps it was a product of their situation, of hormones or stress. It didn't matter. For that moment, his heart was hers.

He kept his hands on her upper arms until the wounds were closed.

"Thank you," he said, feeling the gratitude to his bones.

She turned and looked up at him wide-eyed. She touched his lower lip with her fingertips. "Why are you thanking me?"

"I know it's hard for you to let people be nice to you. I know you don't trust them to stay that way."

She blinked, sudden moisture glittering in her eyes. "Adam—"

He stepped back before she could voice whatever warning she seemed about to make. "We should return to the roof. The gargoyles will be waiting to do their ritual."

Her gaze dropped when she nodded, and then a little smile tugged her mouth. "Um," she said, "I think you'd better put your power tool away first."

∞

Considering the exciting lead-in, Ari found the ritual itself anticlimactic. The gargoyles circled Adam as he stood in the center of the library roof. Without a word, they lifted their wings together, closed their eyes, and went stonelike. The only sign that something was happening was a shimmering in the air, like gas fumes rising from asphalt. Adam hissed in a breath as a pale blue fire sprung to life around his wrists. He held his hands out in front of him, turning them back and forth, but the glow didn't seem to burn. It guttered out after a minute, and the gargoyles' wings rustled down.

"Done," said the matriarch. "You sleep. Tomorrow flower bloom."

Ari was still enjoying a private snigger at the thought of the big bad wolf with a flower in him.

"Cut it out," Adam said, holding the yellow cab's door for her.

She slid into the back seat biting her lip. Adam followed and slammed the door. The boy gargoyle was a hulk on the library steps, having arranged to fly home with them. Their cabbie looked up as he took off, but didn't flinch otherwise.

Just an ordinary city sight, she supposed.

Adam gave the driver his address, then slid the privacy window closed. The simple act made her pussy squirm, though what he said next wasn't terribly sexy.

"I stuck your depowering charm in my coat pocket. You should put it on again."

With an inward sigh, Ari dug it out from behind his folder and dropped the chain back around her neck. The silvery gold medal nestled between her breasts. The hum she'd almost stopped noticing quieted.

Adam grunted in approval and sat back on the black seat. Seeming immune to the night's lower temperature, he'd rolled up his cuffs. His palms rested on his thighs, the marks the gargoyles left ringing his strong wrists. They resembled good quality tattoos: eye-catching red and orange flame bracelets, like you might have custom painted on a motorcycle. Adam was holding them as if they needed to dry.

"Do they hurt?" she asked.

He shook his head. "They're just tingling."

"Did the ritual feel weird?"

"It hardly felt like anything. I'm hoping it actually did something."

"Maybe the gargoyles are like the Mayor. You know, so much mojo they don't have to shove it in your face."

"They're the Eights," he said. He shifted on the seat to face her. "On the Bunscombe Scale."

His legs were long enough that his knee bumped hers. Ari tried to pretend the contact didn't make *her* tingle. "That makes sense. Since they invented it."

Adam curled his hands into fists, then forced them to relax. "Most people postulate that faeries are Tens."

"And you're sure the Mayor isn't one?"

"I've met fae." The flattened line of his lips suggested it hadn't been an undiluted pleasure. "Purebloods are both more beautiful and more aloof than him. They're like the Parisians of Resurrection. They don't let you forget who built this place."

Ari smiled at the analogy. Adam stared at her.

"I would kill," he breathed, "to have your mouth on me now."

He shifted on his haunches, his once again fisted hands rubbing up and down his thighs. A giant hard-on bulged up between them, pulling the cloth of his slacks tight across his lap.

Ari's nipples beaded so fast they stung.

"Crap," he said, twisting so he sat facing front again. "I knew this would be hell."

He might have known, but the immensity of the lust that seized her took Ari by surprise. He'd warned her their desires would become contagious. He hadn't said it would be a tidal wave of longing. She didn't need his jacket to warm her. She broke into a sweat just from thinking about making love to him. She'd happily have done it in this cab, just yank down his zipper and straddle him. He'd be thick and hot, and he'd thrust into her really far. It would be heaven. She thrust and grind and thrust and grind until they screamed with pleasure.

"Ari," Adam said in a strangled tone. "Whatever you're thinking, stop."

She blinked out of her daydream to look at him. The muscles of his face were tight, and his nostrils flared with quick breathing. "Oh my God, did you read my thoughts?"

"No," he said through clenched teeth. "I'm just feeling what they did to you."

She blushed as hot as he usually did. "Sorry."

"It's okay. Maybe think about the weather instead."

She meant to, but ended up picturing him sunning naked on a tropical beach, his long muscular body sprawled in sensual abandon across the sand. His skin would be brown, his graceful legs fuzzed with hair. The throbbing rod that thrust from his groin would be a thousand times more tempting than a drink with an umbrella.

"Ari," Adam complained, gripping his knees white-knuckled.

She bit her lip and tried to wrestle her imagination under control. Her labia were swollen, and her clit felt like it swam in hot cream, its steady pulse rolling up into her pussy. Could a person come from a pulse, or was that wishful thinking? Her insides needed something to rub against, something thick and warm to stretch their walls and pump between them really hard . . .

"Crap," she said, echoing him. She snuck a look at him and saw his face had broken into a sweat. His gorgeous mouth looked like it was covering fangs. "How long are we going to feel like this?"

Without turning to her, he grasped her hand and squeezed. "Oh, only until the next full moon forces me to turn. Or until we do something about it. That'll make us feel better for a bit."

A bit was better than nothing. Grateful for his hold, even if in some ways it made things worse, Ari returned the grip of his fingers. The next time she glanced at his profile, he was smiling a little.

She realized she wouldn't have wanted to feel this sex-crazed with anyone but him.

∞

The fifteen minute cab ride to Adam's house gave them both a chance to calm down. Once there, Adam went up to the roof to meet the gargoyle, to show him around and help him do whatever gargoyles did to set up housekeeping.

Seeing how excited he'd been to live here made Ari regret screaming like a banshee the previous night.

She returned to her room. Well, not *her* room, but certainly the nicest she'd ever stayed in. It was just right, she thought, with its granny chair and its hand-stitched quilt. Flea market-type paintings hung on the walls in cheap frames. She saw street scenes of city life in Resurrection, three wolves who might have been Adam's relatives, and one picture of a big blue moon reflected in a lake. None of the paintings were sophisticated, but all stirred her emotions. Ari felt like she was peering into the window of a house she wished she were invited to.

"Maria paints those," Adam said. "They make Ethan feel more at home when he sleeps over."

Ari turned and found him leaning in the doorway, his hands in the pockets of his gray slacks. The top two buttons of his shirt were undone, and the pose made his shoulders appear incredibly broad. His slightly shaggy hair fell over one eyebrow. Ari struggled not to focus too hard on how good he looked.

"Is the gargoyle settled?" she asked.

"For now. He asked us to call him Grant, by the way. He said he chose the name to be easy to remember."

Adam's grin called up one from her. "Grant the gargoyle?"

"Yes. From his mother's reaction, I gather he's considered eccentric."

Ari knew how that was. "Were you ever?"

He rubbed one foot on the threshold. "Was I ever what?"

"Eccentric."

"Ah. Not so much. Because my parents were, I think being normal was my way of rebelling."

She realized her hands were twisted together with nervousness.

As she drew breath to speak Adam moved, shoving his hair back from his forehead. "Look, Ari. Maybe this is presumptuous, but I stopped in the corner store after I talked to Grant."

He pulled something from his pocket: a small embroidered bag that was folded into a flat roll and then tied with red satin cord. The bundle looked pretty but inexpensive, like a mini-gift from an import store. When he held it out, she took it. Chinese characters she couldn't read mostly covered its ornate label. The English letters at their center spelled out *Tiger!*

"I'm afraid I don't know what this is," she said.

Adam's cheeks went pink. "They're enchanted condoms."

Ari burst out laughing, which caused him to turn redder. "I'm sorry!" she said through her snorts. "I'm sure it's a cultural thing. That just sounds so funny to me. And the brand is Tiger! Don't they have any Wolf?"

"Tiger! is the best," he said grumpily. "They come in more sizes, and they're 99 percent effective—even for alphas."

Ari pressed her hand over her giggles.

"You wouldn't think it was funny if you'd spent two weeks' salary on six rubbers."

"Sorry," she said, her amusement receding. "Really? Two weeks? That's very flattering."

"I thought—" He dropped his gaze to his feet, which were clad in black dress socks. His toes bunched and straightened on the floor. When he looked up again, his soft green eyes glowed from the inside. "I thought it would make things easier if we had actual sex before we laid ourselves out as bait. Once we're undercover, we're bound to be watched closely. You do want to have actual sex, don't you?"

Oh, she could fall for a man like him.

"I want to," she said.

His eyes darkened and then flared brighter. "Good." His gaze slid to her breasts and he wet his lips. "Good."

Taking the hint, she began undoing the front of the flowered dress, which had buttons all the way down. "I do have a condition."

"What?" he asked hoarsely, his gaze now glued to her hands.

"You get naked for this too."

She'd never seen a man undress so quickly. Of course, Adam wasn't just any man. He was a werewolf with supernatural strength and speed. She dropped the simple dress to her ankles as his last sock went flying behind him into the hall. The only thing he wore then was his saint medal.

Ari was trembling in all the right places.

"God," he said. "Ari."

He came toward her like a man with a serious do-or-die mission, his cock bouncing thick and red before him.

"Wait," she said, her breath gone short and her pulse pattering in her throat. "Give a girl a chance to admire the view."

He groaned, but he stopped a full stride away from her.

"Half a minute," she promised, moving to circle him. Oh, he was pretty. He had a swim trunk tan, his legs brown from the sun, his butt white and high and narrow as its strong cheeks clenched with tension.

"Ari . . ."

"Sh." She touched the plane between his shoulders to keep him from turning. "Those rubbers aren't the only things I'm finding enchanting."

His fingertips dug into his palms, his nails slightly longer than normal. "I need you."

"And you'll have me. I only want a few seconds." She trailed around to his front, where she took in his strong pie-wedge chest. Its cloud of hair narrowed to dive down his belly, then spread around his groin. His six pack was so shredded it had a few extra cans. His erection was just flat out phenomenal. When she stopped to stroke both thumbs around his navel, the heat of his swollen tip beat back at her like a candle flame.

"You," she said, "are a very good-looking man."

"I can't even describe how beautiful you are. Now could you please take off those damn panties?"

She'd forgotten them in her distraction at seeing him naked. She backed up and sprawled on the bed with her hips at its edge. "You take them off," she taunted.

He moved to her so fast she gasped. His fingers curled into the waistband above each of her hipbones. Some primitive part of her wanted him to rip them free. Instead, he pulled them slo-owly down her dangling legs. He went to one knee to finish, his eyes burning straight up her reclined body. Ari wasn't the shyest girl on the planet, but more than her usual was displayed. When she blushed for him, his grin was 100 percent Grade A male.

Gaze still on hers, he took her knees in his hands and pushed them apart.

"You smell hot," he said.

He went down on her like he had at his kitchen table, only this time it was better. He knew her sweet spots: where they were, how hard to rub or tongue them. He also knew the signs that she was about to come. Twice his talented mouth took her to the brink, and twice he stopped right there.

"Shit," she gasped the second time he did it, a bit too tempted to yank out his nice thick hair.

He kissed the inside of her thigh, then rose to loom over her on his elbows. He was furnace hot, especially at his groin, which might have been a were thing. He ran his tongue around fully erect canines. "Want me?"

His voice rasped like sandpaper, making her shiver. "You know I do."

"I want to hear it."

She ran her hands up his hard torso, fingernails scratching lightly through his hair. "I want you, Adam. I want that big cock of yours shoved up in me to my throat."

A shudder rolled through his frame. "Do you want it now?"

"Yes, Adam. Please."

He liked her pleading. His heavy eyelids narrowed his gaze. "Touch yourself first. Rub your juice on me and then roll on the condom."

She jerked, because she'd forgotten the blinking thing. She'd have ridden him bareback without a second thought.

Adam smiled knowingly. "Touch yourself," he said again.

For him, she did it, though she was reluctant to put the private act on show. He must have liked shy girls, because her hesitation only aroused him more.

"That's it," he rumbled, pushing up on his hands to watch. Maybe it was her imagination, but the gargoyles' tattoos seemed to grow brighter. "Work two fingers all the way in."

This felt good in spite of her self-consciousness. "I'd rather this were you."

"It will be. Oh yeah." He fought against his eyes closing. "Deeper. Do it again. Ari, your fingers are so shiny."

She drew them out to rub the shine on him. He made swallowed noises as she caressed his impressive length. Up his shaft she went, around his flare, back and forth across his sensitive tip. His slit was leaking excitement almost as freely as she was. As long as the moisture was there, she rubbed it around him too.

"Mmm," he said, his spine wriggling with pleasure. "You petting me is magic."

She wanted him so much she was starting to vibrate. "Ready for the condom?"

He looked at her and let out a breathy laugh. He must have noticed how hopeful she sounded. "More than. You felt too good rubbing me to stop."

Aside from their packaging, the Tiger! rubbers had the same construction she was used to. They were big enough for him and appeared to have a generous receptacle tip. He moaned some more while she rolled them down, a process she might have dragged out a bit.

"Bitch," he laughed when she finished.

"Is that an insult to a werewolf?"

He sank down to rub her nose with his. "Nuh-uh." He moved one hand between them, his finger searching her furrow before setting his rounded crest in place for entry. Just that felt so incredible her back arched uncontrollably off the bed.

He stretched the arm that had reached between them to the side and got a firm grip on the mattress. "Ready, sweetheart?"

God, he got to her with his endearments. About to combust, she pulled her knees up and set her heels. "Whenever you are," she panted.

The first long push seemed to last forever. This was a claiming with a capital 'C.'

"Mmm," he hummed, going in and in and *in*. "Oh my God, Ari."

She gripped his back hard and tried to help. He was huge, but her body wasn't stopping him. It creamed for him and twitched and tried to suck him farther by tightening. When he was all the way in, he switched the mattress-holding to his left hand and shoved his right underneath her butt. That held her pelvis nice and tight to his. He looked at her, just for a second, the fire in him blazing like the sun.

He had to have felt how ready for this she was. He let go of his control, just rocketed from zero to sixty—as if his cock were a jackhammer.

Ari came the first time in under a minute.

He grunted at her contractions and shoved them both higher on the bed, though his feet were still on the floor. "'gain," he demanded.

She didn't quite come on cue, but within the next dozen thrusts. This orgasm was harder than the first. She threw back her head and arched.

"Shit," he said, going faster and pumping in at a new angle. The bedsprings squeaked like frenetic mice, but she barely noticed. He was pummeling a spot so incredibly sensitive it made her eyes want to cross. The feelings were almost too good to bear. Little helpless wails began breaking in her throat. To judge by the way his face suddenly got darker, her excitement excited him.

"Sorry," he gasped. "God."

He crammed into her and held, so obviously ejaculating that it sent her into a bliss of spasms for a third time. Surely this was a record. She was a girl, but usually she needed some recovery time. Still shooting, Adam groaned, pulling his pulsing shaft halfway out and then jamming it in again. Six more times he did this, as if he couldn't decide whether he wanted to stay as deep as possible inside her or savor the friction. Her pussy certainly was very tight around him, though it didn't hurt anywhere. Truthfully, she didn't think its nerves had ever registered so much pure ecstasy.

"Man," he groaned, pulling out one last time.

He rolled off her onto his back. His hairy calves dangled off the mattress, his eyes covered by one arm. Ari went up on her elbow to enjoy what their energetic screwfest had done to him. Though his cock was still thick enough for the rubber to be secure, the receptacle tip drooped from the weight of the seed in it. Ari was more intrigued by this than she might have been with another man.

"I'm peeling this off," she said.

Adam grunted, which she took as a *yes*. She disposed of the condom without spilling, then brought a hot wrung-out washcloth from the bathroom.

"Don' haff do," he mumbled, sounding like the gargoyle.

Since Ari was having fun, she cleaned his cock anyway.

"Ow," he said as she worked the cloth—she thought—gently around his base.

"Sorry," she said, pulling her hand guiltily away.

Adam blinked sleepy eyes open. "'s okay. You didn't know I'm sensitive there."

"Okay, well, I'll just—"

He caught her wrist before she could move off the bed. "Come back. I'll show you the spot you hit. You'll want to see it. It's big kinky werewolf stuff."

She laughed. He *was* getting to know her a bit. She sat again and he pulled his nearly limp cock up along his belly. Even relaxed, it was substantial. "You see that swollen bit at the base?"

She wanted to touch it but wasn't quite ready to. "Where it's redder?"

"It's the werewolf version of a *bulbus glandis*. It's mostly vestigial, but it swells up sometimes when we ejaculate. It adds . . . an extra kick to the business, I guess. Makes everything more urgent."

"But you can't get stuck in me?"

He shook his head, measuring her reaction to this rather exotic sexual detail. He was still holding up his shaft, his pinkie finger fanning back and forth on the flushed gland thing.

"It can't feel bad to rub it. You're doing it a bit now."

For once, he didn't blush—probably because she was. "It doesn't feel bad to rub it. When I'm coming, getting more pressure there feels great." His eyes darkened. "You were perfect, Ari. Your pussy was so tight on me you nearly sent me out of my mind."

She remembered how he'd kept thrusting even as he shot. She clenched her hand on the washcloth she'd forgotten she was holding. "Can I kiss it?" she blurted.

The subtle tension in him eased. He smiled and sprawled back for her.

She crawled over him and licked him right where he'd been fingering himself. It seemed natural to cup his balls while she did it, and even more natural to start giving him head when he hardened. She loved the way he moaned for her, the way his body heaved and both sets of fingers kneaded her scalp. He was as sensual as an animal would have been, and she found that incredibly erotic.

He was gentle too, and that just made her chest ache.

When his thighs began to quiver, she knew they'd soon be on to the next course.

"Man," he said, shoving across her tongue one last time as far as he dared. "Those enchanted condoms aren't going to last long."

∞

Ari sure knew how to help him regroup. Once she'd brought him up with her mouth, she'd let him take her doggy style, which—not surprisingly—was one of Adam's favorite positions. His wolf instincts activated, he slammed into her so hard they both had to brace on the headboard. It was a struggle not to let his claws jut out, but he figured he'd given her enough to adjust to. Her responsiveness made him hot all over, her increasing surrender to pleasure. He saved one hand to rub up and down her front: from her sharp-tipped breasts to her rounded belly to the slippery button of her clit. Her cries got looser, her orgasms more intense. He didn't want to come himself, because the spells on the rubbers were only good for one go. He held back until he shook, then shouted like a berserker as he let loose at last.

She reached under herself to rub him where his gland had swollen up like a crazy mother again. The extra pressure sent him through the roof. He came so hard he stopped breathing, absolute stabs of pleasure bolting up his spasming cock. When the cataclysm finally ended, he gasped for air and moaned.

This spelled the end to his consciousness. He fell asleep like a stone, barely waiting to go under until his face hit the bed. When he woke, hours later, he was curled so tightly around Ari you'd have thought she was trying to escape. Alarmed by that, he returned to his own room.

# CHAPTER SEVEN

A̲ri and Adam met up with his team early the next morning, gathering in the alley beside Nate's loft. Nate had parked their unmarked black response van there. Its double back doors were open as they walked up. Rick, Carmine, and Tony were setting up a listening post in the bay, the various desks and pieces unfolding from compartments inside the walls. Aloof from their bustle, Nate leaned cool as a cucumber on the back fender. He wore a tight black T-shirt, artfully faded blue jeans, and a tailored black leather jacket that filled Ari with envy. The fact that the jacket wasn't overshadowed by the hotness of the man inside it really said something. As if he knew how fine he looked, he was smugly sipping the contents of a tall Starbucks cup.

Actually, make that *Star's Brew*. The logos were so similar the resemblance must have been intentional. Ari guessed Starbucks couldn't sue for infringement here.

"Got yours, boss," Nate said, reaching behind him for another cup. "Yours too," he added to her. "Since I was guessing, it's a cinnamon cappuccino with two sugars."

Flattered, which was probably what he'd intended, Ari accepted it. "I like any kind of coffee as long as it isn't black."

Nate smiled down at her lazily, clearly pleased with himself. The long black hair he'd combed into a ponytail shone as bright as glass. Ari wondered if his styling products were magical.

Beside her, Adam rumbled out a low growl.

"Sorry, boss," Nate said cheerfully. "Couldn't help admiring. I forgot how pretty some girlies look at the crack of dawn."

Adam muttered something under his breath.

Ari smiled at the lid of her cappuccino. If she looked pretty, it was because Adam had worn her out enough to sleep well.

The memory of him bucking into her from behind tightened her pussy. The hoarse cries he'd made had been arousing and unforgettable—as was the feel of his thick organ. The skillful way he used it was enough to turn any woman into a size queen.

When her tongue went around her lips, it wasn't only to lick off foam.

"Stop," Adam said in an undertone, touching the back of her hand lightly.

Ari started. She'd forgotten he could feel her reactions. Before she could apologize, a shadow blocked the sky above them.

"Wait for me," cried a soft voice from overhead.

They all looked up to see Grant the gargoyle gliding down from above. Between the van and the dumpsters and the fact that Grant was nearly as wide as the alley, landing was a challenge. He did it neatly, tucking his wings so they didn't scrape the brick walls.

"Grant," Adam said warningly. "This is police business."

"I know," Grant said, his cute goblin's head bobbing. "The Eunuch is my people's enemy too."

Tony had stepped out of the van and was gaping. "It has a name?"

"*He*," Grant said, drawing his head higher. "I'm a person just like you."

Tony looked embarrassed, but Adam believed in rules. "Person or not, you aren't an RPD officer."

"I can be useful," Grant insisted. "No one notices my people. We're as ordinary as pigeons. I know you're going undercover. I can be your eye in the sky."

"He has a point," Rick said, also stepping from the van. "Even with the wires, he might see things we can't."

"I won't *do* anything," Grant promised, sounding as if he were trying not to plead. "I'd just watch over you and report. You can't deny my people have experience at that."

Adam dragged one hand down his mouth—his thinking gesture, Ari was learning. "You'll wear an earpiece," he said. "You'll take orders from Rick and obey them to the letter."

"Agreed," said the gargoyle, bouncing a tiny bit on his giant paws.

As if already regretting the concession, Adam trailed out a sigh. He waved the other men ahead of him toward the van. Ari saw her presence wasn't required yet.

"I like your hair painting," Grant said in a polite aside to her. "That's a powerful character."

Ari's hand went to her pointy platinum locks with their red dyed swirl. "A friend of mine drew this for me. A human friend from Outside. I'm pretty sure it's just a design."

"It's an old rune," Grant said firmly. "For concentration. It focuses mental powers. Perhaps your friend found it in a book?"

Perhaps he had, though Maxwell hadn't mentioned it. She was about to ask Grant more when Adam leaned out of the van. "We're ready for you," he said.

Ari's nerves abruptly coiled twice as tight. She hoped she was ready too.

∞

After they assured themselves the subdermal bugs were in working order, Nate drove them out to Poughkip where Adam could practice using his new skill. He'd accidentally set his toothbrush on fire that morning, so he knew it was active. Although his cover didn't require him to be a good firebug, the sanctity of his eyebrows would benefit from him learning to ignite objects on purpose.

They parked in an empty cornfield, out of sight of houses or paved roads. Poughkip was still the Pocket, but it was rural. Rick expressed his faith in his alpha by forcing Adam to don a firesuit. He followed that by setting up a barrier for the others to crouch behind.

"The gargoyles gave me a *small* gift," Adam reminded him. "They didn't turn me into a character from a Stephen King novel."

"Sure." Rick handed him a fire-rated helmet. "But better safe than sorry."

Grant put the icing on the annoyance cake by landing in the stubbled field to watch.

The next half hour was quite possibly the most embarrassing of his life. He tried to concentrate. Then he tried to relax. He visualized different types of fire so vividly his brow broke into a sweat. No matter what he did, he couldn't raise so much as a spark.

Finally, he yanked off the helmet to take a break. "Crap," he said. "Maybe I'm only good with toothbrushes."

Seeing he'd stopped, Grant took two flapping four-footed hops toward him. To Adam's relief, the gargoyle had been a mute peanut gallery. The way he smiled down at Adam led him to believe Grant wasn't as young as he'd thought. Gargoyles had long life spans. Maybe youth was relative.

"You're not entirely off track," Grant observed pleasantly.

"Do you know what I'm doing wrong?" Adam was desperate enough to ask.

Grant closed his yellow eyes to consider this. "What were you thinking about when you set the toothbrush alight?"

A hint of heat crept into his cheeks. "Um, I was thinking about Ari."

Grant's mouth split into a giant grin. "Perhaps you should try thinking of her again."

Adam had been trying not to think of her, so he could concentrate. Thoroughly sick of the helmet, he tossed it to the ground. Right about now, he was willing to try anything.

"Your hands are your emitters," Grant said. "The bracelets we put on your wrists are designed to channel your power through them. Stretch them out and, er, maybe thinking about touching Ari somewhere nice."

Adam stretched out his hands and thought about caressing her pretty breasts.

The power whooshed through his palms like it had been storing up. A patch of dried cornstalks, maybe a foot across, *phoomed* alight a short distance in front of him. Adam watched the merry flames dance with his jaw hanging.

"Good," Grant said. "Now slowly, gently, close your fingers again. You want to think *cool, cool, cool,* and imagine it going out."

It took two tries, but the fire snuffed out as promised.

"Wow," Adam said, doubly amazed for having tried and failed at first.

A chorus of cheers broke out from behind the fire barrier.

"Awesome, cuz!" Rick called. "Now do it again."

∞

One he'd picked up the knack, Adam learned quickly. It wasn't yet noon, and he could set most things he wanted ablaze on the first try. The fires weren't big, but they'd be enough to catch Henry Blackwater's eye.

Ari loved watching his face light up each time he succeeded. Alpha responsibilities notwithstanding, Hot Cop had a boyish streak.

She shoved her hands in her jacket pockets to keep from clapping. That morning Adam had returned her clothes. She had a feeling the mysterious Maria had been at them, and that Ethan's mother was a clean freak. Ari's oversized white T-shirt was now stain free, the worst rips in her black jeans had been mended, and all her mementos were once more securely fixed to her de-sleeved Yankees jacket. She looked a little too tidy, to be truthful, but was glad to have her own garments back. The way Adam tugged at her, she could use the reminder of who she was and where she came from.

He wasn't her forever boyfriend. He was her partner for now.

With that in mind, she reminded herself not to take her Yankees jacket on their hunt for Blackwater. No matter what happened with the Eunuch, she wanted her favorite link to happier times to survive unscathed.

"You just need one more item for your disguise," Tony said. He pulled a pair of black horn-rimmed glasses from the pocket of his gray hoodie.

Adam took them and put them on. Now he looked like a hot egghead.

"So," he said, mugging for them, "would you mistake me for an Outsider?"

This was when Ari realized she hadn't seen any people in glasses here.

"Hey," she exclaimed. "How come none of you guys need them?"

Tony and Rick snickered.

"It's a citywide school program," Adam said. "Every kid gets his vision fixed by the elves for free."

"That's cool," Ari said.

Rick and Tony laughed louder.

"There was a scandal some years back," Nate explained. "A group of high school students were caught using enchanted eyeglasses to cheat on tests."

"And to surf the net in class," Tony added. "Even as a youth, I was scoping out guy candy."

Rick's laugh trailed off on a sigh. He clapped his brother on the shoulder, but his face was a little sad.

"One other thing," Carmine said, sounding reluctant to bring it up. Adam's only married team member was stocky but not fat, his brown curly hair almost as thick on his arms as it was up top. Ari concluded his wife must like bearlike guys.

"What other thing?" Adam asked.

"Uh, well, you marked her," Carmine said, "and you're supposed to be a human Talent, not a werewolf. Maybe you ought to take away those bruises."

"Oh," Adam said, seeming startled that he'd forgotten.

"I can do it," Ari offered. "You don't have to bother."

Adam's men suddenly got quiet. Was this because their lieutenant had marked her in the first place? Or because she'd volunteered to heal herself? Or maybe Adam's team was staring at the ground because she hadn't done it already.

Just how serious was this marking thing?

"That's fine," Adam said, nodding at her gravely.

Though he wasn't acting like she'd insulted him, she still had the impression she'd put her foot in it.

∞

"Have you been Outside?" Ari asked Adam.

They sat together in a booth in the same crowded coffee shop where she'd found Donnie West. Because the gofer was currently in secure lockup, this seemed as good a place as any to dangle themselves as bait.

Adam leaned closer to her across the table. "I lived in New York for two months as part of my Academy training, so I'd understand the criminals who cross over. We shouldn't talk about this here, though. It's noisy, but some creatures have sharp ears."

"Right," she said and then couldn't speak at all. She tried to picture Adam in Manhattan. Riding the subway. Running in his wolf form in Central Park. Could they have crossed paths without knowing it?

Her Converse-clad feet tapped restlessly on the floor. Adam caught them between his boots, stilling them. "It's okay to be nervous."

She nodded. Of course it was okay. Anyone who was hoping to be grabbed by the Eunuch would be nervous. Nervousness was perfectly consistent with their cover.

Adam covered the hands she was using to ball up her napkin.

"If anything happens to you because of me . . ." she said.

He smiled and leaned in. Suddenly, he was kissing her, his mouth sealing over hers as his tongue slid in. He kept the kiss going for a good half minute, his probing gentle but delicious. Ari was breathing quicker when he backed off.

"See anyone you know?" he asked.

It took a moment before she was able to move her eyes from his. She didn't know how to be subtle, so she just looked around. "Maybe," she said. "That guy sugaring his coffee seems familiar."

Adam didn't follow her gaze. "Okay. Time to put on a show. Drop that crumpled napkin on your saucer."

Ari put it where he asked. Adam stretched out one finger and set its edge alight. He extinguished it a moment later, but his action was enough to draw attention.

"Hey," said the mother elf at the next table. "That's not allowed in here." She pointed sternly at the *No Flaring* sign hanging on the wall directly above their booth.

"Sorry," Adam said, his wolfish grin undermining it. "My girlfriend is making me hot. Love your ears, by the way."

The mother elf slitted her eyes at him, then returned to scolding her two toddlers. Adam pushed his sexy horn-rim glasses farther up his nose, which caused the littlest elf to gape at him. The boy was about Ethan's age. His miniature pointy ears were the cutest thing Ari had ever seen.

"All right," Adam said, pushing up from his seat and digging in his jeans pocket. "It's probably time to go."

He dropped some wadded bills on the table beside their cups.

"You're sure?" Ari asked, rising with him. "We—" She lowered her voice. "We don't know the right person saw."

Adam put his arm around her and steered her to the door. "I paid our bill in US dollars. Trust me, the waitress won't let that pass without setting up a stink."

If there was a stink, they were outside before it broke. Adam snuggled her to his side, ambling around the corner to Chinatown as if they had all the time in the world. Ari dreaded seeing the skinned gnomes again, but Adam stopped in front of one restaurant's window like his shoes had been bolted there.

"You're right," he said a bit more loudly than he had to. "These things are complete freakouts."

Ari didn't notice anyone watching them, but maybe Adam knew better than she did. There were a lot of windows to either side of them. Farther down the street, a shadow that could have been Grant the gargoyle changed the shape of one roofline.

"Want to go in there?" Adam asked, pointing toward an import store. "Maybe they've got something cool we can take back home."

Ari discovered how effective obfuscation spells could be when a long white limo literally came out of nowhere. It squealed onto the sidewalk in front of them, bouncing slightly before stopping. The nearest door sprang open and a man with dark gray skin and tusks leaped out of it toward her. Dressed in a double-breasted gangster suit, he had to be eight feet tall.

Out of instinct, Ari grabbed Adam's hand and ran the other way. Two more goons in suits blocked their escape from that direction. They were joined a moment later by the Eunuch himself.

Henry Blackwater was an elegant man—smooth-skinned, strawberry blond, with a partiality for cream-colored Italian suits. He was slender and not quite a six footer. He strolled toward her like a dancer, pulling thin tan gloves from his long-fingered hands. His sharp fox-like features kept him from looking completely effeminate.

Ari's throat threatened to close. Their fishing expedition had worked faster than she was prepared for.

"Ari," Blackwater said in his favorite slightly mocking tone. "I assume you're looking for me. How silly of you to run."

"How silly of you to bring your goons if you didn't want me to."

It wasn't the greatest comeback, just the best she could do right then.

The giant gray guy with the tusks was holding Adam from behind by the arms. Adam wasn't struggling, but he jerked like he wanted to.

"Nice of you to bring a friend," the Eunuch observed. "I'm always looking for new talent."

Ari didn't like the way he smiled at Adam. Adam was considerably bigger, but Blackwater wasn't afraid of him. He didn't even seem to view Adam as a person. He was . . . speculating about him, like he might an item on a new menu. When Blackwater had first found Ari, he'd at least pretended to care for her well being.

"Put them in the limo," he instructed his cohorts. "We need to get out of here."

Ari couldn't stop herself. She didn't want to be shut up in that car. She lifted her hands to fight. Maybe she could take him out here and now. She drew up power from the ground so fast her feet went numb. It wasn't fast enough. Before she could release her gifts, one of Blackwater's men slapped her in the same silvery-gold handcuffs the police had used.

"None of that," their boss reproved. "Not if you hope to strike any sort of deal with me."

Because she had to, Ari controlled herself. His men shoved her and Adam in the limo. They weren't too careful about it. Ari would have fallen on her face if her hands hadn't been cuffed in front of her. Adam fared a bit better. He only got a bonked elbow.

"Watch the goods!" he protested to the gray skinned man.

Tusk Man bared the rest of his teeth and pulled a gun from a side holster. He sat on the seat opposite with it trained on them. Blackwater slid in beside him, followed by a hunk of more ordinary muscle in a suit. Ari thought he was human, though she couldn't be sure. Ordinary Goon shut the door, then rapped on the partition for the driver to pull away. As they rolled into motion, he set a small brown rock on the limo floor. He closed his eyes, extended his hands, and muttered a foreign word.

A shock wave made of light burst out from the rock. Ari's brain went completely fuzzy for a second. When it cleared, the rock was gone and a slick of wavering brown light clung to the outer surfaces of their vehicle. It could be seen through from inside, though she doubted the reverse was true.

*Huh,* she thought, intrigued in spite of herself. That's what an obfuscation spell looked like. She wondered if Adam's team would be able to track them when it was on. Their plan didn't depend on them doing so, but it would make her feel better. Possibly Grant would be able to if they couldn't, given his Level Eight mojo.

That thought ran through her brain in a twinkling. It occurred to her the ordinary looking goon wasn't that ordinary after all. She didn't recognize him, so maybe he was Resurrection-only staff. When he noticed her attention, his mouth curved like he wanted to do not-very-nice things to her.

"You wish," she said, at which both Adam and Blackwater laughed.

Their masculine amusement was a tad disturbing. Blackwater's elegant legs were crossed. He flapped the strangely supple gloves he'd removed earlier on his upper thigh.

*Shit*, Ari thought. She just bet those things were gnome skin.

She couldn't keep her muscles from tightening. As they did, Adam's arm shifted beside her, not an actual gesture of reassurance so much as a hint of one.

She realized she was glad he was there. She didn't like depending on other people, and she didn't want him getting hurt on her account. That said, she couldn't deny one important fact.

Adam knew what he was doing.

Willing though Ari was to go to the mat for her friends, the Eunuch had her outclassed. While she might have more power here in Resurrection, so did her enemy.

∞

The limo carried them north and east for about forty minutes. The reason Adam knew this was because his wolf side had an innate sense of direction, one he didn't think the obfuscation spell could mess with. Looking out the window was less informative. Presumably, the driver could see clearly. From the back of the vehicle, the brown tinged landscape was fuzzy and confusing.

The strength of the spell impressed and concerned him at the same time. He doubted his team would be able to track the car. Maybe Grant would, but that wasn't a sure thing. For certain, the Eunuch wasn't pinching pennies when it came to security.

Resurrection's foremost criminal kingpin sat flanked by his men, calm and relaxed as the drive drew out, a sleek golden-haired serpent without a care in the world. He fondled those poncey gloves of his now and then, but that seemed pretension rather than nervousness. One of the few things they knew about Henry Blackwater was that he'd been born to the owners of a tiny cleaning supply store, the sort where people could rent equipment to get stains out of their carpets. He doubted it was coincidence that they'd died in suspicious circumstances soon after Blackwater established his first cross-border trafficking enterprise.

The Eunuch had wanted to erase his humble beginnings.

*He's a drug dealer*, Adam reminded himself. *He may strike terror everywhere he goes, but he isn't anything fancier than that.* Magic-wise, he wasn't much of a power. Barely a Level Two—and who knew how weak he'd been before doing his alleged demon deal? He bought the spells he needed with his profits from exploiting other's weaknesses.

Adam's eyes had gone hard. Blackwater noticed and lifted his brows at him.

"Just admiring the apps on your ride," he said, tapping one knuckle against the clouded brown window.

"Resurrection does offer a special brand of wonders."

"So I'm seeing," Adam said.

The Eunuch's smile was small but satisfied. Adam had just given him something he wanted: implied credit for the mojo his money bought. This might be one reason he collected his entourages of Outsiders. Insiders wouldn't be so easily misled.

Insiders knew a lot of things, including that the difference between Talents and sorcerers was that talent was natural. Sorcerers forced magic to behave in a certain way. Thanks to their training in rituals and spells, they could pull off amazing things—precise, powerful, dangerous things most Talents couldn't dream of. Sorcery was the closest humans came to wielding the power of the fae. The downside was that sorcerers paid a price.

A big spell—say if someone wanted to recreate the Washington Street Bridge disaster on purpose—would cost a sorcerer a year of his life. Activating the obfuscation spell for the limo probably stole a week from the Eunuch's sorcerer-goon. Whoever created the rock that contained the spell likely gave up a month.

With only so much life to spend, sorcerers charged a premium for their services. To do everything he needed, Blackwater probably kept a dozen on retainer.

Adam revised that estimate upward as the limo approached its destination. He was relatively certain they'd entered Clifton Bluffs, a wooded and affluent area overlooking the wilder reaches of the North River. Here every house was a compound, and the neighbors didn't invite each other to barbecues. Some faeries kept residences here, or simply maintained the forest version of no man's land. You wouldn't want to stroll through those spooky trees at night, not unless you were high up in the fae yourself. Adam might be a big bad wolf, but the thought of it was enough to make him suppress a shiver.

If Grant had managed to follow them, Adam hoped he'd be all right out there.

"Home sweet home," Blackwater said as they rolled through an automatic gate that resembled something out of Versailles. The last of the obfuscation spell dissolved, revealing a large white block of a house with narrow Moroccan style windows.

Adam wasn't at all surprised to see every one of them was electrum barred.

The tall gray spink demon with the tusks took charge of Ari, ushering her from the vehicle with more care than he'd initially shoved her in. Spinks could be aggressive, but as demons went, they were reasonably self-controlled. Many worked as bouncers in clubs, a career track that could lead in less savory directions. The human sorcerer-goon looked like he wanted to take Ari into his personal custody, but didn't dare ask his boss for favors. As the spink demon pushed her forward, Ari shot Adam a wide-eyed look over her shoulder.

Adam hated her fear more than he could afford to show. At least he'd warned her they might be separated. From what he knew, the Eunuch was a divide-and-conquer boss. On the semi-bright side, Ari was no burned out Talent like the ones who had disappeared. Her potential usefulness to Blackwater ought to keep her safe for a while.

"Where's the weird guy taking her?" Adam thought it appropriate to ask.

"Oh, no worries," Blackwater said, facing him on a roundabout paved with shiny obsidian stones. "Your girlfriend will be taken excellent care of. We just want her to be . . . secure."

Adam grunted, pursed his lips, then met Blackwater's amused violet eyes. "How come you don't care if I'm secure?"

"I've yet to decide your value. Or the risk you might pose to my operation."

"I won't let you hurt her," he said, but not like he was passionate about it.

Blackwater's thin lips curved up, the idea that Adam had the power to defend her ridiculous to him. "I'm Henry Blackwater," he said, offering his hand.

"Adam," he returned, shaking it. He wasn't going to offer his last name. Full true names could be used in too many spells. Blackwater didn't push. Perhaps he assumed Adam had a history in New York he didn't want him researching.

"You strike me as a sensible man," he said. "Why don't we go inside and discuss your prospects over a drink?"

Adam's touch of Sight allowed him to spot more magic being used inside. The halls of the compound were white and still, their marble floors as shiny as hockey rinks. Here and there, the walls showed glimmering signs of spy runes and magical alarms. He knew they were searching him for weapons and surveillance devices.

The weapons—a knife holstered at his ankle and a set of brass knuckles—would be spotted and probably ignored. He'd have seemed more suspicious if he'd left them at home. By contrast, the tiny subdermal bugs were well camouflaged. Without the right sort of scanner, Adam might not find them again himself. They'd remain inactive until he turned them on, which he wouldn't do unless Blackwater appeared about to incriminate himself. Once he'd recorded what seemed prosecutable, Adam would send the data to his team in one lightning burst. Because the transmission would set off alarms, he'd have to be strategic. That the message would get through he felt confident.

Resurrection's police force had its own magical personnel.

After a heated debate among the squad, they'd decided not to wire Ari. She had an emergency transmitter and that was it. Adam hadn't wanted to risk even a remote chance that the bugs would be discovered on her. She was his ticket in here. That was more than enough risk for her.

A brief flash of heat at his neck informed him his saint medal had just been scanned. He was grateful he'd never had it charmed Any protective qualities it had came from faith alone.

Apparently, this concluded Blackwater's magical gauntlet. The hall they'd been walking down ended in a pair of shiny white paneled doors. Blackwater opened them.

"Please," he said, gesturing Adam ahead of him.

Cautious, Adam stepped into a large high-ceilinged office. Three narrow windows were spaced along one wall, their view blocked by overgrown yew trees. Some light filtered in, revealing a space decorated in unrelieved white and gray. Even for Nate, the decor was overdoing the cool. Adam's detective liked plenty of color to spice up his modern style.

"Drink?" Blackwater offered.

Without waiting for an answer, he poured two glasses of an insanely expensive single malt. He handed a glass to Adam, who sipped it like he didn't want to let on this booze was more sophisticated than his usual.

Given his salary, he didn't have to pretend hard.

"Nice," he said and continued wandering the office with his tumbler in hand.

He tipped his eyeglasses back into his hair, which he'd seen Outsiders do on TV shows. Blackwater watched everything he did, his hips resting on the front of a bleached-looking driftwood desk. Ari had mentioned he disliked computers, and there were none in sight. Did he keep handwritten ledgers? Maybe in that long white wall of locked cabinets? The man seemed vain enough to want to store the records of his financial victories close at hand. Maybe he fondled them during his down time.

If the stories were true, ledgers were all he had for that.

"So," his host began, taking a sip himself. "You and my old friend, Ari . . ."

Adam allowed himself a laugh. "Ari doesn't call you her friend."

Blackwater didn't like that, but it wasn't enough to make him angry. "I'm curious to know how you met. If you'll forgive my saying so, you're more . . . mature than her usual boyfriends."

That was a nice double dig: calling him old *and* reminding him Ari had a romantic past. Though he bristled inside, Adam shrugged. "Some girls dig older men."

"Some girls always fall for users."

Adam smiled with one corner of his mouth. "Ari's nice. A guy like me could hook up with worse."

Distaste flicked across Blackwater's features. He pulled himself back on track. "And you met . . . ?"

Adam threw off another shrug. "I was doing my thing in the park one night. Lighting trashcans on fire. I like to practice. Ari saw and realized we had an interest in common."

Blackwater set down his drink. "She never mentioned you to me."

"Why would she? You and she were on the outs by then." Adam dropped into a white horsehide chair whose sides were wrapped in riveted aluminum. The tightening of Blackwater's lips betrayed how little he appreciated Adam sitting without an invitation. Adam threw his vanity a bone. "I gotta say, this is a sweet set up."

Blackwater considered him coolly. "Why did you come to Resurrection?"

"Ari told me about this place. She said I'd have more juice here, and described the elves and shit. I thought it'd be cool to see. Of course, I also thought she might have been confused by an acid trip."

"And now?"

"Now I think it's freaking awesome. I hardly have to work here to do my thing."

One of Blackwater's fingertips tapped the rim of his glass. "Ari didn't bring you here just to entertain you."

Adam leaned back in the hide-and-aluminum chair. Maybe Nate should get one of these. It really was comfortable. "Ari seemed to think she could use backup when she came to discuss your issues."

Blackwater rose and paced to the middle of his three windows. Adam didn't think his feelings were hurt by Ari's precautions. He seemed more like he was worried. It was the first real crack Adam had seen in his confidence. Maybe the Eunuch didn't just *want* Ari back in the fold. Maybe he *needed* her for something.

He stood where he was, looking out at the tangled yew, not speaking. After a minute, he turned back to Adam. "What sort of 'backup' are you interested in being?"

"Well, that depends," Adam said. "I like the girl, but as you pointed out, I'm a sensible man. Seems to me you've hired people with my sort of skills before."

Blackwater might not have known it, but his face got smoother when he relaxed. "You'd be more valuable to me if you could convince her to cooperate."

Adam's mouth stretched into a grin. "Cooperative women are my specialty."

Blackwater didn't look convinced. Mostly, he looked faintly disgusted. If he had sacrificed his genitalia to a demon, maybe he made himself feel better about it by looking down on people who still enjoyed the use of theirs. For the moment, that didn't matter. Any plan that put him and Ari back together, where Adam could watch over her, was inherently better than a plan that kept them apart.

Ari's cuffs had been removed, but the room she'd been put in might as well have been a cell. It had no handle inside the door, one small barred window too high to see out of, and a gray futon with no frame and no bedding. What she'd thought was a closet turned out to be a cramped bathroom.

*En suite!* she joked to herself. *You must be a VIP.*

What truly bugged her, of course, was that the room was charmed to damp her power. She couldn't use her telekinesis to break out. Then again, with all of Blackwater's guards, she wouldn't have gotten far. She'd just have felt better sneaking out, and she'd have poked around.

That was why they were here, after all. To get the goods on the Eunuch so the law could put him away.

God, she should have killed him back in Manhattan.

She paced to keep herself from going crazy. After a bit of that, she noticed the floor tingled in its center, straight through her sneaker soles. Curious, she hunkered over the spot.

Was this where the depowering charm was placed? The smooth white tile appeared featureless. Ari patted it, then cocked her head.

Did she hear chanting?

She pressed her ear to the floor. Yes, that was chanting, and whoever was doing it hailed from New Jersey. Her cell was being charmed by a fellow Outsider.

She sat back on her heels as the chanting stopped, both offended and befuddled. The spell caster had done something. The walls felt subtly tighter around her.

The puzzle would have to wait. Her door was opened by a guard, and Adam strolled in like the Lord of Flatbush. His hot geek glasses were on top of his head. He folded them, then tossed them onto the bare futon.

"Hey, babe," he said cockily.

The door clicked closed again as she rose.

"C'mere," he said, putting out his arms. Ari wasn't sure what script she ought to follow, but she went to him anyway. Though she knew they were being watched, possibly with more spells, his strong embrace felt like heaven. The smell of him equalled comfort, the heat of him and the size. He buried his nose in her neck and groaned.

"You kill me, babe," he said.

She felt his arousal, that he couldn't suppress it even now. His hands slid up and down her back, a ridge beginning to harden within his jeans. Ari leaned back before she lost the strength to. "What did Blackwater say?"

His hands locked behind her waist, keeping his hips on hers. "I think maybe you haven't given him a fair shake."

"What?" She knew he was feigning this attitude, but her outrage came naturally.

"He's only trying to run his business. He needs you to help him out."

"He hurt my friends. He's holding us prisoner."

"Do I look like a prisoner?"

She tried to fling away from him, but he held her secure. His strength did funny things to her hormones. Heat flashed through her pussy, thickening its walls and slicking them with wetness. Nostrils flaring, Adam growled and kissed her.

She must have kissed him back too well, because his canines lengthened. When he pulled back, he kept their foreheads together. "Your friends aren't here, babe. I am. Sometimes you have to be practical."

"You dick!" She shoved him—possibly for the secret pleasure of being unable to budge his hard muscles. "I asked you to come with me to back me up."

"Sometimes plans have to change." He stroked the side of her cheek. If she hadn't known what it would cost her, those soft green eyes might have made her forget right and wrong. They were awfully seductive. "You could do the man a little favor. He's not asking for the moon."

"He starts with little favors. He ends by me murdering someone."

"Don't be a drama queen." His hand slid under her jacket to cup her breast. His canines had gone back to normal, but the brush of her budded nipple darkened his eyes. "We could do all right here, Ari. You and me, playing around with our special gifts. We wouldn't even be freaks."

"Blackwater is a bad person."

Adam palmed her butt with his second hand and dragged her hips closer. God, he was hard now. And big. Her pussy was melting, her nipples tight and hot. When he plucked one with his thumb and fingers, she couldn't help moaning.

"That's more like it," he said.

He kissed her like he wasn't going to stop this time, like this was going to finish with his giant hard-on rammed up inside of her. He lifted her, urging her suddenly shaking legs around his waist. The huge bulge behind his zipper rolled against her deliciously.

Ari wanted him, but she drew the line at screwing him in front of Blackwater. She struggled, which Adam put an end to by slamming her into the wall.

She really shouldn't have found that a turn-on.

"Trust me, babe," he said huskily, beginning to push up her shirt front. "I'll get us through this."

She wore a bra today, but he pushed that up too. He ducked and his lips sealed warmly around her nipple, sucking and flicking it with his tongue. She told herself at least he was hiding her from view, but that was only useful if he didn't undress her more.

"Adam."

He stepped them onto the futon, where he dropped to his knees. His eyes were very close to burning as he laid her back under him. She felt him work the front of his jeans open. The metal button, the zipper . . . Her excitement spiked so high she knew she needed to stop this now.

"*Adam*," she said more insistently.

"Sh." Holding her with his gaze, he unzipped her jeans and wedged his hand down the opening.

She forgot everything but him. His longest finger cruised into her red-hot folds and all she could do was feel. She writhed for him, trying to get the finger to curl inside her sheath. He wouldn't do it. Groaning, he rubbed her clit from side to side *almost* fast enough to make her come. She stretched up and kissed him again. Her eagerness seemed to push him over some edge. Grunting with impatience, he picked up his hips to shove his jeans and underwear further down. His pelvis came back naked, his erection long and hot on her denim-covered thigh. Ari moaned her approval into his mouth, caressing his now bare ass.

Without warning, the bond his bite had created became ten times more alive. Suddenly, the urges that gripped him bombarded her. He could take her. She was ready. His cock was leaking excitement onto her skin. He wanted to claim her in the most basic way males had. He wasn't going to be happy until he impaled her.

*Yes*, she thought, her thighs straining wider.

Adam tore his lips from hers.

"Okay," he panted. "The watching spells have turned off. We should be able to talk, though probably not for long. Blackwater will check again when he thinks we're done. Hopefully, he doesn't take me for a five-minute guy."

"What?" Ari's brain was sluggish from the way her body was jangling.

"I figured he'd turn them off. He seems to find the idea of sex repugnant." He rolled off her with a sigh. "Are you all right?"

Apart from being yanked back an inch short of bliss, she was peachy. To be fair, he didn't look so happy about pulling back either. His face was strained and glistened with a light sweat. He started to tuck his cock away, then winced.

"Sure," she said, squirming into a more comfortable position on her side—or as comfortable as she'd get with her pussy pounding like a marching band. His expression softened as she came closer, which sort of squeezed her heart. Ignoring that, she shared what she'd found out, little though it was. "There's a room under this one. I heard someone chanting. Someone from New Jersey."

"Are you sure? Some of Resurrection's accents are pretty close."

"I know my Jersey shore," she said.

Adam rubbed her shoulder as if touching her helped him think. "If Blackwater is training Outside Talents to cast spells, maybe that's how he burns them out. He could be promising them they'll up their juice that way. They might not realize what it's costing them."

Despite the rock-hard rod that continued to throb from his unzipped jeans, he explained how sorcerers paid the bill for the rituals they performed. The idea creeped her. She'd stick with her Talent the way it was. Or at least she'd stick with whatever improvements plain old practice could bring her.

"These spell things have to be recharged?" she asked, thinking that might have caused the walls to feel more closed in.

He nodded. "That's one of the reasons Blackwater sometimes turns them off. He doesn't want the batteries running down. What I'm wondering is why didn't he burn you out like the others? What's he saving you for?"

The question gave her a chill, which Adam soothed by chafing her arm. "I have no idea," she said. "I don't know of any way I'm different from the others. Outside, lots of them were better with their gifts than me."

"He's worried about something. I could tell when he so graciously invited me to be a part of his team."

"What favor did he want to ask me?"

"He didn't give details. All I know is it has to do with some club he's going to tonight. He wants us to come with him."

"I guess we're going then," she said resignedly.

Adam kissed the tip of her nose. "Do you want me to finish you?" he asked, nodding toward the gaping zipper of her jeans.

She did, but the implication that she was the one who needed it frosted her.

"I'd like it if we both went," he said softly.

His mind-reading would choose then to kick in.

"You kill me, babe," she said wryly, and wrapped her hand firmly around him.

As cheap thrills went, the blazing heat of his cock definitely rated.

They were both businesslike about getting off, considering how little time they were likely to have. Adam's hand worked faster than hers, but he was really ready to go. His body tensed and he blasted off maybe ten seconds before she did.

The little sounds he made as he shot his load drove her crazy: not quite grunts, not quite moans, but like going with her hand on him was extremely enjoyable. Those noises were the best soundtrack ever to come by.

She had the sinking feeling the memory of that soundtrack was going to keep many future climaxes company. Adam's wolfy libido was the stuff fantasies were made of.

# CHAPTER EIGHT

The club was in East Elfyunk, a mixed-income, mixed-race suburb outside the city core. They drove there in a massive tricked-out black Hummer. Blackwater didn't bother with an obfuscation spell, though he did bring along the spink demon and two more hunks of muscle for bodyguards. One of them was the beefy sorcerer, whom Adam learned was named Francis. He probably preferred Frank, but that would just make Blackwater enjoy calling him Francis more.

Given how he'd eyed Ari earlier, Adam didn't feel too sorry for him.

He forgot him entirely when he saw the sign for the worn down two-story building that housed their destination. Adam had heard about this place. He had an immediate inkling why they'd come.

Evie's was a supper and music club that had been popular since the 1930s. Criminals liked it, but so did succeeding generations of Resurrection's youth. For them, the air of danger added to its cachet. Though it was Tuesday, a slow night for many places, the graveled parking lot that surrounded the club was packed. Their driver handed a bribe to the attendant and got them a reserved spot.

"Who's Evie?" Ari asked as Adam helped her climb out. This was more than politeness. The dress Blackwater had sent to their room wasn't designed for getting in and out of large vehicles. The slinky gray satin number was spared from baring the hooch in her coochie only by its final layer of fringe. Ari grimaced as the strappy heels he'd included wobbled on the gravel, but Adam had to admit she looked amazing.

This was a different sort of dress from Maria's. In it, Ari was a woman and not a girl, one with the power to turn heads. Blackwater might not be personally interested in that, but his pride would enjoy being seen with a female other men would admire.

"Evie isn't a who, my dear," he said now. "Evie is a what."

When the Eunuch stepped out of the Hummer, one of the goons brushed his spotless cream linen suit for him.

"Okay," Ari said. "*What's* Evie?"

"Evie is Mariska Andoor. She owns the club, and she's an elf-vampire, hence E.V."

"What does that even mean?" Ari asked. "She only drinks blood on St. Patrick's day?"

Blackwater laughed lightly. "Ah Ari, how I've missed your sense of humor."

His tone gave Adam a turn, reminding him there'd been a time when the Eunuch and Ari might have been if not friends at least friendly. He'd saved Ari and her companions from starving on the street. She must have felt grateful to him, until she figured out how dark his nature was.

Maybe Ari was remembering too. She frowned and smoothed her dress's fringe down her upper legs. "How do you make an elf-vampire? Do the vampires bite them?"

Blackwater enjoyed playing teacher, which she likely knew. "Elves can't be turned, but they are one of only two races who can breed with vampires. Vampires can't breed amongst themselves, of course, not being alive anymore."

"Who's the other race?" Ari asked, clearly curious in spite of her dislike.

"Faeries," he said. "But there aren't many who'd stoop to it. Reproducing with anyone but themselves—and never mind the undead—generally isn't their style."

Blackwater said this differently than Adam would have. He could tell the Eunuch approved of their elitism.

The conversation had taken their little group around the side of the brick-clad building to the faded red awning that sheltered the front walk. A blue elf, one of the more solidly built subspecies, was vetting the night's customers. He looked dubiously at the Eunuch, who he obviously recognized.

"Just visiting," Blackwater said, his palms exposed and his mouth gleeful. "You know how I admire Mariska's talent."

That the blue-skinned man wanted to turn him away was clear. That he didn't dare to, equally so. "Lord Grygir is here tonight," he said stiffly. "We don't want trouble."

Blackwater's teeth seemed to sparkle, he'd bared them so broadly. "When have I ever caused trouble? I assure you, I'm delighted Lord Grygir is in attendance."

Adam wasn't sure *he* was. Lord Grygir, a pureblood fae, ran most of the strip clubs in Resurrection, a business Blackwater had been trying without success to encroach on. His own disinterest in sex aside, he'd have been happy to cut a slice of that lucrative pie. Adam didn't believe for a moment Blackwater hadn't known the fae would be here.

"Fine," the blue elf surrendered. "Just remember, we will call the cops if you give us cause."

He waved the rest of Blackwater's group through without comment. As they passed inside, Ari took Adam's hand and held on. She might not know the players, but she'd be no stranger to her old boss's mood. Adam suspected she knew more was on tonight's agenda than a pleasant evening of listening to music.

∞

Evie's was exactly the sort of club she and Max and Sarah would save their nickels to go to. Music was their shared passion, part of what had drawn them together. The performer wasn't on stage yet, but the recording coming through the speakers inspired a smile: Jamaican reggae with a head-bobbing beat. This wasn't big-label music; this was home grown imported stuff.

The main room was a sea of, well, not exactly humanity but certainly people. Drawn together by their air of anticipation, they sat at round white-clothed tables, vampires next to elves next to who knew what. Candles flickered in glass votives, wisps of smoke rising to a stamped tin ceiling. Underneath the fresh table cloths and the flowers, the atmosphere was a little divey, though not so divey it would stick to your feet. Ari imagined the decor hadn't changed much since the place had been built. Its very datedness made it cool. Lots of good music had soaked into these age-browned walls.

Seats were found for Henry Blackwater's party at a small corner table near the front. To Ari's dismay, her chair was squished close enough to Blackwater's for their sides to bump. Blackwater didn't seem to mind or even notice. His trouser leg brushed her calf as he tapped his foot to the beat. Then again, he might have been messing with her on purpose, because he knew she'd dislike him touching her.

At least Adam was on her other side.

The chairs' backs were turned toward the table so they could see the stage. Ari tried to distract herself from Blackwater by checking out the groups next to them. Surprisingly, no one was checking out Blackwater. He was sufficiently distinctive to draw eyes, but tonight everyone's attention seemed directed toward a table front and center before the stage.

Ari craned forward to see who sat at it.

There was just one man. He was tall and lean and dressed very much like Adam in a casual business shirt and jeans. A carafe of orange juice—chilled to judge by its condensing sides—sat behind his elbow with an empty wine glass. Maybe fruit juice was his species' version of alcohol. If it was, he wasn't imbibing. Positioned to face the stage, he leaned forward over his knees with his gaze on the floor. His hands were clasped together as if he were praying. He seemed too deep in thought to be aware of the eyes on him.

Ari understood why they couldn't look away. He was the most beautiful being she'd ever seen.

Adam was a handsome man. So was Blackwater, in his skin crawly way. This male threw off beauty like pollen. He was angel-gorgeous. Polished and buffed, his masculine splendor was touched with the perfect dollop of sweetness. Just staring at him gave her a little high.

This had to be the fae Lord Grygir. When Adam slid his hand to lightly rub the back of her neck, the reminder that any other man existed came as a shock.

She snuck a glance at Blackwater, whose gaze was also locked on the fae. His expression was . . . illuminating. If she hadn't believed him to be incapable of attraction, she'd have said he was staring at the object of a crush—one he fiercely resented experiencing.

She wrenched her attention away before Blackwater could see she'd noticed. Her hand was on Adam's kneecap, clutching it like she needed a lifeline to steady her. A lifeline wasn't all she needed. The flowery scent that lent Resurrection its trademark aroma wafted strongly from Lord Grygir. It smelled so good she wanted to hang her tongue out and pant.

Adam nuzzled her ear, teeth closing over her lobe in a gentle nip. "Faerie dust," he whispered. "It's a mild aphrodisiac."

If this was mild, she'd hate to see intense. She was perspiring from arousal, and they'd barely been here five minutes. Adam released her ear and patted the hand she'd clamped on his knee. For a second, she wanted him so badly she couldn't think.

It was a relief when the faerie lifted his head, his focus drawn to the room's wide door. Then she saw the arrogance Adam had mentioned the fae having, but maybe *pride* was a better word. Lord Grygir's spine was as erect as a general's, his shoulders born in review posture. No woman with a shred of sense would fall for a man like that. He'd grind her into powder under one autocratic heel.

And then Mariska Andoor entered the room.

Ari didn't know how to describe Grygir's reaction except to say that joy washed through him. His eyes lit up and his proud mouth went soft. His beauty simply hurt then, the cool superiority gone from it. He was a young man in love, maybe for the first time. Her knowledge that his people probably disapproved only made him more romantic. His love was forbidden, but he loved anyway.

Ari gave the elf-vampire a heap of credit for not leaping into his arms. Instead, she nodded at him warily, circling him a bit further off than necessary to reach the small raised platform at the front of the room. Ari was amazed to find a quartet of musicians sitting there with their instruments. She'd bet she wasn't the only one who hadn't seen them come in.

Mariska pulled the microphone from its stand. "Good evening, everyone," she said.

For the first time, Ari really looked at her. She wasn't breathtaking like Lord Grygir, but she was really cute. Slender and vampire pale, she lacked elf ears but did have elfin eyes. They were green and slanted and fringed thickly with dark lashes. Her brunette hair was cropped very short, her nose was a button, and her little bowed mouth was as red as a kewpie doll's. Her tatas were small but knockouts, a pair of peaches nestled in the low cut bodice of her blue velvet dress. Ari could see why the stuck up faerie would go for her. She looked like someone who'd be a hundred times more fun than him.

Mariska turned slightly, signaling to her band. They struck up an old jazzy tune. The elf-vampire swayed, drew a breast-lifting breath, and then she began to sing.

Every hair on Ari's arms stood up. Maybe the faerie liked the club owner for more than her cuteness. Mariska's voice was amazing, like Lena Horne crossed with Rihanna. She knew how to use her pipes, for real, her delivery not just deft but emotional. Ari didn't recognize the song, something about dark alleys and the ill-fated women who wandered into them. Possibly the composer was from Resurrection. She found herself wishing Max and Sarah could be there to share her pleasure.

When Adam's fingers rubbed hers, it was almost a good enough substitute.

Blackwater let her enjoy two songs before pressing a piece of paper that had been folded into an origami pocket into her hands. Ari squeezed it open, dread gripping her. Two locks of hair lay inside, one of them Maxwell's russet brown, the other Sarah's honey gold. Tears she couldn't control swarmed into her eyes.

Blackwater leaned closer to her ear. "I just want you to know," he murmured, "that even though you and I are here, it's always possible for me to reach out and touch your friends."

She'd known that. She just hadn't thought he would. Always before when he'd disappeared from Manhattan, no one would hear from him. Ari swallowed the lump in her throat.

"What do you want from me?" she asked.

"I want you to sever her vocal chords."

He didn't look at Mariska, but Ari knew which her he meant. She understood immediately that the singer wasn't who Blackwater was striking at, he was striking at Lord Grygir. That was the Eunuch's MO, to hurt his opponents through the people they cared about.

"I might kill her," she objected—stupidly, no doubt.

"Not if you're careful," Blackwater said silkily.

"Will she heal?"

The Eunuch smiled with only his violet eyes, which were too avid for comfort. "Magically inflicted injuries tend to leave terrible scars on vampires."

So she'd never sing again. Not for the enraptured crowd made one by her magic voice. Not for the man who loved her. Not even for herself. Ari could tell what singing meant to the club owner, how it was the true expression of her soul. Severing her vocal chords would be like cutting off Jimmy Hendrix's hands, a theft the whole world would be poorer for.

No matter how much they wanted to live, neither Maxwell nor Sarah would approve of her doing this.

"I can't," she began to plead, but Adam chose then to lean across her shoulder.

"I'll fry the bitch if you want," he said.

His werewolf hearing must have picked up their conversation.

"That won't do," Blackwater said primly.

"The fuck it won't," Adam said. "Ari ain't gonna cave for you."

Before either of them could stop him, Adam extended both index fingers and shot two shimmering lines of power from between his knees toward the stage. The carpet to either side of Mariska's heels ignited in foot-high flames. The singer let out a shriek that actually shattered a few wineglasses. Despite this feat, Ari gawked at Adam, stunned by the image of the blazing fire reflected in his horn-rimmed lenses. He was a cop, sworn to protect and serve. What the hell was he doing?

"Shit," he muttered. "My aim is crap."

Her sanity recovered. He'd missed the singer on purpose. He'd been trying to spare Ari a terrible choice. As soon as relief welled up, terror swallowed it. What if Blackwater figured out what he'd done?

Adam must have known this was a concern. He furrowed his brow and squinted behind his glasses, his fingers straightening to try again.

Blackwater seized his fire-tattooed wrist before he could. "Idiot. I told you that wouldn't do."

At least the crowd wasn't watching them. They were screaming, the ones in front jumping to their feet, the ones in back trying to reach the exit as an assortment of shrill alarms went off. Growling curses, Blackwater grabbed Ari and Adam by the scruff of their necks. He pushed them ahead of him into the panicked mass of people. Ari saw Lord Grygir leap across the flames to where Mariska was cowering. Ignoring the musicians, he scooped the singer up in his arms—her knight in faerie armor, she supposed. He took a second to stare deeply into her eyes, then whizzed away with her like a special effect out a movie. A wake of sparkles trailed after him.

"*Move*," Blackwater ordered, clearly incensed by the rescue.

They moved and kept on moving, even when some bright soul found a fire extinguisher and doused the flames into submission.

By the time they and the bodyguards reached the Hummer, Blackwater's curses had sunk into brooding. From experience, Ari knew this wasn't a good sign.

He didn't speak during the ride home, just wedged himself beside a window and drummed his long fingers on his thigh. With his other hand he pinched his lower lip. His gnome-skin gloves made this especially creepy.

"Boss," said the one called Francis, "do you want us to—"

Blackwater shut him up with a glare.

The tense silence reigned until they pulled up in front of the house. The roundabout's obsidian pavers were shiny enough to reflect the moon.

Blackwater craned his neck to consider the satellite. Like a poster for a horror movie, the moon illuminated the edges of a window in the clouds. Its phase wasn't full, but it was past three quarters. Ari wondered how close it needed to be before it tugged Adam into turning. Could he resist it? Would they be gone from here by then?

The state of the moon seemed to weigh on Blackwater too. His jaw tightened as he stared at it.

A distinctive winged silhouette crossed the glowing edge of the clouds. Ari's heart leaped to recognize it. Grant had found them. He could tell Adam's team where they were.

"Fuck," Blackwater spat. "Darius, shoot that down."

Darius was the tusked demon. He pulled out a silver pistol and steadied it on his thick gray wrist.

"No!" Ari cried, running toward him without thinking.

The gun went off as she hit the spink. Darius was eight feet tall and quite a few feet wide. Ari wasn't going to knock him over. She barely made him move, though the jostling ruined his aim. Grant wheeled away, apparently unharmed, disappearing over the neighboring woods.

Darius turned to gape at her, clearly having trouble believing she'd just done that.

"Gargoyles are pests," he said in a slow deep voice. "Giant gnomes with wings. And they spy."

Ari wasn't sure she should admit she knew they were sentient beings. "They're cute," she said. "And I wouldn't watch you shoot gnomes either."

Eyes rounded with amazement, he looked over her head to his boss, obviously seeking instruction. Ari knew she didn't want to see the Eunuch's expression.

"Get her out of my sight," he said through gritted teeth. "And post someone on the roof to take down that gargoyle if it returns. I don't care if they need a bazooka."

Orders received, Darius caught her upper arm in his massive hand, his grip more than swallowing its circumference. He pulled her fast enough to make her stumble, especially in the stupid strappy heels she wore. Each time she fell, he simply lifted her off the ground and set her down again. Ari had had nightmares about things like this, about being a child and too small to fight being dragged along. To her surprise, once they were out of sight and inside the house, Darius moderated his pace to one closer to her own. Ari panted to catch her breath, too afraid to ask him to slow more.

"Human," he rumbled when they reached the door to her cell room. "You'd better stop doing crazy things. I've seen that man kill girls like you for less."

This was quite a speech for someone she hadn't heard say a word until tonight.

"You can't *like* working for Blackwater," she burst out impulsively.

"He pays," said the demon. "And I'd rather live here than home."

This was all the explanation she was going to get. He propelled her into the room as if her comment had angered him more than her spoiling his shot. The door closed with a resounding thud.

A prisoner behind it, Ari rubbed her arm where it felt like the demon had crushed her muscles.

*Way to go,* she thought dryly. *Always making friends and influencing people.*

∞

Adam no longer had to wonder why the gargoyles had a grudge against Blackwater. The paranoid crime lord must have killed a few already. Adam's heart had just about stopped when Ari rushed Darius.

She hadn't known Grant wasn't in real danger. It *would* take a bazooka to kill a gargoyle from that distance. She probably thought Adam was a dolt for standing there with his mouth open. But at least his inaction was consistent with the role he'd assumed.

He consoled himself that she'd know he'd meant to miss setting Mariska Andoor on fire.

"Look," he said to Blackwater, judging it time to speak. "I'm sorry I didn't hit your target back at the club, but I know Ari. She wouldn't have gone along. She's got a thing about hurting innocents."

Blackwater's jaw worked with rage, his elegant profile to Adam. When he turned to face him, Adam didn't have to fake a flinch. There was more than a hint of crazy behind his glare. "I suppose it's too bad for you that I needed *her* to do as I asked."

This was an interesting emphasis, almost as interesting as Blackwater ordering Darius to get her out of his sight, presumably before his anger drove him to injure her.

"I can talk to her again," Adam offered, nudging his borrowed glasses to the bridge of his nose. "Try to make it up to you."

Blackwater slitted his eyes at him. "Oh, you'll be making this up to me, one way or another."

On that ominous note, he stalked to the compound's entry, leaving Adam to trail behind, which he did reluctantly. One of Blackwater's human goons was holding the door open.

"Where's Vito?" the big boss demanded.

"Uh," said the suited man, looking highly uncomfortable. "I'm sorry to be the one to tell you, but that last spell shorted Vito out. He dropped and went an hour after dinner."

"Dropped and *went*?" Blackwater repeated dangerously. "Vito is dead?"

Such was Blackwater's authority that, if they'd been wolves, the hulking goon would have been groveling on the floor. Instead, his shoulders hunched and his head ducked lower. "I'm sorry, sir. We didn't know he was that bad off."

"*Didn't know?*" Blackwater screamed at him. He lashed out, taking the cringing man so harshly across his face that his gloved fist split the skin over one cheekbone. "What do I pay you idiots for?"

His employee put up no defense, just covered his bloodied cheek and bowed nervously. "Do you want me to call in another of the trained Talents?"

"I need them," Blackwater huffed, his fit of rage easing. "They've still got plenty of juice left."

The frightened goon's eyes cut to Adam.

*Uh, oh,* Adam thought, not liking that even before Blackwater's cool gaze joined in.

"Hey," Adam said, hoping to head off whatever this was. "I've got juice left."

"Yes, you do," the boss man agreed. "But since you're currently proving less useful than I'd hoped, I'll squeeze a bit of it out early."

∞

Ari had been correct about the house having a basement. In contrast to the sleek white and gray ground floor, the basement was unfinished, low of ceiling, and wired like a spaghetti factory. Who needed a firebug when they had incompetent electricians? If the place hadn't been built mainly of concrete block, Adam would have worried about them burning up in their beds.

The code violations couldn't quite distract him from the fun he knew was coming.

The Eunuch's hired muscle shoved him through what looked like the door to a utility room but turned out not to be. Adam fell to his hands and knees not on more cement, but on a smooth and tingling electrum floor. The alloy of gold and silver was ideal for holding magic, which was why security grills and charms were so often made from it. The more electrum got used, the better it worked—not unlike seasoning a cast iron pan. This electrum was warm under Adam's palms, so it must have been used a lot. Adam concluded Blackwater's pet sorcerers performed the majority of their rituals here.

As his eyes adjusted to the flickering florescent light, he discerned faint chalk lines on the burnished metal—probably the remnants of the spell that had killed the unfortunate Vito from New Jersey.

"Chain him," Blackwater ordered from behind him.

Adam struggled, but not as hard as he could. Avoiding what was coming wouldn't gain him much. Blackwater had more muscle to throw at him, some of it equal to his greater than human strength. He'd simply have betrayed an advantage he preferred keeping to himself for now. In any case, escaping before he had an exit strategy for Ari wasn't an option. Whatever value she had for Blackwater, Adam couldn't count on him not hurting her while he went for the cavalry.

On the other hand, Adam didn't hesitate to give the door-goon and Francis a few oven-fresh bruises.

In the end, they chained him to eyebolts in the wall with four lengths of iron chain, his wrists and ankles spread like daVinci's Vitruvian Man. The wall he was fastened to was bare but for water pipes. Metal storage shelves lined the others, holding items in mason jars and bowls that were best not examined closely. Many ingredients for ritual magic were every bit as disgusting as non-practitioners had heard.

More prosaic but hardly less alarming were a garden hose attached to a spigot, a handsaw, and a drain cut into the silvery-gold floor. Rust-like stains splotched the area around it. That they weren't rust Adam felt pretty sure.

"Open it," Blackwater said to his sorcerer.

Adam smelled Francis's sudden anxiety. Nonetheless, he obeyed his boss's cryptic order. He grabbed two raw quartz crystals from a shelf, plus a bowl of ingredients.

Adam's stomach clenched when he recognized the new chalk pattern Francis knelt down to draw.

The sorcerer was opening an illegal portal, a door to a different dimension. It wasn't a benign bunny realm either. The protective runes he worked into his circle were designed to contain highly unsafe energies.

Francis was no bunny himself, but he was sweating when he finished. He didn't like the idea of opening this gate any more than Adam did. Adam was glad he'd activated his subdermal recorders back at the club. The Eunuch could get quite a few years in prison for what he'd asked Ari to do. For this act, if the dimension he was accessing was dangerous enough, he could get the needle.

The hidden bugs were designed to see and hear through Adam's skin, and to survive his death by any number of gruesome means. Being grateful for that wasn't the most heartening reaction he could have had.

"Ready, boss," Francis said nervously.

Blackwater waved for him to proceed, the tension that had also come into him less than reassuring. Blackwater's nerves were steelier than his employee's, but he wasn't calm either.

Francis knelt outside his circle, bowed his head, and began murmuring in the language of the high fae. Adam wasn't fluent, but he knew enough to realize he was addressing an intelligent entity.

*Great,* Adam thought, sweat breaking out underneath his outstretched arms. Francis was summoning a demon.

Francis set fire to something black and squishy that had lain in the bowl. The two quartz crystals sat inside the chalk circle, maybe four feet apart. As the foul black thing burned, light streaked up from the quartz, inscribing the shape of a door frame. Francis chanted louder, beads of sweat rolling down his temples as he began to shake. This spell was going to cost some sand from his hourglass, knowledge that wasn't comforting Adam much.

"You sure your boy should be doing this?" he rasped. "He doesn't look so hot."

Not surprisingly, no one bothered to answer him.

The air within the light-door darkened and rippled. Adam smelled the tang of eucalyptus oil and sulfur. True to lore, sulfur rarely signified pleasant guests.

*Crap,* he thought. He did not want to die tonight, not when he'd finally found his twin flame.

In spite of his situation, his thoughts shocked him. He'd tried to deny what Ari was to him as superstitious nonsense, or as something too rare and fine for a down to earth wolf like him. Maybe he'd been afraid to hope for what his parents had. Maybe he'd thought he didn't deserve it. Now, as he faced his death, those denials were stripped from him.

Ari was the mate to his spirit. Given a choice, he'd have chosen her. She was the whole package: brains, heart, a body that made him ache just to think about being holding it. How many cops would have been as good an undercover partner as she was? Nate was the best he knew, and Ari was nearly as quick-witted. Yes, she could have blown it big-time when she'd charged Darius to save Grant, but that just proved how brave and decent she was.

The only thing that could have made him prouder than loving her would be having her love him back.

He'd never know whether that could happen if he bit it tonight.

*Cuz,* he thought, *your timing could be better.*

"Who summons me?" uttered a voice like doom itself. The spink demon would have shivered had he been there, and that guy's voice rivaled James Earl Jones.

"'tis I, Henry the Eunuch," Blackwater answered formally.

A head materialized in the gloom of the door. The demon wasn't hideous, merely foreign, its skin the color of indigo. Scarcely any flesh lay between its skin and skull, giving it a starved appearance. It had two large dark eyes, one sharp nose, and a wide lipless mouth full of white pointy teeth. Its ears were holes and its scalp was hairless. Black veins branched in strangely graceful trees through its dark blue skin. Though Adam had seen stranger creatures, he couldn't recall feeling worse. This demon radiated malevolence and hunger, even through the protective wards. It made Adam glad Francis appeared to know what he was doing.

It also made him wish Francis didn't currently look like Death warmed over.

"Where is my payment?" the demon asked.

"It's almost ready," Blackwater said with admirable sang-froid. "Only a few details remain to put in place."

"You're cutting it a little close," the demon observed. "You know what I'll take instead if I don't get it by your full moon."

"I am aware," Blackwater said, bowing.

The demon's use of slang sent unease skittering down Adam's spine. Blackwater must have been summoning it for a while, long enough that it had become familiar with their realm, long enough that it probably hoped to gain entry. Call Adam crazy, but he didn't think this particular demon could meet the Department of Immigration's qualifications for a work visa.

"In the meantime," Blackwater continued, still in his bowed posture, "I thought you might accept a token of my respect."

As Blackwater waved toward Adam, the demon seemed to notice other people were in the room outside its portal. Its eyes narrowed and its nostrils flared. The latter worried Adam more than the former.

If a non-were knew what to look for, it was possible to identify a were by smell. Once a year, at their annual checkup, Adam and his detectives had a spell renewed to reduce the chance of that happening. So many wolves went into police work that being "sniffed out"—as it was called—was tantamount to flashing their badges.

Fortunately, the demon either couldn't read his underlying nature or didn't think it worth mentioning. A long blue tongue flicked out of its toothy mouth. "There in the chains?" it asked.

Blackwater confirmed the guess.

"It looks strong," the demon said, an extra huskiness entering its voice. "You could hurt it quite a bit without it losing consciousness."

Blackwater straightened, relaxing now that his gift had been accepted. "I shall endeavor to please," he said.

Again, the blue tongue licked out. "Your magician must cut a hole in the portal. So the pain can flow in."

"He will cut a small one," Blackwater said.

"Not too small."

The demon was panting now, which caused Blackwater to smile as he turned toward Adam. "Do it," he said in a low aside to Francis, who was hollow-eyed and sweating. "But no larger than the last time."

Blackwater took the cat tails to Adam with his own hand, whipping him as firmly he would any strong human. Though skilled, he seemed unmoved by the procedure, neither hating nor loving it. Adam supposed the Eunuch's sadistic bent was more psychological. The same could not be said of the demon. Its enjoyment of Adam's pain, as it drank it through the coin-sized hole in the portal, was unabashedly sexual. It moaned when Adam did, though for different reasons. When Blackwater laid one final lash across Adam's nipples, the demon groaned like it was coming.

"Again," it pleaded, its breathing harsher than Adam's. "Do that to it again."

"I don't think that would be wise," Blackwater cautioned. "You might become overly excited and forget your judgment before your peers."

The demon snarled, baring its many sharp white teeth. It stopped after a moment and shook itself in a distinctly animal fashion. Evidently, Blackwater had chosen the right warning, though he might not want to hold his breath waiting to be thanked.

"You are cleverness itself," the demon said, and it didn't sound like a compliment. "Next time, Henry the Eunuch, you'd better bring the pureheart with you."

# CHAPTER NINE

A ri had paced so much she'd gotten tired of it. She was sitting with her knees clasped to her chest in the corner opposite the door when it swung open.

Darius and a guard she hadn't seen before dragged Adam in between them. Adam was moaning softly, his head lolling. His shirt was so red that for a second she thought he'd been given a different one.

Realizing he hadn't, Ari leaped to her feet. "What did you do to him?"

The guards lowered Adam to his back on the bare futon, more or less carefully. His shirt was in ribbons. His bloodied skin had made her think it was new color. His jeans weren't as ripped up, but the denim was black and wet. She didn't know what had happened to his glasses. Then she noticed he wasn't moaning any more.

"Oh my God," she said. A terror like none she'd ever felt gripped her. Her parents kicking her out when she was seventeen hadn't been this bad. If Adam died . . . If she lost him . . .

Darius cut through her panic. "The boss is careful about this stuff. He won't die."

"You mean he won't die tonight," she exclaimed angrily. "When the Eunuch wants him to, he will."

Darius didn't avoid her gaze, though his expression was impassive. "If your friend will let you, wash out his wounds. You don't want them to get infected."

He turned and walked to the door with the other man. Ari ran to the futon where Adam lay.

"Bring blankets," she snapped at the departing guards. "He could go into shock. And he'll need clean clothes to wear."

The door shut without either man responding. Ari pressed her hands to her mouth.

"'s okay," Adam rasped in a rough whisper. "Only whipped me as hard . . . as an ordinary man."

Ari laughed a little hysterically. As long as it had been an *ordinary* whipping, that was all right. At the sound of her choked amusement, Adam worked his eyes open. His pupils were contracted, his soft green irises brighter than normal. Ari was afraid to touch him.

"What can I do? I don't know first aid."

"The blankets were a good idea."

Ari swiped at her damp cheeks. "They do that for people on TV."

He smiled at her, his head turning slightly on the futon. "Take my hand. That part of me doesn't hurt."

His wrists must have. They were bruised from yanking hard at something. "Did they chain you?"

"I let them." He squeezed her fingers. "Didn't . . . want to give the game away."

He'd done this for her, so she wouldn't be left in danger if he escaped. More tears rolled from the corners of her eyes. Adam tried to lift his hand to them but winced. "Ari, you don't have to cry for me."

"Sure," she agreed. "I'll stop any second now."

His smile made her feel like her ribs were being squeezed. "God, I love you," he said.

That shocked her into drying up. Her breath caught in a hiccup. The only people who'd ever told her that were Max and Sarah. Her parents hadn't even said it to each other.

"I—" she said, then had to close her mouth.

"I know," he soothed. "Sometimes it's hard to say."

"I like you," she said, unaccountably defensive. "A lot."

"I know." His smile broadened.

This was ridiculous. She wasn't going to discuss her feelings while he was lying there bleeding. A knock sounded on the door. She jumped up and went to it, reaching for the knob before she remembered there wasn't one. When it opened, Darius handed a stack of blankets and clothes to her. An orange prescription bottle sat on top.

"The pills help fight infection," he said.

Ari gaped at him.

"It's all I can do. If the boss decides to kill him, that's going to be that."

The spink sounded as defensive as she had. He pulled the door toward himself. "Thank you," she said before it shut.

She walked back to Adam in a daze. His eyes were closed, and he was breathing more deeply, but not as if he were sleeping. His big chest went in and out like he was trying to calm himself.

"You okay?" she asked.

"Pain's kicking in. I think . . . you could take me into the shower."

She hardly knew where to grab him to help him up, but somehow she managed it. "You're burning up," she said as he leaned heavily on her. It had to be a were thing. He was way hotter than a fever could account for.

"Uh-huh," he said, his jaw gritting. "Think I need cold water."

They were at the little bathroom's threshold when he bent forward and groaned alarmingly. Was Darius wrong? Had Blackwater unintentionally injured something crucial?

"Shit," Adam gasped, one arm clutched around his stomach. "Get me in there and shut the door."

She got him in and lowered him to sit on the rim of the tiny tub. Her fear that his answers might be direr than she could handle kept her questions inside. He started to undress, which seemed stupid to her, seeing that he was in pain.

"All right," she said when he wouldn't stop. "Just let me take over."

He let her remove his shoes and peel off the scraps of his shirt, a process that made her suck in her breath more than once. He was stoic compared to her. When she reached for the waist button of his jeans, his bowed head lifted.

His green eyes glowed like they had lasers behind them.

"Oh God," she breathed. His canine teeth had slid out, and she didn't think the reason was arousal. "Adam, are you going to . . ."

She trailed off. She didn't know if the watching spells were on, or if they worked in here. She guessed the room's anti-spelling wards wouldn't stop this particular form of magic. What would happen if he turned into his wolf? Would he try to eat her?"

He panted, and it didn't sound quite human. Perhaps he heard the strangeness as well. He swallowed, fighting back the transformation. "My body . . . wants to," he said, low and gravelly. "I'd heal faster if I did. Just—" He screwed his eyes shut, some invisible force seeming to roll through him. "Just turn on the cold water. The urge will . . . ease off if I cool down."

Ari rose and turned on the spray, figuring this would be faster than running a cold bath.

"Are we being watched?" she asked as low as she could. Since he clearly couldn't stand, she helped him sit in his jeans on the tub bottom.

Adam hissed in a breath as the icy water hit the wounds in his chest. The streams were pink where they ran off him. He shook his head tightly. "Not here. Not now."

"Then maybe you should, you know, let yourself go."

He jackknifed forward like a pregnant woman having a contraction. Muscles moved beside his spine that really shouldn't have been there. "No," he said once he'd stopped groaning.

"Are you, um, afraid you'd eat me?"

He laughed in spite of his agony. "I wouldn't do that. I'm still me inside my wolf form. The problem is the moon isn't full. It'd take too long to turn back. We can't afford for me to be outed. Werewolf equals cop for most people."

"Oh," she said. "Well."

He opened his eyes, the last of his spasm seeming to have passed. His canines were still longer than normal, but his eyes weren't glowing. "Talk to me," he said. "Give me a distraction."

The threat of being eaten might have been preferable. "Um, does changing form usually hurt?"

"No." His fingers gripped the tub's rim. "When the moon lends its power, it happens very naturally."

"So a little kid like Ethan isn't going to be writhing around in pain?"

Adam's nailbeds whitened. "Ari, this might not be the best topic to calm me down."

"What should I talk about then?" she asked.

He leaned gingerly back against the tub's sloped end. "Tell me a story from when you were little. Maybe how you found out you had your gift."

The shower had washed his dark hair in front of his eyes. Ari reached out to stroke it back. Because this seemed to soothe him, she kept it up. "I was four or so. I'd been misbehaving, and my mother took away this little stuffed dog I had. I made it float back to me. She screamed like she was auditioning for *Saw XII*."

"Mm," Adam said, his eyes closed now. "Then what?"

"I didn't use my gift again until I was six. I think my mother convinced herself she'd imagined it, but that time my father saw it too. My parents were . . . religious, but not in a nice way. Uptight religious. They said I had the devil's mark on me. They ordered me not to do it anymore or they'd send me away."

Her voice had gone husky. Adam gathered her hand in his and rested both on the tub rim. "Could you not do it?"

"I managed not to where anyone could see. In private, though . . . It was like an itch. I had to let it out sometimes."

She shivered, but that might have been the cold water—and the fact that she still wore the short fringed dress. Adam's thumb caressed her knuckles. Touching her seemed to relax him, which certainly relaxed her. "How did you end up on the street?"

Ari let out a long sigh. "I had a friend. Her name was Liv, and we'd been best friends since kindergarten. We did everything together, even got dumped by our first boyfriends on the same day."

"Did she know about your gift?"

"No." Ari fell quiet, and Adam didn't push. He still looked tense, so after a moment, she continued. If he'd wanted a happier story, he should have asked for it. "Liv and I were in our senior year of high school. She was way more popular than me. Straight A's. No trouble with the principal. But she always stuck by me anyway. I was meeting her after cheerleading practice. I wasn't on the squad. I was kind of a Goth by then. She was teasing me because she claimed the quarterback had a crush on me, and that was going to put this other cheerleader's nose out of joint. We were crossing the grass outside the practice field, laughing, when out of nowhere this tree fell on her.

"There must have been too much rain, because it hadn't looked sickly. The trunk pinned her underneath. There were a few other kids around. One called 911, but a branch stub had gone into her and she was bleeding bad. She was so scared. And paper white. She held my hand the way you are. She couldn't talk, but her eyes were locked on mine, like she was pleading for me to do something. I thought maybe she *knew*. And then I realized whether she did didn't matter. She was my friend. I could help.

"I'd never moved anything that big, but I moved that tree. I healed for the first time too. Blood was pouring out of her where the branch had gone in. I closed my eyes, and I made it stop. It was like that adrenaline strength they say mothers get who lift cars off their children. I needed to help her so badly somehow I could."

"Did Liv survive?"

"She did." Ari blew out her breath. "She walked again and everything. And she never spoke to me after that." She saw from Adam's expression that this surprised him. "We were a little God-fearing community. Football and God, in about that order. What I'd done frightened people. I suspect most of them approved of my parents kicking me out."

"That's— That's just wrong," Adam said, clearly having forgotten his own troubles. "Your parents were stupid, but that girl Liv was your friend."

Ari stroked Adam's still-warm cheek. "I like to think she still is. I like to think she only stopped talking to me because other people put so much pressure on her. Iowa isn't Resurrection. The things I can do aren't normal there."

Adam's mouth quirked unexpectedly. "You said you were from Kansas."

"I lied. Habit. There were a couple stories in the local papers. I didn't want to risk anyone connecting them to me."

"So your friends in New York . . . ?"

"Are the only people who know the truth. To be honest, they're my only friends in the world."

His eyes flared softly. "Not your only friends. Whatever you do or don't feel for me, I am a friend to you."

∞

Ari might not love Adam back, but he could tell seeing him hurt upset her. When his body cooled from the shower at last, she helped him out of the tub, dried him gently with a towel, and bundled him into bed with the blankets Darius had brought. She made him take the antibiotic before she crawled in too, curling herself carefully next to him. Her presence was as comforting as if she'd been pack. She found an uninjured spot on his arm to nestle her head against.

He was childish enough to enjoy all of it. Exhausted from the whipping as well as fighting off his change, the mightiness of his yawn shook him. He was lucky he wasn't human. The energy the demon stole would have taken much longer to restore itself.

"Sleep," she said, stopping herself from patting his wounded chest at the last moment.

"I need to tell you something," he said, knowing he couldn't rest just yet. "Before the watching spells go back on."

She went up on her elbow, one hand coming up to stroke his hair. That was almost too soothing, but he fought past the languor rather than ask her stop.

"Blackwater thinks you're a pureheart. He wants to sacrifice you to a demon."

If he hadn't been running on fumes, he'd have put this more delicately. Ari sat straight up and stared at him. One side of her spiky platinum mop was wilted, where the shower spray had doused it. White showed around her eyes. "A demon?"

"He's been summoning one in the basement. He's got a balloon payment coming due at the next full moon, which is also when he must be getting whatever prize he bargained for."

"And I'm the balloon payment."

"It sounded that way to me. It would explain why he wanted you to injure Mariska Andoor. Purehearts can only be sacrificed after they've been led into sin."

Ari coughed out a laugh. "If Blackwater thinks I'm pure, he hasn't been paying attention."

"It doesn't mean *pure* as in virginal." Adam pulled her nearer hand into his. "Pureheart refers to someone who's true to their own sense of right and wrong. It's about personal integrity, not a particular moral code. You could sleep with every man you met, but if you didn't think that was wrong, it wouldn't sully your energy. You being a Talent and a believer on top of that makes you the trifecta of tasty demon treats."

Ari was shaking her head. "I'm sorry. Me pure? Or a believer? That sounds like the opposite of who I am."

"Does it? Despite what your parents told you about your gift, your password is Godlovesme2. You came here to face down a dangerous crime boss because you don't want to kill people. Even threatening your best friends couldn't make you harm Mariska."

"My friends wouldn't have wanted me to. They're the goodhearted ones."

"Ari, you said yourself Blackwater's gift is finding valuable people. He's betting his own life that you're this thing."

Ari tried to pull away from him, but he kept her hand firmly caught in his. He needed her to take this seriously. After a bit, she stopped tugging.

"If I'm so valuable pure, which I'm not saying I believe, why does Blackwater want me to sin?"

"There are different theories about why, but sinning seems to gives a demon magical permission to take the pureheart's soul. Too many sins, and your soul loses its mojo. If there's only one big transgression, you supply a demon with so much juice he might jump a couple ranks among his own people. Demons are no different from other species that way. They enjoy being top dog."

Ari shuddered, and he decided not to tell her this particular demon siphoned off power through pain—a drug Blackwater seemed to be encouraging it to crave. Ari shifted uncomfortably on the futon. "What does Blackwater get out of this?"

"I don't know yet. Probably a spell only a demon can do. Maybe being kicked up to Level Two in power wasn't enough for him. Whatever he wants, he's burning through an awful lot of resources to accomplish it."

Ari gnawed her lower lip.

"I'm sorry," he said. "I don't mean to alarm you, but you should be forewarned."

"No, you're right." Her eyes focused down on him. "I needed to know this."

"It's important you don't give in. No matter what or who he threatens you with."

"Right," Ari said, nodding.

"Even if it's me, sweetheart. This demon isn't the kind any reasonable person would want to get more power. If it got loose in this realm, it would be bad. Lots of people would die in very unpleasant ways. I wouldn't want to be the one who had to catch it."

A look crossed her face that touched his heart and made him uneasy at the same time. She did care about him, maybe more than she was prepared to admit.

He brought her hand to his mouth and kissed her knuckles. "Promise you won't do anything you know is wrong just to protect me."

Her eyebrows puckered above her nose. "I can't promise," she whispered.

Her words jolted him. They had to be both the best and the scariest anyone ever said to him. The temptation to reach through their moon bond to read her emotions proved too much to resist. The love and worry he found inside her knocked him on his metaphoric ass.

She cared so much it frightened her.

"Ari," he said, breathing her name in awe.

He sat up, ignoring the pulling of the healing wounds on his chest. His own love had swelled big enough to drown him. When he cupped her cheek, she tensed.

"What?" she asked warily. "Why are you staring at me like that?" Her pretty little face took on a look of horror. "Were you snooping inside my head?"

He smiled and brushed one fingertip along her soft cheekbone. "Don't be afraid, darling. Your heart is safe with me. I'd break my own before I hurt yours."

She shrank away in alarm. "Adam . . ."

He caught her jaw and kissed her softly.

"Adam, don't—"

Evidently, if she was still talking, that last kiss wasn't good enough. He slanted his head, covered her lips, and slipped his tongue in too. She moaned as it cozied alongside hers. Encouraged, he massaged her neck and went deeper. After suffering so much pain, his nerves were ready for pleasure. Waves of lovely sensations rolled through his body as her mouth tentatively answered his. When he'd gotten out of the tub, she helped him drag off his wet jeans. Now he was naked under the warm blankets. His penis rose freely as the kiss drew out, stiffening in delicious little surges until it stood straight up. Adam groaned and pushed Ari backward, knowing exactly where he wanted to bury the aching rod.

"You'll hurt yourself," she gasped as she toppled back.

He reached under the short fringed dress to pull her tiny panties down her strong legs.

"Adam . . ."

"You just keep saying my name," he teased.

Her legs spread as he crawled forward over her, her body telling him what she wanted no matter what her mouth said. She started to put her hand on his chest to stop him, then remembered his injuries. The feelings that fought for precedence in her expression were comical—concern and annoyance being the biggest two.

The story she'd told him was very fresh in his mind. This girl deserved much more than she'd been given.

"I love you," he growled. "You're my mate whether you want to see it or not. I need to show you how much I care."

Her gaze settled on his mouth where his upper fangs had dropped. His cock throbbed hard when her tongue snuck out to wet her lip. The ache in Adam's chest shifted to amusement once more. His mate had a nice little wolf fetish going there.

"I don't want you to start bleeding again," she said.

"I won't if I'm on top. I know how to be careful."

He knew her sense of humor had returned when she let out a muffled snort. "You like being on top regardless."

"I like doing everything with you. Every fucking goddamned thing."

Her eyes widened at his fierceness, their lust mingling together in the most wonderful aroma. To him, the smell was better than faerie dust. He dropped his head to nuzzle her neck. Her hands tangled in his hair.

"*A-dam.*"

Oh yeah, he liked hearing her saying his name. Balancing on one elbow, he followed his cock's pussy radar straight to the hottest, creamiest part of her. He knew this was where they both wanted him to be.

Her back arched as he pushed the head in. Bliss closed his eyes, but only for a second. He wanted to watch her, but God she felt good. Tight. Hot. Her inner muscles rippling in reaction. He was big compared to her, but the generosity of her wetness meant he didn't have to stop, just take his time pressing into those satiny clinging depths. Halfway in, her nipples tightened. Not wanting to miss that, he tugged the top of her dress down to admire them.

She moaned as he seated himself balls deep. Her legs moved restlessly with pleasure, her hands fisting in the blankets to either side of her.

Adam thought he'd never in his life seen anything so hot.

"You can touch me," he panted. "Only my front was whipped."

Her eyes were dazed when she opened them. "You fill me," she said. "Like nobody ever has."

It wasn't *I love you*, but right then it was close enough.

"Touch me," he repeated hoarsely. "I need you stroking me."

She put her hands on his back. Something in her face stilled him where he was. "Thank you for loving me," she said shyly.

That was it then. He had to move, though he thrust in and out as gently, as tenderly as he could. They both groaned at how incredible the slick friction felt, their bodies joined in that intimate spot, their pleasure twice as intense for being shared. He wanted it to go on forever, to fuck her just like this till the end of time.

About ten minutes into nirvana, he remembered he needed protection.

*Oh. . . fuck*, he thought, wanting to groan aloud. He knew he ought to pull out. He must have been seeping precome since before he entered her. He certainly would be now. He was way too worked up for his dick not to be leaking up a storm. Weres had great immune systems and weren't prone to STDs, but the very vitality of their constitutions insured even small amounts of semen might hit a bull's eye.

Naturally, since he was at *that age* for baby hunger, the mere thought of impregnating his beloved hardened him even more.

*I will pull out*, he swore to himself. *Just five more thrusts. Nice long slow ones. Or ten. Or maybe—*

Ari nearly shattered him by shoving her hand in between their groins. "Sorry," she said, her middle finger working hard on her clit. "You're so sexy it's killing me. If I don't come soon, I'm going to die."

"I could do—"

"No," she interrupted, her face twisting as she fingered herself faster. "You need bo . . . both hands to hold up your weight. So you won't hurt yourself."

Maybe he did, or maybe she was turning him on too much not to be glad she wanted to do this herself. She came in under a minute, groaning and shaking for longer than it had taken her to go over. He kept gliding in and out, giving her something to contract against. As she settled, she blinked up at him and squirmed around his next thrust. When he smiled at her, the orgasmic flush on her cheeks darkened.

"You want another," he guessed.

"It felt so good with you moving like that inside me. Adam, you're just so *hard.*"

She sounded like she was apologizing for wanting more pleasure. He dropped his head and kissed her, growling his denial into her mouth. Their tongues battled in the sweetest possible way. The way she sucked his canines stood up his hair with lust. A pulse like an alarm bell tapped the base of his cock, warning him his *bulbus glandis* was activating.

That only happened when he was very close to shooting.

"Give yourself another," he rasped. "Just make it quick and, whatever you do, don't get in the way of me pulling out at the end."

Ari's eyes widened as his meaning registered. "Oh boy, I completely forgot."

"Me too. But I think we'll be all right—or not any worse—as long as I don't come inside of you."

If she'd asked him to pull out, he would have. She bit her lip in indecision, her pelvis rocking a restless inch up and down his immensely swollen shaft. As snugly as she fit him, the pressure of her entrance did impossibly pleasurable things to his bulbus gland. That pleasure spread deep into his balls, now tight enough to hurt. The tip of his penis felt like it was stretching.

"I should pull out," he said uneasily.

"No." She shook her head, her hand moving decisively on her clit again. "I promise I'll be quick."

He wasn't certain she could be quick enough. He thrust again, because it felt so good, and because he knew she loved it. Those long slow probes pressed him to his climactic edge. He bit his lip to keep from going over. Nerves that normally would have long since exploded held onto ever sharper sensations. Holding back strained him worse than the whipping had.

"You're close?" she gasped, her hips rocking more wildly against his.

He couldn't speak. Tears were squeezing from his eyes at the pleasure and the need rocketing through him.

"Fin—" *ish*, he tried to say. Obeying some instinct stronger than he was, he shoved his cock inside her as far as it would go.

She went with it jammed up against her womb, the contractions that marked her climax bliss and torment as they gripped him.

He couldn't last until they ended. The pressure in his balls went critical a second before his gland contracted. He yanked out without even breath for cursing and fisted himself madly. He had to rub fast, or he'd shove back in her. As it was, he was pointing his cock at her, his grip clicking in the wetness her pussy had left on him. Ari pulled her rumpled dress further up her belly, baring it to him, and that plain sent him into crazy land.

He was going to mark her. With his seed. With his scent. With his white hot come all over that silky perspiring skin. He kneed up closer to her belly and propped himself on one arm, desperate to get every drop on her. Ari knew what was coming. She cradled his balls and thumbed his *bulbus* at the same time.

He lifted off like the freaking space shuttle. His head flung back as the orgasm roared from him. He needed every scrap of self control he had not to howl like the wolf he was. For about six seconds, his thoughts were completely blanked by ecstasy. Then he wrenched his head back the other way.

He had to watch the rest of his seed spurt on her.

He milked himself until no more came, his ragged breaths practically sobbing out of him. When Ari rubbed his emissions into her skin, the satisfaction that swelled inside him was as strong as an orgasm.

To his wolf side, this meant she accepted him.

"I love you," he sighed, his weight dropping wearily to his heels.

The whip marks on his chest were bleeding a bit, probably from tensing to hold off his orgasm. Ari sat up, her legs splayed around him, her hands stroking soothingly up his arms. She couldn't have known it, but her touch felt the same as if she were pack. She was inside the circle of the folks who belonged to him. Her big blue eyes stared gravely into his.

"You're the best man I've ever met," she said.

This wasn't *I love you* either, but Adam liked it nearly as much.

Trembling from exertion, he lay down beside her with his palm spread possessively over her navel. She pulled up the blankets to cover them. Her head turned toward him. "You okay?"

"Uh-huh."

"Really? 'cause you look kind of wrecked."

He laughed through his nose. "The last bit of 'wrecking' isn't something I'd take back. I'll be fine once I sleep an hour or two."

"Okay." Her smaller hand covered his on her belly, which was a bit sticky. "Don't be upset if I get up later to shower."

She understood him better than she realized. He dropped into slumber with a smile on his face.

He was flying. Wings stuck out from the fire tattoos on his wrists. As he flapped his arms, he wheeled in lazy circles around the Eunuch's boring white block house. His mind was very strong for his age, maybe because he asked it to act in ways his people didn't usually attempt. He thought if he concentrated, and if he got close enough, he could reach the person he was concerned about. There ought to be some link between them. He *had* participated in the spell that gave the other were the gift of creating fire. Plus, his new friend did have a touch of Sight.

*Grant?* Adam thought confusedly through his dream.

*Yes!* he cried exultantly in his own head. Weirdly, it felt like both sides of this conversation were originating from him.

*Grant,* he said, in case he wasn't imagining the communication. *You shouldn't have come back. The Eunuch's men have orders to shoot you down.*

*I'm fast,* he seemed to think to himself. *I wanted you to know I told your team where you are. If you have what you need, they can pick you up by morning.*

Adam's gratitude was extraordinary. *Yes,* he thought to his internal image of the gargoyle. *Tell them I have the evidence we need. And that they should come with back up.*

*Ari is okay?* Grant asked.

*She's fine,* Adam assured him, amused by the fondness he sensed through the connection. The gargoyle seemed to have a small interspecies crush, one that thankfully wasn't big enough to raise his hackles. *Now get out of here before you're spotted.*

A sound like a muffled gas explosion yanked him out of his dream—if that's what it had been. He reached for Ari, but she wasn't on the futon. The shower was running, which explained where she was. Adam stretched out his Sight to see if he could perceive Grant's presence. Instead, he found the watch spells running. With an unpleasant lurch, he realized he couldn't remember when they'd gone on.

Had they been active when he fell asleep? And before that? While he and Ari were making love? He'd told Ari he loved her. He wouldn't relish Blackwater having heard that, but at least Ari hadn't said it back. Blackwater was hoping to manipulate her behavior, not Adam's.

Then again, if Adam could read the signs that she might love him, would a sharp tack like Blackwater be blind to them?

The muffled *whump* of a second explosion reverberated through the walls of the house. Adam was alarmed enough to jump to his feet. Grant must be under attack.

Ari burst out of the bathroom a second later in hastily drawn on jeans and a damp T-shirt. Her wet blonde hair was plastered to her head. "What was that?"

"I'm afraid Grant's in trouble," he said.

∞

Ari didn't have sufficient curse words for this. She'd been hoping Darius wouldn't follow Blackwater's orders too closely. He didn't seem like he wanted to hurt people.

Of course, if someone else was handling shoot-down-the-gargoyle duty, Darius's semi-reluctance would be moot.

"We have to help him," she said, dashing to the cell room door. She pressed her hands to the surface where the handle was on the other side. "I can't let Grant die for me."

Trying to get her telekinesis to work was like trying to force super-glued gears to turn. Pain throbbed in her temples as she struggled to pull power past the wards. She'd moved that damned tree all those years ago. She ought to be able to break through a damping spell. There was magic to draw on here. She just had to get to it. She ignored the warning tremor in her right arm, but an odd crackling sensation in the cartilage of her nose broke her concentration. When she brought her hand up, she was bleeding.

She pushed her dismay at that aside. A nosebleed was an improvement over an all-out fit.

"Ari," Adam said, his grip warm on her shoulder. "You can't get through these shields. Blackwater's sorcerers are experts."

She wasn't going to cry. She was too damned angry. "I'm going to kill that fuckhead."

Adam pulled her against him. His chest was hard and broad, and she was instantly, irrationally comforted. His skin was warm velvet beneath her cheek.

"You're naked," she pointed out.

He smiled into her hair before pushing back from her. "Right. No more nakedness when we might have to fight something."

He pulled on the clothes Darius had brought, his beautiful body disappearing into baggy gray sweats and a white T-shirt. Evidently, everything Blackwater's employees wore had to match his house's color palette. If Ari got out of here alive, she was going to wear lime green and purple for a whole year.

"Want to see if you can peek out the window?" Adam offered.

The square of glass was barred and set high up in the wall. By kneeling on Adam's shoulders, Ari could steady herself with the silvery-gold bars. It was dark outside, but the security lights were on. Through the branches of a tree, she spied the gated end of the drive. Since the turnabout was empty, this was not helpful. On the other hand, if she got the bars off and broke the glass, she thought the window might be big enough for her to squirm through. Now if only she could find some way to get at the power out there . . .

"Don't," Adam said before she could do more than inhale. "The spells are twice as strong on the window. You can' t help Grant if you give yourself an aneurysm."

Ari frowned, not sure she liked such sensible advice. "Maybe I could try to—"

The room's door banged open, startling both of them. What looked like a horde of guards burst in. These goons were in black camo rather than the usual gangster suits. They carried the same crazy rifles the cops had used, which they pointed at Ari and Adam.

"Away from the window," one of them ordered. "Hands where we can see them. Don't try anything funny."

"Whoa," Adam said. "Just let me help her get down."

After barking out a few more mistrustful orders, they let him help her to the floor. Ari had a perverse sense of satisfaction at being considered dangerous.

"Walk ahead of us," said the lead soldier.

He and his companions prodded her and Adam with the tips of their rifles, forcing them through the house and up a set of utility stairs.

"What's wrong?" Ari asked their captors, unable to keep silent. "Where are you taking us?"

The muzzle in her back jabbed harder.

Despite the weaponry, she didn't get the impression they were going to be shot. The soldiers could have done that back in the cell. Adam shrugged at her when she sought his eyes. He seemed relatively calm—not happy, but not like he thought the end was nigh.

Naturally, they both could have been wrong about that.

They were pushed out onto the compound's flat walled roof, where more soldier-guards were gathered. Apparently, Blackwater had quite the tin pot dictator's army—maybe five dozen in addition to his regular personnel. She wondered if this meant something big was happening. From the rueful twist of Adam's mouth, he hadn't expected these numbers.

The armed crowd parted as she and Adam emerged from the stairwell.

Their movement revealed a shape on the roof, bound down against it by steel cables, like an unstable load on a big rig truck. One of the soldiers poked a spear at the small mountain. Electricity crackled from the metal tip. The big shape *whuffed* like it was too weary to make any other sound. The back of one batlike wing lifted.

"Oh my God," Ari breathed.

They'd caught Grant. He was still alive, which was good, but the heavy bondage: not so much. She bit her lip as the soldier tasered him again. She suspected it wouldn't help if she protested.

When she tore her attention away from Grant's suffering, Henry Blackwater's gaze was waiting. He stood behind Grant, partially hidden by the gargoyle's bulk. Blood had splashed the front of his trademark cream linen suit. Ari couldn't remember ever seeing him dirty. For no reason she could explain, she was suddenly aware of the stars twinkling in the deep black sky that stretched above him.

"Ari," he said pleasantly.

Her jaw worked for a second before she could speak. "I'm fucking going to kill you, Eunuch."

His smile jerked and faded. She didn't think she'd called him that to his face before. Maybe no one had in that tone. He recovered too soon for her taste.

"Everyone needs a dream. Why don't you come see what we caught in our net?"

He beckoned her toward him. Since he could force her, she didn't see the point in dragging her feet. She ordered herself to keep her temper under control. She knew Blackwater and his games. She would need a clear head for this.

As she stepped around Grant's body, the gargoyle opened his eyes. She'd never have guessed goblin eyes could be beautiful, but his were. Within his stone-gray face, they were as yellow as polished citrines, with vertical cat pupils. They sparkled in the roof lights, tears of pain adding to their luster. She couldn't speak to him. She hoped he knew she was sorry.

Blackwater's hand dropped heavily onto her shoulder. "You're going to kill this for me," he said.

A sound broke in Ari's throat. When she twisted to look at Blackwater, his little pleased smile was back. This was the sin he hoped she'd commit. He must have thought it wouldn't seem as bad as maiming Mariska Andoor: the death of an alleged pigeon versus a talented singer lost forever. If Adam was right about her being a pureheart, as long as she thought the lesser evil was bad enough, it would suit his purposes.

She knew she'd brought on this confrontation the moment she tried to defend the gargoyle from Darius.

"I won't," she said quietly.

Blackwater's grin broadened. "Are you truly so tenderhearted? It's nothing but a pest."

Grant was a person, one who'd risked his life to help her and Adam, one who'd crowed with excitement at gaining his first home. God knew Ari didn't want to die, but she couldn't kill Grant to save herself.

"I won't," she repeated.

Blackwater beamed. "Ari, Ari, Ari, you've no idea how elated I am to hear that, especially since I'm going to give you a choice. Kill the gargoyle, or I'll kill your lover. You know, the fellow who swears he'd sooner break his own heart than hurt yours? Truly, I'm insulted you didn't think I'd notice you were in love. Haven't you learned I make a point of knowing all my employees' weaknesses?"

Adam made a sound as if he would speak.

"Oh, do!" Blackwater cut him off chirpily. "Do tell her to let me kill you! It's so delightfully trite. It won't save the flying squirrel, of course. You're the only one I'm offering to let live tonight."

He was rubbing his hands together, practically giggling. Ari noticed she wasn't the only person looking at him askance. Henry Blackwater didn't express joy this way.

Grant's low moan pulled her from her amazement. She fell to her knees beside him. No one stopped her. Perhaps they knew she couldn't do anything for him. The surface of the roof was warded, as was the net of cables that held him. She couldn't free Grant without magic, or heal the wounds she now saw scoring his wings and side. His blood smelled like it was spiced. Ari's palm had landed in a pool of it.

When she patted his front lion leg, she felt like she was trying to comfort an old-style Volkswagen minibus. Grant's tired eyes were as big as hubcaps.

*Level Five!* she heard as a faint echo in her mind. *Hello, Ari.*

Ari jerked in surprise, and immediately tried to hide the movement. Her fingers clenched deeper in his warm gray fur. Grant was communicating telepathically. Maybe them being so close together gave him that ability. She was pretty sure most people in Resurrection wouldn't have guessed he could.

*I'm sorry*, she thought as forcefully as she could. *I never meant to get you in trouble.*

*Hush*, came the answer. *You. Me. Words not good head. Watch picture.*

Did he mean he couldn't communicate to her mind-to-mind with words? And what picture was he talking about? She didn't see any—

Her vision disappeared as images slammed her. She saw herself standing over Grant, one of the soldier's spear things gripped in her upraised hands. She plunged the blade downward into his heart, the location of which Grant sent her. Grant lay still, blood spreading out under him. Blackwater bent to check his pulse, seeming to pronounce him dead. Like a silent film unreeling, everyone left the roof. Alone then, a glow began to surround Grant's body, until he was bathed in radiance. He burst through the cables that held him and flew up into the sky.

*No sin*, Grant's voice came more weakly. *You still pure. Demon be mad. My people enemy die.*

Did Grant mean it was okay to kill him because he believed he'd go to gargoyle heaven? Ari was no atheist, but she was far from certain about an afterlife.

*I forgive*, Grant said. *No sin you. This . . . only way.*

She felt the connection between them shut off. Maybe Grant closed it. Maybe he'd run out of strength. The furry foreleg she petted was very still.

"Well?" Blackwater said, breaking into her thoughts. "Let's have a decision."

Ari rose shakily. She didn't look at Adam. She didn't want what was on his face to influence her.

"I'll take the spear," she said.

# CHAPTER TEN

Adam forced himself not to look at Ari, in case his expression gave away his thoughts. He'd done enough of that already. Though he wasn't in on it, he'd sensed a communication between Ari and the gargoyle. Could Grant speak in her mind the way he'd spoken in Adam's dream? He hoped Grant had a plan—like breaking free of his bonds and blasting Blackwater's men to bits with his Level Eight magic. That would probably be too easy. Gargoyles worked in teams, and who knew how well even they could function in this warding?

He hoped Blackwater wasn't thinking along these lines. He seemed to take the common view that gargoyles were powerful and annoying, but not the most intelligent species.

One of Blackwater's soldiers handed Ari an electrified taser-spear.

"You probably want to stand over here," Blackwater pointed out helpfully. "To ensure the proper angle to hit the heart. Assuming you'd like to kill it on the first try."

Adam had to look at Ari then. The clenching of her jaw was grim but determined. She stood where Blackwater had directed her. Grant lay quiet, like a dumb beast in truth, watching her with his big yellow eyes.

"Put your back into it," Blackwater added. "That blade is sharp, but it'll be similar to harpooning a whale."

Adam winced at the description. Ari set her feet in a wider brace and wiggled her shoulders. She was wiry, the spear taller than she was. She'd probably have trouble wielding it.

*Any time now, Grant*, Adam thought.

Letting out a grunt like an Olympic shot putter, Ari plunged the spear into Grant's lion chest. Blood fountained up the shaft, the scent a combination of copper and cinnamon. The blood was as red as Adam's would have been.

*Damn it*, were the only words he could think. She'd hit Grant's heart. Blood wouldn't pump from the wound that way otherwise. Grant's paws twitched, and then he went stonelike. She'd killed him. Ari had actually killed the gargoyle.

Adam hoped saving him was worth it.

"Well," Blackwater said into the stunned silence. "That was . . . to the point."

Ari jerked out the blade and handed the gory spear back to its owner. He was more openly stupefied than Blackwater.

"Check its pulse," the Eunuch ordered another man.

The soldier bent for a moment, gingerly touching the gargoyle's neck. Grant didn't spring to life and attack. The soldier straightened and shook his head. "It's dead. No pulse. No breath."

Blackwater turned to Francis, who looked steadier than a few hours ago but not exactly good. Considering the dangerous tasks he'd been entrusted with, Adam would have welcomed a return of the man who'd had the energy to leer at Ari. Like his boss, Francis wore a suit, though his was a gray pinstripe. He shook his head the same way the soldier had.

"There aren't any spirit signs, just fading life essence. The girl definitely killed it. Would you . . ." He hesitated, for what reason Adam couldn't guess. "Do you want me to harvest the valuable parts?"

Ari gasped in horror. She couldn't have known gargoyle organs were used in rituals. Blackwater glanced at her briefly.

"Someone else can do that," he said. "I have other duties for you right now."

Francis gave a tight-lipped nod of acquiescence, and Adam realized he relished those *other duties* even less than he'd have enjoyed cutting open a still-warm animal the size of a minivan. Then the lightbulb clicked above Adam's head. Sweat broke out underneath his arms, the scent of his alarm sharp to his own nose. Blackwater must intend to give the demon his final payment tonight. With Ari's decision to kill Grant, he had all the pieces in place. He wasn't waiting for the full moon.

*Oh Ari*, he thought. *What were you thinking?*

He seemed unlikely to get an answer. Beneath them, from the direction of the front of the house, came the sound of a vehicle crashing through the entrance gate. Half the soldiers ran to the wall on that side of the roof. They knelt the moment they reached it, bracing their rifles on their shoulders. He gave them credit for being disciplined. Blackwater hadn't given them an order to shoot, and all of them refrained.

"Henry Blackwater," roared a male voice so mellifluous despite its anger that it must have belonged to a noble fae. "Come out here and face me like a man!"

"Ah," Blackwater said, his air of satisfaction clear. He tugged his blood-splashed linen suit straighter. "Come on, everyone. Let's go down and welcome our final guest."

∞

Faeries weren't strangers to hubris. Lord Grygir hadn't come alone to Blackwater's party, but the dozen men who'd jumped out of the troop transport with which he'd rammed the gate weren't going to do him much good—even if they were faeries. The Eunuch's troops simply outnumbered and out-armed them by too much.

The hubris became most obvious when Lord Grygir flung up one hand and started chanting in his kind's high tongue.

Absolutely nothing happened. The air didn't even ripple.

"Ah, ah, ah," Blackwater admonished. "None of that *Stop! In the Name of Love* nonsense here. I've been preparing for your visit for quite some time." He spread his long-fingered hands to indicate the roundabout's shiny black pavers. "You see my lovely obsidian cobbles? They're set into an inch-thick electrum plate. My pets have been feeding power into it for nearly a year—storing up for a rainy day, you might say. I anticipated I might need a little extra warding tonight."

"What's your game?" Grygir demanded, either too stupid to be afraid or too self-controlled to show it. "I know you practically choke on your envy every time we cross paths, but you could be more of a man than to attack me through my girlfriend."

"Your girlfriend!" Blackwater laughed. "Is that what you call women you pine after? Trust me, your unrequited hybrid crush couldn't matter less. I did think you'd figure out I was behind it quicker, but I only moved against Mariska so you'd come storming here." Licking his thumb, he wiped a smear of blood off one jacket button. "Faeries can be challenging to track when they don't want to be found."

"You wanted me here?" Grygir said disbelievingly. "You don't dare injure a faerie lord. You'd bring the entire weight of the fae crashing down on you."

Blackwater's smile gave the proud fae lord pause. "That would be suicide," he agreed. "Fortunately, I don't intend to harm a single hair on your head. Francis, please do the honors."

Francis cleared his throat as Grygir gaped at him. "By the power of Earth and Air I bind you, Grygir Aloysius Burke Err-Elian di Spaña."

Though the charged electrum plate prevented Grygir from using magic, it wasn't designed to stop Francis. Grygir didn't have a chance against the invocation of his true name. Adam didn't doubt some black deeds had been required for Blackwater to obtain it. Power flashed through the air to whip around the fae lord's torso, a long wrist-thick eel of barely visible energy. It trapped his arms against his body more strongly than any rope. Sputtering, Grygir struggled against it. As he did, his faerie bodyguard sprung belatedly into action.

Like a scythe through grass, the Eunuch's men mowed them down.

The soldiers must have been firing electrum bullets, a general-purpose ammo that could take down most supes. Adam discovered faeries smelled like lilacs when they crossed over.

"Shut the gate," Blackwater ordered, businesslike once more. "And hide the bodies. We don't want the neighbors seeing them if they drive by."

If they smelled them, they'd think the Eunuch was a really good gardener.

Another snap of Blackwater's fingers bought Grygir a two-man carrying team. Adam was certain he and Ari could be given one as well. He was so shocked by the events of the last few minutes, he was having trouble catching his breath. Training forced him to ask if he could have done something to head this off. Right that second, he couldn't imagine what. Grygir had a hell of a lot more power than he did, and Blackwater had snapped him like a twig.

He looked at Ari, who stood a few feet away from him. Her eyes were as sad as a pieta. She hadn't liked seeing those faerie bodyguards die either.

"So," Blackwater said, drawing their focus back to him. "Shall we raise the curtain on the next act?"

∞

As they were herded into the house, the scent of lilacs clung thickly to Ari's nose. Those faeries had been so pretty, a sparkly bouquet of strong male beauty. She knew that shouldn't have made her mind them dying. What mattered was that they might have left behind faerie families and faerie friends—maybe faerie children as well.

Could a person like her learn to heal the sort of injuries they'd died from?

The idea didn't have time to flower. They stumbled at gunpoint down the basement steps, too many bodies trying to go down at once.

The men who carried Lord Grygir nearly fell when they reached the bottom, earning themselves a scathing insult from Blackwater. They looked abashed rather than irritated. Didn't they realize they were stronger than their boss? And that they had the guns? Maybe it didn't matter. Maybe they liked being a cog in a powerful criminal machine. Maybe—just as Adam was alpha to his pack—Blackwater was a born leader. Why Ari hadn't broken to his will was a mystery she probably wouldn't live long enough to solve.

Francis the sorcerer followed the downward migration. He, Blackwater and four guards joined Ari, Adam and Grygir in the metallic-floored spell room. Blackwater instructed another dozen men to remain outside the door with their weapons drawn.

"You know what to shoot if it comes through that door," he said.

Ari didn't enjoy noticing that a couple of the soldiers looked frightened.

She wondered what was happening on the roof. Was Grant's spirit ascending like he'd hoped, or was he simply dead? She couldn't tell if she felt guilty about what she'd done to him. For the moment, her emotions were numb.

"Don't let the Outsiders interfere," Blackwater instructed, inadvertently pulling a thrill across her shoulders. Blackwater still didn't realize Adam was a were, and that he'd been born here in Resurrection. "You don't need to chain them unless they fight."

As aces in the hole went, Adam's true nature remaining hidden was a small one. All the same, Ari sensed a note of hope vibrating in him as well.

They were pushed back against the wall where Adam must have been whipped. His blood hadn't been washed off. Two hulking spink demons, neither of whom was Darius, took charge of Adam—which might have been a compliment. A human who looked and acted like he could have been Secret Service guarded her. He'd already slapped magic-damping cuffs around her wrists, which were in front of her. Adam had a pair as well, on account of his firebug power. She could tell there weren't any wards against using magic here. Grygir could too, because he began to whisper under his breath. His guard shoved him to his knees and gagged him with a cloth that looked like silver lame, but was probably woven and warded electrum thread. Silenced, Grygir glared at Blackwater. Blackwater was lucky the fae lord couldn't strike him dead with his eyes.

Through it all, Francis was hastily drawing three symbol-decorated circles on the gleaming floor. The patterns meant nothing to Ari, but Grygir must have recognized their purpose. He roared at Blackwater through his gag, his words unintelligible, his sentiments obvious.

The faerie would have wriggled up, except the guard who had charge of him pushed him back to his knees. Blackwater smiled down at him pleasantly.

"Don't worry, Grygir," he said. "While I fully intend to fuck your 'girlfriend' once I'm inside your lovely body, I promise not to enjoy it."

Knowledge lit up Ari's mind even as Grygir went wild with rage. This was what Blackwater wanted from the demon: for him to swap their bodies. No wonder he'd stared so avariciously at the fae in Mariska's club. The Eunuch literally wanted to *be* him.

Finally, Blackwater would have everything he wanted. No more barely Level Two power for him, he'd stand on the tippy top of Resurrection's supernatural heap, a genuine lord of enchantments. Prestige would be his, plus a beauty so radiant no one could outshine it. The Eunuch would cease to exist. Lord Grygir would supplant him as the head of Blackwater's criminal empire. Details of the transfer might need to be finessed, but Ari was certain Blackwater had planned for them.

He'd planned everything else perfectly.

Except for Adam. Except for Grant and possibly her.

*God*, she prayed. *If I'm right about You, and if I really am this pureheart thing, please help us find a way out of this.*

She didn't know what response she expected, but Adam's head jerked to her. The softest glimmer of green fire shone in his eyes. The emotion that rose inside her might have been love, but it certainly wasn't soft. What it felt like was incredibly resolute. She wouldn't just give her life for him. If she had to, she was willing to give her soul.

She kind of suspected he was thinking the same thing.

"Ready, boss," Francis said, his expression tight and resigned.

"Strip him," Blackwater ordered Grygir's guard.

The barely visible magic that trussed Grygir's arms to his sides didn't prevent a pair of shears from cutting off his clothes. When his business shirt fell free, Ari sucked in a breath. His wings were both unexpected and a rapturous sight: filmy dragonfly sort of things that grew from his shoulder blades. They overlapped so closely to his back they hadn't affected the drape of his shirt. Even folded up, colors sparkled and danced across their transparent iridescence, forming shifting patterns that mesmerized. Though delicate in appearance, she sensed they weren't fragile.

For all his beauty, nothing about Grygir seemed fragile.

He'd been great looking in his clothes. With them gone, he was so gorgeous he dried her mouth. Like, Greek god gorgeous. Like, Michelangelo would have wept to sculpt his rippling muscles. His shape was perfect—broad shoulders, tight narrow hips—and his flawless skin shimmered all over.

He was also pretty darn well endowed.

Adam cleared his throat beside her.

She pulled a *sorry* face in response to his raised eyebrows. So sue her. She was human. If it came right down to it, she liked Adam's rough looks better.

Out of nowhere, the thought came to her that babies with faerie wings would be seriously cute. That was weird. As a rule, Ari rarely remembered infants existed.

Her reaction to the faerie's beauty had prevented her from noticing Blackwater undressing too. His nudity was an eye-opener, but in a different way.

The man people called the Eunuch really was. Between his legs, he was featureless. No hair, no genitalia, nothing but smooth pale skin. Ari imagined this precluded chats with underlings in front of urinals. Blackwater must have had to sit down to pee.

Had he known he'd look like this when he made his initial deal? Would it have mattered to him? More than anything, his choice made her realize how committed he was to his goals. Nothing was going to keep Blackwater from being who and what he aspired to.

Lord Grygir looked away from him. He didn't seem disgusted, more like he just didn't want to see. Blackwater didn't notice his aversion. Possibly, he didn't care.

"Open the portal," he said to Francis.

Ari's heart clenched tighter. Opening a portal suggested she was about to meet the demon who wanted to eat her. She remembered Adam mentioning his parents worked in Portal Management, and that they'd died in an explosion. She found herself half wishing this one would explode. At least they'd all die clean.

Francis looked like opening one wasn't easy. His face broke into a sweat as he knelt and chanted. Ari was no expert, but she thought it was the same language Lord Grygir had used earlier. The hollows under the sorcerer's eyes grew darker by the second, and his hands trembled where he'd rested them on his thighs. If she'd ever doubted the stupidity of learning sorcery, watching Francis struggle to get through the spell put an end to it. He couldn't have been more than thirty. By the time he finished, he could have passed for twice that age. Finally, like a laser show at a concert, the shape of a door shot up from the two hunks of crystal he'd set in the main circle.

Blackwater now stood in the smaller circle to its left, while Lord Grygir's guard forced him to remain on his knees in the right. As the portal appeared, the atmosphere took on the scent of a locker room . . . lots of males perspiring before a game they weren't certain they could win. When the odor of rotten eggs joined the sweat, Ari had to fight not to gag.

The smell eased off as she noticed the next development. The rectangle inside the frame of light was changing color and moving. A tall dark figure materialized within it, seeming to stand behind slightly wavering glass—the barrier between the dimensions, she assumed. The figure was humanoid: two arms, two legs, and one extremely erect penis. Its hands and feet sported claws, and its skin was deep purple. Its very visible veins were black. As it finished becoming, its great dark eyes zeroed in on her.

Ari couldn't stop herself from shrinking back to the wall.

"Ahh," it said, a deep and creepily sexual groan. "You bring my tribute."

"I do," Blackwater said. "Precisely as we agreed."

A dark tongue swept across the demon's sharklike teeth. "Give it to me."

"When you fulfill our bargain."

"I will not be tricked," the demon warned.

"I wouldn't dream of trying, but if I give you your payment first, you will be . . . too distracted to hold up your end of the deal."

"Hah," the demon laughed. He jerked his hairless skull toward Grygir. "I expect you don't want to miss your chance to live in that body. You'll finally have a fuck-stick after all these years."

Blackwater inclined his head, hiding—from the demon at least—that his lips were thinned with distaste. "Who wouldn't be eager for that, my lord?"

The demon's amusement faded. "You need to let me taste the sacrifice. I must know she's a true pureheart."

*Oh boy*, Ari thought, knowing her personal moment of truth was coming. Were Grant and Adam right about her? Was she good enough, and did she believe enough to fail this test the right way?

"Ari," Adam murmured, but she couldn't look at him.

She'd want to live too much if she did.

"Bring her closer," Blackwater said, his voice just a little hoarse now that his dream was a hair's breadth from fruition. "Francis, open a hole in the door."

Ari recognized Francis's pretty ritual knife as an athame. Under other circumstances, she'd have been proud for remembering the arcane word. Under this one, she was too busy trying to struggle neither too much nor too little as Secret Service man dragged her forward across the floor. She had to sell this, or they'd lose the element of surprise.

The portal surface made a thick ripping sound as Francis pulled his knife through it, reminding her of raw meat being sawed. It felt like raw meat when the guard shoved her cuffed hands through the opening.

She noticed he was careful to keep his own outside when he did.

The dimension her hands had been thrust into was icebox cold. Frost began forming on her fingers.

And then the demon took hold of them.

She cried out because the pain of his touch was incredible, like every bone she had was being ground into the one next to it. Even worse was the sucking sensation—and never mind the crude hungry noises the demon was making. Some fluidlike essence was being pulled from her, something important to her existence. Ari's head spun with nausea and dizziness.

"*Ari*," Adam said, his voice sharper than before. "Look at me now."

Ari looked. Away from the demon. Away from the odd bony hands that clutched and sucked at hers. Knowing she had to, she let Adam be her fortress.

It seemed her fortress was close to turning. Framed by his thick dark lashes, his eyes beamed phosphorescent green. Fortunately, no one but she was paying him any mind. Her struggle with the demon had everyone's attention. *I love you*, he mouthed to her, those three small words any woman—including her, apparently—knew how to lip read. She gave her head the tiniest shake to let him know he didn't need to rescue her.

The demon coughed like it was politely hacking up a hairball.

Ari didn't move her gaze from Adam, and she saw him grow more alert. He was breathing faster, crouching slightly between the spink demons who gripped him. His eyes narrowed on what was happening behind her.

The demon suddenly pushed her hands from him. Ari yanked them back to her chest, not surprised to find them coated in ice crystals. Thankfully, all her fingers were there.

"Poison!" the demon roared like thunder. "You dare to—" It broke off to retch and then recovered. "You dare to poison me!"

"I wouldn't," Blackwater protested.

"The pureheart is *too* pure," the demon accused, then had to vomit again. Thick white light issued from its mouth.

"She can't be," Blackwater said. "I oversaw her sin myself."

A number of important things seemed to happen at once. Adam let out his own roar, his shoulders straining massively as he yanked his cuffed hands apart. The charmed restraints snapped open and fell from him, a feat Ari hadn't thought possible. Brute force and familiarity with the things from his job must have allowed them to exploit their weak spots. Hands free, he cracked his gaping demon guards' skulls together. Their heads must have been hard, because both were knocked unconscious. At the same time, the demon squeezed his clawed purple hands into the slit in the portal and started pulling it bigger.

"Seal the hole!" Blackwater ordered Francis.

Francis barely looked capable of crawling. She saw the realization finally enter his face: that Blackwater had always intended to use him up to the last cinder, that he was going to die tonight. A second later, his horror was erased for him. The demon stretched through the widened slit, caught the sorcerer's neck and crushed it.

He was dead before he hit the floor.

Blackwater didn't miss a beat. "You," he said to Secret Service guy. "Patch it."

Evidently he was yet another Talent who'd been trained in sorcery. He must not have studied as hard as Francis. Though he immediately started chanting, and at a safer distance than his peer, the demon continued to rip the hole wider.

Meanwhile, Adam finished tearing off his clothes. He fell to his hands and knees and started growing fur. In a night of wonders, this was possibly the most amazing one.

"Shit," breathed the guard who'd been holding Grygir in the third circle. "He's a werewolf."

The fae lord took advantage of the guard's distraction to throw his weight back and knock him over. This was a good thing, because Adam was still transforming, an act that didn't seem conducive to fighting off attacks. Ari guessed he couldn't shift rapidly without a full moon. She winced at the way his skeleton wrenched and popped, though he made no sound but panting. She had the impression he was concentrating on changing as fast as he could. To her dismay, the spink demons whose heads he'd cracked together were recovering consciousness.

It was a partial consolation that they focused on her.

"Get the girl," one said to the other.

Ari didn't know why they wanted her, and she didn't care. She didn't kid herself that she could fight off two eight-foot tall tusked demons, but she did want their attention. With this in mind, she seized the athame from Francis's cooling hand. Hopefully, she was holding it like she meant business. The anti-magic cuffs probably ensured that she wasn't. The spinks were grinning as they approached.

"Stay back!" she ordered. "I'll stick this right in your family jewels."

"I'll show you my family jewels," both demons said in unnerving unison.

Ari retreated so fast she coshed the back of her head on a metal shelf loaded with specimen jars. She would have said there was nothing left to do then but pray, except one of the spink demon's necks abruptly disappeared in a spray of blood. Adam had completed his transformation. His wolf had bitten through the demon's throat from behind. The head dropped and bounced off the demon's foot.

Adam's balance was so perfect he rode the headless body to the ground, then used it as a springboard to attack the other spink. The demon was considerably bigger than the oversized timberwolf, but Adam was both ferocious and lightning quick. He darted in and out at his opponent, snapping like a crocodile and ripping big bites from him. Ari guessed spinks weren't tasty. Adam was spitting out the bites.

In another corner of the room, Lord Grygir was rolling on the floor with his former guard. Despite being gagged and bound, he was putting up a fight by using his head and legs as weapons. Blackwater ran over to them and dragged Grygir back by his binding.

"I'll give you the faerie!" he cried to the purple demon. "He's got plenty of juice."

The demon had his head and one arm squeezed out of the portal. He seemed unimpressed by this offer. "I'll take you all," he swore.

He wasn't going to get the chance just them.

The second spink demon had succumbed to Adam's vicious bite-by-bite assault, freeing Adam to make quick work of Secret Service guy. He was just a human, and Ari swore that only took two seconds. Then, with his wolfish lips curled back and his eyes afire, Adam streaked toward Blackwater. His furious snarls stood Ari's hair on end. The Eunuch didn't like them either. Clearly terrified, his grip on Grygir faltered. The fae lord wrenched free, and Adam's wolf leaped straight for his target's chest.

Kareem McKenzie couldn't have executed a better tackle. Blackwater literally toppled into the demon's hand. Adam twisted in mid-air, neatly squeaking out of danger. Blackwater screamed as the demon hauled him through the portal's slit and into its own realm.

The sounds that followed were indescribably awful.

"Well," panted a beautiful male voice. "That ought to keep the demon occupied for a few minutes. Too bad I can't close this thing."

Lord Grygir was on his feet but none too steady. His magical trussing still bound his arms, though he'd worked off his gag. His eyes were red-rimmed, either with sorrow or anger at the loss of his men. His former captor was lying very still—dead, she presumed—leaving her, the fae lord and Adam alone with the ripped portal.

Adam padded to her with his tongue lolling, wolf claws clicking on the electrum floor. He stationed himself between her and the faerie, as if he felt a need to guard her. The bloodied fur on his back came up as high as her waist. Ari went ahead and buried her cuffed hands in it.

"Um," she said, feeling a little shy what with one sexy man leaning into her all furry while another stood before her naked as a jaybird. "Do you mean you're too weak to close the portal or that you don't know how?"

She must have insulted the faerie. He answered a tad stiffly.

"I mean it takes a specific sort of magic to close a door someone else opened, a magic I personally don't have access to right now. Blackwater probably intended the spink twins to be backup to perform the spell."

"They were twins?" she said, surprised she actually had the energy to be startled.

Before the fae lord could answer, Adam whined softly and nudged her thigh.

"Oh!" Ari exclaimed. "Adam knows how to close it. At least, I think he does. His parents used to work in Portal Management. Maybe you could help him change back to human form? I don't think he can shift soon enough without the moon."

Grygir studied her with more attention than she expected. "You and the werewolf are lovers?"

"Yes," she said, then blushed for no good reason.

"Very well," said the faerie. "We may have some cause for hope after all."

∞

Adam wasn't surprised the fae lord knew enough werewolf lore to be familiar with the concept of twin flames. Twin flames weren't as rare as—say—unicorns, and many species had similar ideas, but those who were mates in spirit as well as body were mystically special. Though werewolves weren't known for performing magic aside from the change, twin flames working together could accomplish marvels trained sorcerers could not—shutting down portals being a notable one.

Anything to do with magic interested faeries, partly because they always wanted to command the leading edge.

Adam's sweet and eccentric parents had been considered a successful example of a twin flame pair, going into law enforcement from their own unique angle. When he was young, they sometimes took him to empty fields, where they'd practice their special craft. One of the fae who rotated on assignment with Portal Management would call up small doors for them to close. Adam had seen his parents work the tricks of their trade many hundreds of times. He knew how to shut this portal.

The real question was, could Ari shut it with him?

He didn't have time for doubt. The noise of the purple demon rending Blackwater into pieces wasn't as loud as before. Likely, the demon was too angry to draw the process out. When it finished its current meal, Adam was certain it intended to cross into Resurrection for more victims.

Adam waited for Lord Grygir to pull himself together enough to cast off his magical bindings. Faeries didn't have to worry about using up their life force the way sorcerers did. Near immortals, they had too much magic to draw on to ever run out of it. Still, they could momentarily tire themselves. By the time Grygir had freed himself and shook out his tall sparkly wings, he looked ready to collapse.

Perfectly willing to spare his pride, Adam sank to the floor at his feet, his bloodied muzzle resting on his paws. Now the fae could sit without admitting he needed to. He did so with a sigh, laying his hands very gently in Adam's fur.

The touch of most fae was pleasurable. Grygir was a lord, and his magic was especially potent. If Adam had been pure wolf, he'd have wriggled ecstatically. Since he was a man, and not entirely comfortable with getting boners for other guys, he gritted his teeth against the truly wonderful tingles.

Luckily, Grygir was aware of the need for haste and didn't prolong the procedure. He murmured an abbreviated spell for shapechanging, then shot one final big wave of tingles into him.

"Rise," he said. "Walk as a man."

Just like that, Adam was back in his own skin, the shift too speedy to have hurt. He uncurled from the floor and stood. As he'd feared, he had a hard-on stiff enough to pound nails. Ari glanced at it and fought a smile.

"Faerie dust," he said. "It would happen to anyone."

Ari shook her head, her blue eyes twinkling. "Who said I was complaining?"

"What do you need for your ritual?" Grygir cut in politely.

He needed two struts of metal to form an X, preferably long enough to cover the door from corner to corner. He and Grygir pried them from the room's steel shelving, doing their best not to disturb the noisome specimens it held. That done, they brought the bars to the now unnervingly quiet portal.

Stepping into Francis's circle caused tiny jolts of electricity to shoot up his body hair. They couldn't see what was going on behind the barrier. The surface of the portal had reverted to muddied swirls of black and purple.

Adam turned back to Ari. "I need you," he said.

She heard the meaning beyond the moment. Her eyes widened, but all she did was step closer and take the hand he wasn't using to hold the metal bar. Her palms were warm and a little sweaty. Handcuffs notwithstanding, he thought he'd never felt a clasp as nice.

By changing form, he'd broken the moon bond between them. When her gaze met his, that didn't seem to matter. In his heart, in his soul, he'd always be linked to her.

"What do you need?" she whispered.

"I'm going to say some words and cut our fingers. When I tell you, we'll both squeeze a drop of blood onto the center of the X."

"Better hurry," Grygir said, from the other side of the metal structure. "It's awfully quiet in there."

Adam hurried so much the faerie had to correct his pronunciation a couple times. He hadn't quite finished when the purple demon began to snarl. Knowing he must have figured out what they were doing, Grygir grabbed the athame and pricked their fingers.

"Now," Adam said to Ari just as the demon slammed into the interdimensional barrier. The force of the impact caused the strange skin to bulge.

"No," the demon growled in its deep sea voice. "I paid for this portal!"

Again, it slammed the door with its massive shoulder. Adam and Grygir dug in and braced. The X trembled badly enough that their first drops of blood missed the spot. Fortunately, they hit the mark on the second try.

A blinding flash of light swallowed up the room. When it faded, not only was the portal gone, but also the X that had sealed it *and* all of Francis's chalk circles.

"Wow," Ari said, blinking rapidly at the place they'd been. "Now all we have to do is get past the dozen armed goons outside the door."

"They're gone," Adam and Grygir said at the same time. Apparently, both their ears were sharp enough to have heard the soldiers leave.

Ari snickered at their unplanned chorus, a reaction that wasn't quelled by them turning together to frown at her.

"You guys are too adorable!" she exclaimed.

Considering how she'd ogled the fae earlier, Adam's inner wolf didn't like her inclusiveness. It wanted to be the only male she adored.

∞

Adam and the faerie dressed as quickly as they could in what were unavoidably dead men's clothes, though Ari noticed neither of them touched Blackwater's. They were correct about the basement outside the spell room being empty. The house above was a different story. There, a heated battle raged, marked by thumps, crashes, small arms fire, and the shouts and cries of various species. It sounded like a zoo was at war.

Halfway up the cellar steps, Adam cocked his head in a wolfish way. "My men are fighting up there. Grant must have gotten a message through."

Grant's name clutched at her throat. Adam turned to her. "You stay here," he said. "I don't want you getting hurt in the confusion."

"Here?" she said, not liking that idea. This cellar had been creepy before it was scattered with dead people.

Adam lifted his brows at Grygir, who was a step behind her.

"Oh no," the fae lord said, continuing their bromance thing by immediately comprehending Adam's silent message. "I'm not hanging back to guard her."

"Some people would claim you owe me."

"Not that much," Grygir said darkly.

"Fine," Ari surrendered, understanding he wanted retribution for his fallen men. "I get it. Guns bad. Me not have one." She also wouldn't have known how to shoot one if she'd been given it. There was a possibility she could stop a bullet with her telekinesis, but perhaps that theory would be bettered tested under more controlled conditions, and without her handcuffs. "I'll wait out the fighting here. But—"

Adam had been moving upward to join the fray. "But?"

"You will come back for me, won't you?"

And there it was: the whole stupid snarl of fear that sometimes seemed to have replaced the person she was supposed to be. Was there anyone she could truly count on to stick by and defend her?

The craziest thing was Adam's eyes filled with tears. He reached out to squeeze her shoulder. "I'll come back for you, Ari. You can . . . bet your Yankees jacket on that."

She smiled, because he'd understood what the garment meant to her.

He and Grygir paused at the cellar door before going out. "She can bet her *Yankees jacket?*" she heard Grygir ask dryly. "You wolves sure are romantics."

Ari begged to differ with his sarcasm. One wolf at least was the perfect romantic for her.

∞

Ari meant to keep her word. She just couldn't sit on her thumbs in that damned basement. It wasn't the dead bodies that got to her. It was the noise of the fighting over her head.

Though she was no pro, she had some experience picking locks from the days when she and her friends would break into empty buildings to squat in bad weather. Trying to open her cuffs with

155

Francis's athame seemed worth a shot. Actually, it was better than a shot. The magic left in the blade was strong. Ari had barely stuck the tip in the key slot when the things snapped open.

She wished she'd known the knife would do that when the spinks had been closing in on her.

The regret wasn't important now that she was free to sneak out. She told herself she'd be careful; hide behind a door or a corner and use her gift to help. The damping wards remained around the house, but she could feel they weren't as solid as before. There were frayed places to get through them, if she kept her focus. She prayed the rune in her hair did what Grant had claimed. Good concentration was going to be vital.

Just in case it failed, she took the knife with her as well.

Creeping out onto the ground floor was more nerve wracking than she'd expected. She wasn't prepared for the reality of groups of people trying to slaughter each other. Fortunately, there were places to hang back out of the way. The police teams were impressive, and there were more of them than only Adam's men. They were *really* professional, not losing their cool like some of Blackwater's people were now that their leader was dead. She doubted the cops knew she'd tripped their opponents or spoiled their aim. They simply took advantage of any opening. In some ways, the surreptitious fighting took her back to working for Blackwater. Secretly attacking an enemy wasn't much harder than causing a favored horse to flag at the racetrack.

She couldn't worry about the fairness of what she did. Blackwater's people might or might not deserve to die, but they'd signed on to work for an awful man. Ari needed to help Adam's side. Not doing that wouldn't have been a choice she could live with.

∞

It was no surprise to Adam that the demons fought the hardest. Most were only in Resurrection on conditional work visas, and the wheels of Justice tended to grind harder over them. Despite the desperation of their resistance, between Adam's squad, the faerie, and the four tactical response teams Rick and Carmine had wrangled on short notice, many of Blackwater's people were taken into custody alive. A fleet of transport wagons were even then pulling out of the gate on the way to Central Booking.

The rest of Blackwater's men were enjoying a much quieter journey to the morgue.

They had no fatalities themselves, only injuries. In the same good news vein, Adam had hopes the demon Darius could be convinced to help dismantle what remained of the Eunuch's drug empire. He anticipated the city's crime stats taking a dive in the near future. Evil might not be defeated, but Good would definitely survive.

Curiously, Grant's body hadn't been on the roof. Adam hoped this didn't mean he'd been taken elsewhere for harvesting, a desecration he doubted Grant's people would appreciate. He issued an APB for any suspicious vehicles large enough to carry a gargoyle. Grant had died a hero. He deserved a burial his people would consider respectful.

He delegated Nate to notify Grant's mother, a task the laid back cop didn't like but was good at. Then Adam jogged back to the house to collect Ari.

He hadn't quite reached the door when she and Tony came out of it together. Adam's first reaction was that he didn't like how tightly Ari was clinging to his detective's side. His second was remembering Tony was gay. His third was gratitude that his friends would look out for her.

"Look who I found," Tony said to him with a grin.

Adam touched the side of her face, and she unwound from Tony to embrace him. Her cheek squashed against his chest, her arms wrapping his waist with surprising strength. Blood was smeared underneath her nose, as if it had bled again. She had a look on her face he couldn't interpret.

"It got quiet," she said. "I couldn't wait anymore."

Adam pressed his lips to her hair. "I'm sorry I didn't come for you right away. There were things to wrap up out here. I knew none of the fighting had reached the cellar."

"I understand," she said. "You're the boss. People expect you to oversee stuff. I'm just glad you're all right."

Oh, she didn't know how sorry she made him feel, much more than she could have by complaining. He kissed her temple, wanting to kick himself. He was aware she'd been let down by people she loved before.

Ari tipped her head back from him. "Tony told me Grant's body is missing."

"Yes," he said, "but we're doing what we can to find it. If someone's trying to harvest his organs, they won't get far."

"Adam, before I— Before Grant told me I ought to stab him, he sent me some strange pictures. He showed his dead body glowing before it flew away. Is that how gargoyles think they go to heaven?"

He'd figured Grant had given her permission to kill him, sparing her the sin of murder. "I don't know," he said, returning to her question. "I suppose it's possible. And different species . . . decompose in different ways. Gargoyles are very insular. We don't know that much about them."

"He was so cute," she said, her eyes tearing up.

Adam swiped one fat drop away with his thumb. As he did, he became aware that an awful lot of heads had turned to watch them.

"Sorry," Ari said, realizing it as well. "I'm embarrassing you in front of your coworkers."

"Nah." Adam hugged her a bit tighter. "They just haven't seen me getting mushy over a girl before."

She blushed, which he enjoyed right down to his toes.

"I love you," he said, not giving a damn how many sharp wolf ears heard. "Rick's going to be jealous, but you may be the best partner I ever had."

Tony sniggered, proving at least he was listening. "You aren't wrong about that."

"Can we leave soon?" Ari asked hopefully.

Adam groaned at how not soon it was going to be. "I can't, sweetheart. There's going to be a fricking mountain of processing for this number of arrests, even with all the team pitching in. But Tony could take you to his parents' house, so you won't be alone."

"Could I go to your house?" she asked.

Did she mean she'd rather be alone than with other people, or did she want to be around his things—in his territory, as it were?

"Sure," he said, conscious he had a different attitude toward company than she did. She wasn't used to the idea of a pack yet. "Tony and Rick's parents can check in on you there. They won't hover, I promise."

Ari smiled and stretched up his chest to press her lips to his. The kiss was sweet but far too short.

"I'll see you when I see you then," she said.

# CHAPTER ELEVEN

Adam hadn't lied about Rick and Tony's parents not hovering. Neither did their sister, Maria, who Ari finally met and got to thank for the loan of her clothes. Maria's husband had been one of cops on the tactical response teams, and Ethan had been chattering like a cricket about how brave and important his daddy was. Possibly sensing her need for quiet, Ethan's mother and grandparents were now up on the roof helping the three-year-old fly a cat-shaped kite that meowed loudly—and unhappily—when the wind hit it right.

Ethan's delighted laughter drifted down through Adam's open living room windows.

Dogs would be dogs, Ari supposed.

She sat curled up in a comfortable armchair—the only kind of furniture Adam seemed to own—her face turned to the cool autumn breeze. She was tired but not ready to face sleep and dreams.

The Eunuch was dead.

Adam had said he loved her.

It was safe for her to go back to her life in the normal world.

Those three facts chased each other inside her mind. She had decisions to make and no idea how to sort them out. What did she want? What should she? Three times Adam had said he loved her. Or, actually, it was four.

Not that she was counting or anything.

She hugged her knees up against her chest, her precious Yankees jacket warming her. It had been waiting for her in Adam's guest room. She hadn't worn it on their quest to find Blackwater, because she hadn't wanted anything to happen to it. She fingered its attached coins and ticket stubs, mementos from her favorite outings with Sarah and Maxwell. How could she trust Adam, whom she'd only known for days, the same way she trusted friends she'd shared everything with for years?

Then again, he had risked his life for her.

She rubbed the arms of the chair, too restless to be still. Sarah and Max needed to know the Eunuch was dead. She had to go home for that at least. Hell, Sarah had been MIA before she left. Had Blackwater's people hurt her when they clipped that lock of her hair? Had they harmed Max in the hospital?

If Ari returned to Manhattan, would Adam wait for her?

*Stupid*, she thought. He'd said he loved her four times. They'd had amazing sex. He'd wait for her.

But what then? And how did she decide what she wanted the answer to be? She was twenty-six. That ought to old enough to make grown up life choices.

She grimaced at herself, having circled back to the beginning. The sound of Adam's doorbell saved her from going around again.

His friends wouldn't ring, would they? Not down at the front door. Adam would be lucky if they knocked at his apartment before traipsing in. She had the feeling they all had each other's keys.

Curious, she edged her head out the open window. Down below, on the steps of the old brownstone, a UPS man waited with a stack of cartons. He had huge feet and hulking shoulders, but he didn't look scary—more like an overgrown farmboy. His hair was dusky gold, his skin a yummy shade of cafe au lait. From her current angle, that was all she could see. His head was bent over his delivery tablet.

Ari considered the ceiling above her. She could call the Lupones to answer the door. They were wolves and could handle trouble if this was some kind of hoax. She'd feel silly if it wasn't, plus she wasn't catching a danger vibe. Just because she'd had a rough couple days didn't mean she ought to stop trusting her instincts.

Adam's doorbell rang again.

*Fine*, she thought and grabbed the athame she hadn't admitted to carrying out of the Eunuch's house. The ceremonial dagger was probably evidence, but for now she felt better keeping it. It wasn't like she could tell who her gift would work on here, or when she'd get into trouble for using it.

She slid it in her right rear pocket before she opened the door.

"Delivery for Adam Santini and a girl named Ari," the UPS guy announced.

Actually, according to the logo on his brown uniform shirt, he was an **RPS** guy.

"I'm Ari," she said.

"Okeydokey," said the guy, turning to shift the packages into the vestibule. The cartons weren't heavy and this only took a few seconds.

"Holy smokes," Ari said when she saw the printing on their sides. Someone was sending Adam five, no, six cartons of Tiger! condoms. Adam couldn't have ordered these himself. He'd told her a six-pack of the enchanted rubbers cost two-weeks' salary. Six cartons would probably wipe out his bank account.

"Who sent these?" she demanded.

The RPS guy checked his handheld computer. "It says they're a gift from the head of the Gargoyle Council, in thanks for letting her son help vanquish their enemy."

"It doesn't say that!"

The RPS guy turned the screen around to show her. Okay, maybe it did. How was she to know delivery service operated differently here?

"That's crazy," she said, both rattled and choked up. "Her son is only dead because of us."

"I guess they see the bigger picture," said the delivery guy.

Ari narrowed her gaze at him. His tone was odd, and she realized he'd been keeping his head down this whole time, preventing her from getting a clear look at his face. He sounded like he was trying to disguise his voice, a baritone pretending to be a tenor, like maybe she'd recognize it otherwise. Too bad for him Ari had the perfectly normal gift of a first-rate auditory memory.

"Grant?" she said, hardly daring to believe it was him.

The RPS guy looked up and laughed. His eyes were citrine yellow with cat slits, exactly the same as Grant the gargoyle. "Mom warned me you'd see through this."

"But how— You're—"

"Shh," he said, one finger to his smiling lips. "This is the gargoyles' biggest secret. Hardly anyone knows we're a form of were. Most gargoyles don't change if they can help it. It's difficult to shift back without a full moon, and they find it slightly embarrassing to be stuck in a shape so small."

"But you were dead. Even the sorcerer thought so."

"The magic inside me wasn't completely damped by the wards. I couldn't snap the cables that held me, but I could do magic on myself. I created the illusion that I was dead. Then, once everyone was gone, I changed to this shape and slipped out of their net. The shift repaired the damage to my heart—which, by the way, good aim."

"Don't remind me," she said faintly. "Jesus, I thought those pictures you sent me meant you expected to go to gargoyle heaven."

"Sorry," he said. "It's tricky to communicate with a nonreader."

Ari shook her head at Grant, amazed that it was still him inside such a different body.

"Could we hug now, do you think?" he asked.

She laughed and let him pull her off her feet in a bearlike embrace. He might not have much practice, but he was a great hugger. When he held her, she felt like she had a brand new friend.

"Ah," he said, putting her down at last. "That's one good thing about having arms."

Just looking at him made her grin. She did have to ask one question. "Not that I'm complaining, but why the special delivery of the very expensive condoms?"

"Er." Grant scratched the skin of his cheek. "That first night when I was up on the roof and Adam went out to buy them? I noticed this was his brand. And, please, don't worry about the price. Gargoyles handle most of the charmwork for Tiger! brand. We get a big discount."

"Good to know," she said, more amused than she thought was sensitive to admit. One stereotype people believed about gargoyles seemed to be true: They were a teensy bit snoopy.

∞

Much to Adam and his team's relief, one of the backup squads took over processing paperwork a couple hours into it.

"We're claiming the rest of your collars for ourselves," they teased. "So you idiots' heads don't swell up."

If this meant he could go home, Adam was ready to hand them over. He wanted his own shower, his own bed, and Ari—not in that order.

Nate had suffered a dislocated shoulder during the fight. With no small disgust, he handed Rick the keys to the response van. Rick drove fine, but Nate felt a need to "help" anyway.

"You've got to baby her," he was saying, his patient tone so forced it was more like the opposite. "If you punch the gas instead of push it, she's going to stall."

"Maybe you should sit on my lap and work the pedals yourself," Rick snapped.

The riding benches were in place in the back. Tony and Adam smiled at each other across the bay.

"Those two," Carmine sighed, leaning back and closing his eyes.

"I'm not the problem," Rick objected. "He's the one who treats this van like it's girlfriend."

"Guys," Adam said. "Knock it off. The big bad is dead, we're all alive, and our arrest record is through the roof. Try to remember life is good."

"Yeah," Tony seconded. "But Nate could sit on *my* lap if he wanted."

"Do not go there," Nate moaned, though he was laughing. "My acceptance of your lifestyle choice depends on you not daydreaming about me."

The van turned before Adam expected. He twisted forward to see where they were. Rick was driving onto the giant parking lot for Pocket Foods.

"All *right*," Nate said, his anger at Rick forgotten. "Time to stock up for the victory celebration. BBQ and beer."

"I don't know," Adam said, remembering how shaky Ari had looked earlier. She wasn't going to be up for a party. "Maybe we could put this off until tomorrow."

"It's tradition," Rick said, a tad stubbornly. "Everyone will be expecting it. You can have sex with Ari later."

"Dude." Nate slapped Rick's bicep with his uninjured hand.

Rick concentrated on parking. "Whatever. You know that's why he doesn't want to celebrate with us tonight."

Nate shook his head at that. When Adam looked away from them, Carmine was watching him. The older wolf kept watching until Rick got out and slammed the door. "He's your beta," he said quietly. "Sometimes they get possessive."

Adam knew this. He'd just thought Rick would be happy for him. He wasn't simply Adam's second in command, he was his best friend.

"I'll send him back for a chat," Tony volunteered, then jumped out the back doors.

Adam climbed out on legs that felt a century old. Between changing early and the fight and healing that damned whipping, he was ready to drop where he stood. Tony must have been persuasive with his brother. Rick trotted back to him with no foot dragging.

"Sorry," he said before Adam mustered the energy to start in on him. He rubbed the back of his neck, probably trying to coax his inner hackles to stop bristling. "Ari's a nice girl. And I'm glad you've found your mate. It's just weird to see you gaga over a female. You've always been casual about girls before."

"I still love you," Adam said, too tired to make it a joke.

"Jeez." Embarrassed, Rick mopped one hand down his face.

Adam laughed at that, but there was one more thing Rick ought to know. "She's more than my mate. Ari helped me shut the portal."

Rick's eyes got big. "I assumed the faerie closed it."

"Apparently they can't do that unless they opened it the first place."

"Wow. So Ari's your twin flame. Like your parents were to each other."

"Yes."

"Wow." Rick tossed his keys from one hand to the other, sorting this out in his head. "Well, your folks were great together. You and Ari should be happy."

"I hope so."

"You will be." He shuffled his feet sheepishly. "Look, we could postpone the party. People would understand. Sometimes you . . . gotta put your better half first."

Adam considered, then shook his head. "Tired or not, Ari's no weakling. Might as well throw her in the deep end now."

Hearing himself, he wished he didn't sound so dour.

∞

Werewolf strength came in handy for carrying a vanload of food up three flights of steps. As the five of them went into his apartment,

Ari was leaving the kitchen with a bottle of spring water. She looked surprised to see them but not angry. Without a second thought, Adam set down his boxes and went to her. Ari hugged him, and it was like *she'd* become his home; she felt that good to him. She laughed at the intensity of his squeeze, but she also buried her nose in his neck. She smelled of his shampoo, which pleased him. The faint whiff of another male pleased him less, but of course she'd been around a lot of men today.

"Wait till you taste elf ale," Tony crowed as he passed by their embrace with his towering load. "It's the awesomest."

"Don't listen to him," Nate countered, carrying his smaller load with one arm. "Faerie stout all the way."

"Sorry," Adam mumbled into her hair. "This party thing is a tradition."

"That's okay. You had a big win. You should celebrate."

"I *was* hoping for a nap."

She tipped her head back and waggled her brows. "I bet you were, big boy."

This was when he realized he was getting hard. He cleared his throat, knowing that sort of nap would have to wait. He'd never tell her, but she looked like hell. He wanted her to get eight solid hours of lights out. Then he'd lock her in his bedroom. A growl smoked from him at the thought. She laughed and patted his chest.

"You got a delivery. I stashed it in your bedroom closet. Don't let your friends in there unless you want to be teased."

He wasn't really paying attention, more soaking her up through all his senses. "How do you feel?"

"Better," she said, her tired blue eyes locked to his. "I used your shower. As you can see, Maria loaned me another dress. And I think it's finally sinking in for me that the Eunuch is dead."

He stroked her pale hair around her head. She hadn't put the spikes back in, and it was very soft. "She loaned you a party dress. I guess Rick was right. Everyone really is expecting this."

Ari laid her cheek above his heart. "I'm glad you're here," she said.

∞

The crowd at the party wasn't one Ari would have predicted she'd ever hang out with. Adam's roof deck was jam-packed with cops, former cops, cop's wives and cop's kids—most of them relatives. Maria's husband Johnny was playing king of the grill station, with the meat tongs as his scepter. It took some insisting, but Ari finally convinced him that when she said she wanted her ribs well done, she didn't mean half raw.

"Adam!" he cried in the laughing shout so many of the men seemed to use. "You gotta teach your girl here some taste!"

Everyone assumed she and Adam were a couple. More unnerving, they treated her as if she were a princess. Tony switched her chair out for one he thought was nicer, Rick—who'd struck her as a bit standoffish before tonight—built her a plate heaped with cold salads, and Nate—whose right arm was now in a sling—poured her a little glass of his faerie stout so she could sample it. One boy of about fourteen asked if he could run and get her a sweater, because he knew humans weren't as hot as werewolves. He'd blushed right after, which was cute, but the fussing still made her feel self-conscious.

Fortunately, the woman were acting normally. Ari was relieved when Maria plunked down next to her and sighed. Adam's cousin was a pretty woman. Taller and bustier than Ari, she had long curly black hair and the same golden brown eyes as her two brothers. She was also one of the few guests Ari even sort of knew.

"Are they always like this?" she asked in an undertone.

"You mean because they're waiting on you hand and foot? Absolutely not." Laughing, Maria tipped up her beer for a swallow. "You're their heroine tonight. Adam told them how brave you were."

"He did?" she asked, a hint of dismay in it. Would they think she was more or less courageous if they knew what she'd sneaked upstairs to do? Tony had found her near the stairwell. Even he wasn't aware how long she'd been out of the cellar.

"Girlfriend," Maria said. "They hardly needed to be told. You faced down the Eunuch. And a frickin' proscribed demon. I know wolves who wouldn't have done as much. Of course, they're also seriously impressed with Adam. Even for an alpha, he kicked butt."

"It was pretty cool the way he broke those warded handcuffs with his brute strength." She'd spoken without thinking. Evidently, this was a big deal. Also evidently, Adam hadn't been tooting his own horn.

"*No,*" Maria said, her elf ale pausing halfway to her lips. "Alphas are extra strong, but that's the equivalent of you lifting a pickup truck. He must have been very motivated to get you out of there."

"We both were," she said uncomfortably.

Maybe Maria sensed this, because she fell silent. Adam was sitting a little ways off from them, surrounded by a group of laughing, mostly male admirers. Strings of colored lights festooned the roof deck, increasing the festive air. Perhaps because Ethan's father was occupied with the grill, Ethan had crawled into Adam's lap. The little boy wasn't quite asleep, but Adam was rocking him there, patting his butt in time to what sounded like Gipsy Kings music. His wrists no longer bore the firebug tattoos. His change in form had erased them, just as it had snapped their moon bond. Neither loss appeared to trouble him. Adam looked tired but happy.

*This isn't so bad*, she thought. She liked seeing him happy.

Then he turned his head and caught her staring. His arms tightened subtly around his nephew, and the rocking momentarily stopped. Such yearning filled his expression that Ari lost her breath. The absence of the moon bond didn't matter. She knew what he was thinking. It was written across his face. Even though she'd warned him taking care of herself was more than she could manage some days, he wanted to have kids with her.

When Adam said *I love you*, he didn't mess around.

Her heart started knocking against her ribs. She guessed Maria heard the thumping with her wolf ears, because she looked at her.

"They're not as hard as they look," she said.

Ari tore her eyes from Adam. "What aren't?"

"Kids. Well, sometimes they are, but Adam will be a great dad. Just like my Johnny. You won't go wrong with him."

"Maria, Adam and I aren't—"

The men suddenly lifted their bottles for a toast. "To Grant," someone said. "A true prince among gargoyles."

Ari remembered they all thought Grant was dead. Guilt niggled at her, but she didn't think she ought to enlighten them—not when they so obviously were gossips. Grant had said being weres was his people's biggest secret. Ari wasn't sure she even dared tell Adam.

"To Grant," everyone chorused.

Rick rose from his seat awkwardly. "To Ari," he said, gesturing his beer toward her. "May she come to love our pack as much as we're certain to love her."

Coming on top of Adam's yearning, this was too much. Ari's face and chest flashed hot. Maria wasn't the only one jumping to conclusions. Adam's pack seemed to think they were halfway down the aisle. Her mouth fished open and shut. She couldn't deny their assumption. She'd embarrass Adam in front of his friends. Plus, she could see from his discomfort that he hadn't expected Rick to do this.

"Okay," he said, patting the air for quiet. "Let's not rush Ari into anything."

"A-ri," someone started chanting—not a member of his pack. The wolf was immediately joined by a dozen more. "A-ri. *A-ri.*"

"Jesus," Adam said. "Everyone shut up!"

Amazingly, everybody did.

"Ari wasn't born here," he said into the calm. "And she has the right to make her own decisions. Why don't we let her do that?"

This was as good as declaring he wanted to marry her.

Of course, given the way her throat had clenched with emotion, if he'd asked her right that second, she'd probably have said *yes.*

∞

The party wound down soon after that. Though everyone insisted it was getting late, Adam knew they'd felt awkward watching their host be publically rejected by his mate. He knew Ari hadn't meant to hurt him. Nonetheless, most of his guests wouldn't understand her hanging back.

Adam was alpha. And a catch. Why wouldn't she want to marry him and be a part of his pack?

*And have his children*, he reminded himself. Mustn't forget that detail.

He caught her sneaking worried glances at him as they cleared up the trash with Maria, Rick and Tony. Maria's husband Johnny had carried Ethan home, slung sleeping over his shoulder like a puppy who'd played too hard. Adam's last glimpse of his nephew had been a poignant one. As clear as the memory was, it hadn't left him in the mood to soothe Ari's anxiety. He wasn't going to yell at her. She did have the right to her own choices. Just sue him if her choice tonight had left him a bit grumpy.

Finally, the Lupone siblings headed off for their own homes— Rick and Tony only having to walk downstairs. Once Adam and

Ari were alone, Ari didn't beat around the bush. "I really am sorry, Adam. Your friends' assumptions caught me off guard."

"I guess mine did too," he said sourly.

Her hands twisted together in front of Maria's pretty flowered party dress, the picture of vulnerable femininity. Adam wanted to toss his mate's little body over his shoulder and carry her to his cave. His stupid dick began to lengthen inside his jock, totally behind that idea. He couldn't kid himself the cause was pre-full moon horniness. Ari just being Ari did this to him.

A knock sounded on the door. Thinking Tony or Rick must have forgotten something, Adam swore and opened it.

Lord Grygir was waiting in the hall. A hot pink polo shirt with a sprite stitched on its breast in electrum thread draped his model-perfect torso. Dark gray slacks garbed his equally perfect legs. His black dress shoes shone like mirrors, as did his fingernails. He was either on his way somewhere more important, or he was attempting to appear somewhat respectful. Adam presumed his errand had to do with the dark red vacuum canister he was holding between his perfect hands.

"Forgive me for interrupting," Grygir said stiffly. "I waited until your guests were gone."

"How did you—" Adam stopped before he asked a stupid question. A little thing like a front door lock wouldn't keep out a faerie. The idea of Grygir standing in the street, waiting for his guests to leave, was slightly mind boggling. "Never mind. Please come in."

"That won't be necessary. I only came to give you this." With a hint of belligerence, he thrust the canister at Adam. Adam took it dazedly. "I was able to recover some of my bodyguards' remains before they dissipated. If the Talent agrees to marry you, they'll be useful."

Adam was completely gobsmacked. Leaving aside that these were remains, Lord Grygir had just handed him sixteen ounces of uncut faerie dust. Its street value would be next to incalculable.

"I can't accept this," he said firmly.

"You can," Lord Grygir insisted, one eyebrow arching up coolly. "I owe both of you my life, and I value my life highly. Chances are you . . . also preserved the life of a friend of mine. I will email you the contact information of a trusted associate at a pharmaceutical lab. Prepared correctly, the contents of this canister will allow your non-were mate to live as long and healthily as you."

When he put it that way . . . Adam met the proud fae lord's eyes. To his surprise, he saw a hint of envy in them. "Thank you," he said.

"You agree our debt is cancelled?"

"I do," Adam said, understanding his response was contractually binding.

He expected Grygir to leave. Instead, the faerie's face screwed up like he'd swallowed a lemon. "About my true name . . ."

*Ah*, Adam thought. The faerie wouldn't like that he'd heard. "Sir," he said, not prepared to call him *milord*. "You're one of the citizens I'm sworn to protect. I'd never share knowledge that could compromise your safety."

Grygir stared at him impassively. "Others heard my name as well."

Was he worried about Ari? "You shouldn't doubt Ari will honor your privacy. You saw her face down that demon. You of all people understand why it wanted her."

"I don't mean the pureheart." Grygir sighed quietly, some debate decided inside his mind. "I expect it's pointless to ask you to let me kill a few of the men you and your policemen put in jail today. Just the ones who were close enough to overhear."

"Oh," Adam said. He'd forgotten how ruthless faeries could be. "Yes, I'm afraid it is."

"Then I will not attempt to bribe you."

The faerie dust would have made an enticing payoff, if he hadn't given it to Adam already. "I appreciate that," Adam said with dry respect.

Satisfied—or as near to it as he was getting—Lord Grygir bowed and left.

Adam shut the door, then turned to find Ari waving one hand in front of her face. The faerie had left a decidedly heady aroma behind him.

Annoyance flicked through him. Was Ari waving the smell away because she'd rather not be aroused around him?

"Whew," she said. "Looks like everyone expects us to get hitched."

Under the circumstances, he didn't find her attempt at humor very humorous.

"Sorry," she said, her lips twisting. She gestured toward the pressurized container of faerie dust. "Isn't that stuff a dangerous street drug?"

"It depends on what it's combined with. It had medical uses too. Look, Ari, I know we're both tired. Maybe we could leave this aside for now. Talk about it in the morning."

Or never, if she really was going to refuse him.

"Okay." She hesitated. "Would you rather I stayed in the guest room?"

"No," he said, instantly husky with emotion. "I'll always want you with me."

He saw from her expression that he'd pleased her. She wasn't sure of them as a *them*, but he'd pleased her. He promised himself that was enough to build on.

∞

Ari showered again, which was plain nervousness on her part. She'd thought maybe the faerie's visit was what had gotten her wet and squirmy, what with his aphrodisiac scent and all. The cleansing effect of the shower dispelled that theory. Adam made her want him all by himself, no matter how tired she was.

With a sense of anticipation she couldn't quash, she padded back to his room in her towel. Except for stashing his special delivery, she hadn't been in his bedroom. The space was comfortable, just like the rest of his house, with an old-fashioned brass-railed bed, two battered nightstands, and a couple overstuffed armchairs. The walls were beige and the windows big. The only extravagance she could see was that the bed was king size. Adam was sitting up in it with the sheet pulled to his waist. His stomach was lean enough that the only flesh to crease was skin. He had the TV on to the news. Ari glanced at the screen, then did a double take.

"Adam, is that newscaster a talking horse?"

"Strictly speaking, she's a talking unicorn. She's very popular. A little liberal, but viewers consider her trustworthy."

Ari's wobbly knees sat her on the end of his bed. The newscaster—news equine?—did have a little spiral horn sticking out of its—*her*—forehead. Her blonde mane looked like it had been professionally blow dried. Adam clicked the set off with his remote, leaving her blinking.

He put his hands on her shoulders, massaging them gently from behind, which did nothing to put more starch her knees. His lips whispered up her neck to her ear. "There's plenty more marvels to see in Resurrection, you know."

"I wouldn't stay for that. You're the only reason that matters."

"Good," he said and kissed her.

Kissing him was easy to fall into. He did it so well, and he tasted so good. When they touched each other, there was nothing to argue about, no reason for her to worry about disappointing him. Lost in the wet slow pleasure, Ari barely noticed when he tugged off her towel.

"If you're too tired for this . . ." he kind of panted, giving her a chance to stop.

"Nuh-uh," she said and pulled his talented mouth back to hers. She was tired, but this was way better than sleeping. Besides which, she was pretty sure he'd do most of the work. Her hands slid up his muscled back, and he moaned.

Two seconds later, her spine was flat on the mattress and all six foot two of him was over her. His hips came down to hers and pressed luxuriantly. *Oh boy*, she thought, because he turned out to be naked too. He gave a little grunt as he pushed again. His cock felt hot enough to brand her, its thickness slanting to the side to lie across her hipbone. He stretched his gorgeous hard body up her to dig one of his remaining Tiger! condoms from the nightstand drawer. Ari grinned at the thought of how many more awaited unsuspected in his closet.

"What?" he asked, his voice so hoarse it gave her the shivers.

"I'll tell you later," she promised. "But don't put that on just yet."

She pushed him up so that he rose to his knees and elbows. Once his weight was lifted, she wriggled under his body until his amazing cock dangled above her face. The shaft jerked harder as she approached, like a string had been attached to its shiny tip.

"Ari . . ."

"Forget it," she said before he denied himself an indulgence one big part of him clearly craved. "This won't tire me out. I'm still flat on my back. I've been dreaming of tasting you again."

He laughed at her reasoning, then groaned as she pulled his erection down with one hand. She'd never sucked a man off in this position. The angle was a little weird but convenient, because he was doing the thrusting. He was very careful about it, and it wasn't long before she let go of his base and relaxed. His balls were fun to explore, and the firm smooth stretch behind them. He made deep noises in his throat as she played with both. Ari was letting out nearly the same moans. She loved the feel of him on her tongue and between her cheeks—the roundness, the hardness, the buttery smoothness of his skin. She loved the way he trembled as his excitement rose, the way his big thigh muscles bunched with tension. He'd dropped his head down to watch her, and she knew that aroused him too. The flow of his precome grew increasingly salty.

Ari moved the pads of her thumbs to the place where his gland would swell. She rubbed them lightly back and forth across it.

"Christ," he breathed, pushing in almost too far that time.

She could sense him fighting conflicting urges. Keep going and enjoy this. Pull out and shove into her pussy. She let her hands roam up his thighs to the clenched muscles of his ass. Because she could, she smoothed her hands in praise over them. That longing sated, she took his hips in her firmest grip, directing his next thrust and then his next, letting him know precisely how far she was comfortable with him going.

He trembled harder, but he didn't withdraw. "Ari," he moaned. "I don't think I can stand much more of this."

He did, though, for five tremulous, gasping minutes. He was a take-charge guy, but allowing her to guide him was doing it for him. When he gave up, he wrenched out of her mouth as if he didn't have an instant to spare, flopping away from her on his back. His hands were clenched and pressed to his forehead as his lungs labored for control. His cock bounced and throbbed above his belly like a thing possessed. "Don't touch me right now," he warned.

She didn't, but she rolled onto her stomach beside him to watch him struggle not to come from nothing. She thought she'd never seen anything so hot.

"Stop grinning at me like that."

Since his eyes were screwed shut, he was only guessing. She drew one finger around his tightly beaded up left nipple.

"Shit," he said, his cock jerking hard again. A tiny spurt jetted from its hole.

"Want me to unwrap the condom?" she teased.

"Yes," he snapped. "And don't move from the position you're in now."

He was back to giving orders, but she had no complaints. She passed him the opened condom, which he rolled on with gritted teeth.

"Stay," he said, pointing at her like a naughty puppy.

Resisting the urge to giggle, Ari took a grip on the brass bed's bars and arched her bare bottom. She hadn't forgotten doggy style was his thing.

Her blatant tease earned her a nice little curse. More than a curse, actually. As he climbed over her and kneed her legs wider, he leaned down to give her ass a nip. His fangs had descended. She felt their hard curve against her skin. All at once, a gush of cream ran from her.

"God," Adam growled, nuzzling up to her from behind, his tongue reaching between her labia. "Please don't be insulted, but you are the best fucking lay ever."

She would have laughed, except he'd begun sucking and licking his way up her back. He was really tasting her—her sweat, her skin, the scent underneath her arms. He must have liked it. His dick just kept getting harder. Every time he rubbed and rolled it against her, she thought no way could it get bigger.

He kissed his greedy, groaning trail to her nape, where his lips sealed to her skin and pulled. His whole body heaved over hers, shoving her down into the bed. Man, he was into this.

Ari was too. Her spine felt like it was all tingle and no bone. Just the same, she knew she'd better call a halt to this.

"Don't," she said.

He groaned and sucked harder. Ari reached back to yank his hair.

"I have to go home soon," she pleaded. "At least for a while. If you give me another of those moon-bond hickies, leaving will be too difficult."

Adam released her and panted. "You're right. I'm being selfish and stupid."

Ari's eyes burned with tears. "You aren't either of those things. You have no idea what you . . . being so serious means to me."

He rubbed his cheek over hers, seeming to force himself to relax. "Okay," he said. "We'll just do the rest."

He kissed her temple and then her shoulder, his lips as gentle as they'd been fierce before. The *rest* began with him sliding his forearm beneath her pelvis, to lift her hips for entry.

"Do you want me on my knees?" she asked.

"No," he said, his voice as rough as if he were half wolf. "I want to cover you. I want to drive you down into the bed."

She bent one knee to scoot her leg further to the side.

"Oh yeah," he said, his knee coaxing it even higher. His body settled on hers, hot and hard all over. His hips wriggled, and the wide round tip of him touched her folds. Ari reached back to grip the thigh that was spreading her wider. Its muscles tightened as he pushed in.

"Oh *yeah*," he said even lower. His free hand slid up her arm to grip the bed rail above her fist. Right then, Ari couldn't do anything but moan. These slow entries of his killed her. They went on *forever*, allowing her to savor every masculine inch of him. He pushed hard at the end of the thrust and held, his balls squashed tight against her. He stretched her so persuasively she was already coming a little.

"Adam," she whispered.

His hips rocked forward, giving her another pleasure twinge. He dragged his face across her shoulder. "I feel you. I feel how ready you are to go."

He undulated again, not quite sending her over. The arm he'd wedged under her hips pulled back, enabling his hand to engulf her pubis. His fingers squeezed her mound, then parted her labia. So lightly she wouldn't have felt if she weren't hyper-sensitized, he pushed her clitoral hood back and forth.

Ari moaned and dug her fingernails into his hairy thigh. Her neck arched back and he nuzzled it. He was breathing harder, rougher. She knew he wanted to bite her, and she almost gave permission. He grunted, his pelvis hitching deeper into her. Without warning, his middle finger dug in to rub her swollen clit with quick and intense pressure.

The tether holding back her orgasm snapped. She cried out as pleasure shook her, clutching her inner muscles around the hard length of him. She expected him to say something. He could be plenty verbal during sex, and he liked it when she was. Instead, he dragged back through her wet contractions, sucked in a giant breath, and started pistoning into her.

His speed was shocking, the force he used a risk few men could have pulled off. Each thrust's strength was so carefully controlled that it stole her breath with excitement but didn't hurt. Despite having just come, he drove the sharpness of her sensations right to the brink again.

"Ah," she cried, now hanging onto his leg for dear life. "Ah, ah."

Adam shoved her left leg as wide as her right. She was spread like a frog, barely able to move, and she'd never felt any helplessness that enjoyable. She tried to groan his name but couldn't. Adam released the rattling head rail to shove that hand under her right breast. Spikes of pleasure shot back through her taut nipple.

Adam's growl was indistinguishable from an actual wolf.

Too damned turned on not to, Ari came with a wail.

Adam gave her thirty seconds of crazed pumping, then yanked out and flipped her onto her back. She couldn't have stopped him moving her if she'd tried. His strength and coordination were just too great. His speed was as well. She barely had time to miss him being inside her before he plunged in again.

She was lucky she was limber. He bent her knees to her shoulders, using the bulge of his biceps to trap them there. His eyes were glowing, his lips peeled back. She hadn't noticed his lower set of fangs before, but she saw them now. He flinched when he saw her see them.

"I love them," she panted. "I love . . . everything about you."

She hadn't known he could, but he went faster. His eyes squeezed shut, his handsome face straining as he concentrated on the sensation of pumping his cock into her. He pushed up on his hands to give his hips a freer range of motion. His penetrations lengthened, though each drive was just as swift. Ari hovered on the edge again. She couldn't help tightening on him.

He cursed, veins bulging on his brow and neck. His cock got harder, his hips moving desperately now. He wasn't trying to hold off; he was racing for the gold. Ari grabbed his glistening arm muscles and slung herself up him.

He gasped and a glow burst from his tightly shut eyelids. He slammed into her and went.

She went with him, his pleasure the match for her climactic gunpowder. He'd reared back from his waist for the first kick of ejaculation. As she came, he moaned and lowered again, his arms gathering her to him. He wasn't thrusting so much then, more jamming deep inside her. His cock, by contrast, jerked like a spawning fish. The extra gland at his base pulsed wildly.

To her amazement, she actually felt the condom filling as he came. That couldn't be right. Was it part of the Tiger! enchantment? More and more poured from him until his body simply shuddered in her embrace.

"Oh God," he sighed, sagging down on her at last.

He continued to spasm a little.

She soothed her hands up his sweating, still writhing spine.

"Wow," she said and kissed his shoulder.

He held the worst of his weight off her on his elbows. "Sorry. Should have warned you. The closer to the moon we get, the bigger our orgasms."

Ari hugged his butt with her calves. "Not complaining," she said.

He opened his eyes slowly. They looked at each other for a long, quiet time. They'd faced life and death together, but somehow that didn't feel as important as what they were facing now. The green glow in Adam's irises faded but never quite went out.

"I *really* want you to stay with me," he said.

Ari stroked one beautiful lean cheekbone, his whisker bristles prickling under her fingertips. "I have to check on my friends. I have to tell them the Eunuch's dead."

"I could . . . come with you."

For one aching second she wanted exactly that. "I have to be apart from you for a bit. We've known each other such a short time, and you're asking me to make some pretty big changes in my life. I'm not sure I can live up to your expectations."

He hadn't officially asked her to marry him, but he didn't contradict her words, as some men might have to spare their ego. He petted her hair back from her forehead. "I think you can live up to them. I also think—" He stopped to compose his thoughts. "You could never disappoint me so much that I wouldn't count myself lucky to share the rest of my life with you."

He struck her speechless. She wasn't sure he realized she was silent because she found what he said so extraordinarily generous. He pulled gently back from her hold and out of her body, reaching down to secure the condom as he withdrew.

She watched him roll away from her to the side of the mattress, watched his long arm flex as he removed the rubber. The shifting of the muscles in his gorgeous back was a work of art she wanted to memorize. His silky tanned skin gleamed with drying sweat. The intimate tasks were those any man might perform. The fact that he did them made them miraculous to her. Wishing she knew how to put into words what he meant to her, Ari laid her hand where his waist narrowed. Adam reached back to rub it.

"Sleep," he said. "I know you need it."

This was advice she couldn't resist, though part of her wanted to. Adam left the bed, and she curled up around his pillow, which smelled wonderfully of him. Her limbs grew heavier. She heard noises in the bathroom, then the kitchen. She was so tired she felt like she'd been drugged. She literally didn't have the strength to move. Adam came back. The mattress dipped and creaked behind her. A glass of water clicked down on the nightstand in front of her. The lamp that sat on it was switched off. Adam squirmed down and spooned her, his arm a warm hard weight over her.

The sense of safety and comfort that enveloped her could have been a dream. Her second to last conscious thought was that she should never leave this man's side. Her last was that life was rarely that simple.

# CHAPTER TWELVE

For the first time in his life, Adam had zero interest in going in to work. He went anyway, of course. He wasn't irresponsible. He was just incredibly surly.

After a week of being back with no word from Ari, his commander called him into his office and told him to go on leave. "Get your head on straight," he'd said. "You're making your team miserable."

Adam didn't argue. He cleared out his locker and went home. Two days later, he found the special delivery Ari had told him about on the night of their ill-fated victory party. He didn't wear a lot of clothes that required hanging up, and he hadn't opened the closet until then. When he saw what the cartons held, he nearly put his fist through the wall.

Nothing could have driven her absence home harder. He'd known giving Ari time to sort out her feelings was bound to be difficult. He hadn't known he'd miss her enough to hurt.

Every male friend he had asked him out for beers, but Adam turned them down. What if Ari came back and he wasn't there? That she would come back he was sure. She just didn't believe she could have a normal happy life full of friends and family, couldn't trust that Adam's love wouldn't go away. That's why she was afraid to give him her heart. Adam understood that. He wanted her to be certain. He knew she did love him.

Just in case she didn't, he started sleeping in the guest room, where his apartment smelled most like her.

She'd been gone more than three weeks when Maria sent Ethan over to visit for the day. That went fine until the time arrived for the three-year-old to leave. Then Adam had to sit down and cry a bit.

"Unca Adam!" Ethan had wailed, pelting back to him. He'd scrambled recklessly into Adam's lap, his little sneakers nearly emasculating him. "I'll stay! Pwease don't cwy anymore."

Adam had laughed through his tears and hugged him. He thought he could live without his own kids if he had to. He wasn't sure he could live without Ari.

The story of his little meltdown must have traveled through the wolf grapevine. Two nights later, Rick, Tony and Nate barged into his kitchen with a supply of alcohol.

"You're being pathetic," Nate said, twisting open a bottle of faerie stout and sticking it in his hand. "She's your damned twin flame. You have to go after her."

"Seriously," Rick said. "These guys do not like having me in charge."

"You're not so bad," Tony said, probably throwing his big brother into shock. "But Nate is right." He turned the chair next to Adam's backwards, sitting on it with his arms and chin draped over the top rung. "There's a time to be understanding, and there's a time to go after what you want."

Adam took a long swallow of cold dark beer. "She'll come back when she's ready."

"Make her ready," Tony said. "I can't believe I'm saying this, but you need to butch up, cuz."

Adam looked from one of his packmembers to the other. All of them were nodding.

"You can't teach her to trust you when she's there and you're here," Rick pointed out. "All you're doing is letting her run around the hamster worry-wheel in her head."

This struck Adam as surprisingly insightful. Sometimes he forgot his second had more than one side to him.

"Okay," he said, his stomach clenching with nervousness. "I guess I'm butching up."

# CHAPTER THIRTEEN

The full moon floated above the glittering towers of Manhattan like the starless sky was a sea. A month had passed since Adam had walked Ari to the suburban train's Resurrection stop to say goodbye to her. During that time, Ari had sprung Maxwell from the hospital, got back her hostess job at Mikos, and helped Max track Sarah to her parents' house on Long Island. Sarah had run to them when Blackwater's goons threatened her.

Because Ari and Max had been under the impression that Sarah's parents were dead, this was not the first place they'd looked.

As it turned out, Sarah's family had big bucks. Although their free-spirited daughter clearly confounded them, they weren't the monsters Max's abusive folks had been, nor had they kicked her to the curb like Ari's. Whey they'd initially met as street kids, Sarah had been too embarrassed to admit she'd run away simply because they'd been stifling her. By the time Maxwell and Ari found her, Sarah was ready to leave . . . but on better terms. Her parents might be the same as before, but she'd grown up in how she coped with them.

Growing up hadn't stopped her from bursting into tears of shame the moment she laid eyes on Max. She thought she shouldn't have let the Eunuch's enforcers scare her out of the city when he'd been in trouble. Ari shared her opinion a tiny bit, though—to be fair—Sarah might have gotten herself killed if she'd tried to stick by him. It also occurred to her that Sarah could have run home at any time. Instead, she'd shared Ari and Maxwell's deprivations, working just as hard as them to make sure they all got through them.

Everyone had their own way of being brave, she guessed.

As near as they could figure, the locks of hair Blackwater used to frighten Ari had been culled from brushes left behind in their old apartment, which his sorcerers could have tidied up magically. Neither Maxwell nor Sarah saw his men again after Ari left New York. Possibly, they'd all gone to Resurrection with him. With luck, the RPD had tossed them in jail by now.

Aside from sparing her friends some TMI regarding Adam, Ari told them all about her experiences in Faerie. Maxwell seemed to believe her. Sarah pretended to, but Ari had a feeling her friend was humoring her. Ari could live with that. Though Sarah was accustomed to Ari's gift, gargoyles and werewolves and faeries were a big package to swallow.

What she found more difficult to adjust to was the change in Sarah and Max's relationship. A week after they'd rented a new apartment together across the bridge in Brooklyn, Maxwell had moved into the big bedroom with Sarah and handed his off to her. Ari knew he was over-the-moon happy. For years he'd been in love with Sarah, and finally she loved him the same way. They disappeared for long walks nearly every evening and came back starry eyed.

Ari would have envied them if she hadn't known everything they enjoyed was hers for the asking. All she had to do was trust herself to face the things that scared her. Considering she'd gone toe-to-toe with an energy-sucking demon, it should have been easy.

Tonight, Maxwell had his art stuff set up on the table in their combined living room-kitchen. He'd had a burst of creativity once Ari finished healing the broken bones in his arms and hands. The process had taken almost as long as finding Sarah, but Ari was proud to say she hadn't overloaded a single time. Max was good as new—better than, he said. He was working on his own graphic novel, which he hoped to someday make a living at, rather than the more prosaic wall painting that paid the bills.

He was calling his story *Evelyn's Adventures in Elfland*, his heroine being a six-foot tall Amazonian elf-vampire beauty who shot lightning bolts out of her fingers. As her day job, when she wasn't saving the world from demons, she was a wisecracking hairdresser who was being courted by a proud faerie. Sarah insisted the superheroine ought to style people's hair with her lightning bolts. Maxwell claimed to be thinking that over.

Ari smiled to herself from her perch in their miniscule window seat overlooking the fire escape. Sarah sat behind Maxwell now, gently rubbing his shoulders while he sketched ideas. Her presence should have been distracting, but he seemed perfectly content. They both did. All the entertainment they needed was each other.

*They still love you,* Ari told herself. Neither of them had left her in any doubt of that. Besides which, feeling like a third wheel wasn't any reason to run back to a man. How did people make up their minds about being in love anyway? How did they know when they were ready?

She sighed and leaned her temple against the cool window glass. The dark sky outside was clouding over, the glowing moon turning sinister. Ari truly couldn't believe she'd been away from Adam longer than she'd been with him. He felt like the single most important person she'd ever met. Some nights she missed him so badly every bone in her body ached.

"Do you want some wine?" Sarah asked, having gotten up when Ari wasn't paying attention.

"I'm fine," she said vaguely.

A dog bayed in the little park at the end of their street. The sound repeated, then rose and sank in a howl. The quintessentially lonely song dragged a wash of goose bumps along her arms.

Maxwell looked up from his sketchpad. "That sounds like the same dog I heard last night."

Ari opened her mouth but nothing came out.

"What?" Max said, catching her expression. His dark hair was tousled from Sarah running her hands through it. In the brightness of his task lamp, the sprinkling of freckles on his slanted cheekbones stood out. When Sarah looked into his eyes, she saw her beloved . . . at least she did today. Before, had she just seen eyes?

A sudden burst of raindrops spattered against the window. Ari knew they'd be cold. Early winter rains were the dreariest.

"Can I borrow your big umbrella?" she asked Maxwell.

"Sure," he said, "but I can go to the store if you need something."

Ari shook her head more firmly than she had to. "I'm in the mood for some air."

"Take my raincoat," Sarah said. "It's the warmest one."

Ari didn't argue. She took the big umbrella and the good anorak. Shoving her keys in the pocket, she went down the apartment stairs at a run—or as near to as she could without tripping. When the outside door clunked shut behind her, she heard the dog howl again.

*Not a dog,* she thought. God, let it not be a dog.

She sprinted past the corner store with the umbrella furled, the hood of Sarah's slicker enough to keep the worst of the rain off her. The little play park was only a block in size. Lights kept it relatively safe at night, though the swings and teeter totters were empty at this hour. They creaked in the rising wind, sure sign the storm was rolling in for a while.

She stopped at the grassy stretch where the trees began. "Adam," she called, not caring if she sounded stupid. "Adam, it's me!"

A muted bark answered her. Ari's knees gave out from her surge of adrenaline. She fell to the squelchy grass, her blood rushing in her ears. The beast trotted out of the shadows of a big bank of shrubbery. She'd only seen Adam in this form once before, but her heart leaped in recognition. He hesitated when he saw her, too big and wild-looking to mistake for anything other than a wolf—and an overlarge one at that. His silvery-brown coat was darkened by the rain, but his posture was alert. His tail and his ears were up. He cocked his head to the side.

"Please come to me," she said.

He streaked to her at a gallop, judging his stop so neatly he didn't skid. Because she was kneeling, he had no trouble licking her face.

"Jeez." *This* would take some getting used to. Adam's tail wagged madly as he kept up the face bath. Ari tried to stop him by hugging him tighter. "I'm not kissing you until you've got real lips."

He barked and sat on his haunches. He looked like he was silently laughing. Ari buried her hands in his rain dampened ruff and just stared at him. The effect was strangely the same as locking glances with him in human form. Her doubts shook inside her, cracks undermining their foundations. He was her other half. Together they added up to more. She could sense Adam behind those intelligent green wolf eyes: his joy at seeing her, his hint of shyness over whether he was welcome.

"I'm glad you're here," she said, stroking his ears back along his head. "Want to come home and meet my friends?"

He jumped to his muddy feet, then surprised her by dashing back to the bushes he'd emerged from. He returned carrying the kind of leather bag serious bowlers toted their balls in. He resisted when Ari tried to tug it out of his teeth.

"You can't carry that," she said. "You're conspicuous enough already."

He had the nerve to whine when he let it go. When she opened Maxwell's umbrella to cover him for the short walk back, he let out a disgusted huff.

"Shut up," she said. "You think I want my boyfriend getting cold and wet?"

He bumped her thigh with his shoulder, more than big enough to jar her.

"You're crazy, you know. You so cannot pass for someone's pet."

As if to prove it, two black guys gave her wide eyes as they came out of the Korean grocery store on the corner.

"Honey," one drawled, "you need a leash for that."

Adam tried his best to look harmless.

∞

Adam bounded up the stairwell inside her building, bumping through the swinging door to her floor and trotting straight to her apartment. Since the Brooklyn Arms had more than a hundred units, this impressed her. She wondered if he'd used his cop skills to find her or just his nose.

"Show off," she said as he waited for her to catch up with his tongue lolling.

He drew his tongue in and gave her a doggy grin. Ari shook her head to herself as she dug out her keys. This was destined to be more interesting than the usual boyfriend-meet-friends encounter. She noticed Adam's thick wolf coat had shed most of the rain.

"Wipe your paws, please," she said before pushing the door open.

Maxwell and Sarah looked up from the wine and crackers they were sharing. "That didn't take long," Max said. "Who were you talk—"

He gasped as loudly as Sarah when Adam finished wiping his muddy paws and padded into view. "Holy crap," her two friends breathed in unison.

Ari closed the door and locked it, which she belatedly realized might alarm them. "Adam, these are my friends Sarah and Maxell. Guys, this is my friend Adam the werewolf from Faerie."

"Holy—" Max swallowed and shoved back his chair. Once he'd stood, he came around the table to face Adam. Ari didn't think it was a coincidence that this put him between the wolf and Sarah. Adam remained where he was, looking like the most beautiful and intelligent canine in the world. "Should I . . . offer to shake his paw?"

Adam nudged her.

"If you give him a minute," she said. "I think you'll be able to shake his hand."

He didn't need a minute, more like forty seconds. With the full moon to lend him power, his transformation was effortless. He crouched lower on his forepaws, closed his eyes, and let a ring of sparkles roll back from his nose. The effect was like watching him unpeel, except his wolf form simply disappeared as the light progressed over it. He had a human head, then shoulders, then arms and hands. Almost before Ari could understand what she'd seen, Adam knelt on their living room floorboards, his truly fine naked butt resting on his heels. She guessed wolves were comfortable au natural. Adam's palms rested on his thighs, perfectly relaxed, not covering his genitals the way shyer men would have. Not that he had anything to be shy about. Ari fought an urge to press her hand to her mouth. Adam might not realize it, but he had what looked like a half hard-on.

"Wow," Maxwell said hoarsely. "I swear I believed you when you said you'd hooked up with a werewolf, but believing sure isn't the same as seeing."

"Wow is right," Sarah said in a slightly different tone. Ari imagined she'd also noticed the slight boner.

Adam pushed to his feet and immediately seemed to fill the room. Max was no shrimp, but he was on the wiry side. "It's nice to meet you both," he said.

Ari hadn't known how much she'd missed his deep sexy voice until she heard it again. Still not covering up, Adam reached for her hand. The feel of his fingers twining between hers was an instant panty-wetter. Adam's quick inhalation as he scented her reaction was followed by a definite jerk of motion between his legs. Ari suspected his half hard-on had just gone whole.

"Would you excuse us?" Adam asked politely. "Ari and I have catching up to do."

"Sure," Sarah said dazedly.

"No problem, man," Max agreed.

Ari was pretty sure Adam's nose allowed him to tug her straight to her bedroom. She ignored the *omigods* breaking out in the living room.

Ari's room—formerly Max's—was the size of a walk-in closet. A narrow window with a view of a brick wall saved it from being one. Ari had a single bed, a small bureau, and an orange crate for a nightstand. She dropped Adam's bowling bag behind the door, enjoying her rather stupendous rear view of him. He was taking in his surroundings with interest. When he noticed the little painting that hung above her headboard, he froze.

"That's Maria's," he said, amazed.

"Sorry. I know I took it without asking."

"You took the painting she did of me as my wolf."

"I guess you don't all look alike furry."

He turned back to her, his eyes bright with emotion. "Ari," he said as if she'd given him a gift instead of stealing from his home.

Ari smiled at him. He looked down and shook his head, which made her drop her gaze as well. One hot shiver chased another along her spine. Boy, he was hard. His cock stretched straight up to his navel, so thick she wasn't sure her fingers would meet around the shaft. As she watched, a bead of precome squeezed from the slit. When his eyes rose to hers again, his expression was unexpectedly tentative.

"Could we have sex?" he asked. "Maybe before we talk? If the answer is yes, I'd really like you to take off your clothes."

Ari started wrenching free of the anorak.

He was on her before the first sleeve was off, kissing her, squeezing her—as if he had twenty hands instead of two. Ari wrestled with him for the right to shed her garments even as she locked her mouth to his. His tongue felt so good, his lengthened teeth so sexy. She kissed him like a madwoman, thrilling to the hungry sounds he made in response.

"I missed you," he said, freeing her mouth so they could drag her shirt together over her head. "I like your hair that way."

It was black now, except for Max's red design. She'd dyed it back to her real color. Freed of her shirt, she was down to transparent pink panties and a bra—nicer underwear than Adam had seen her in before. He expressed how much he admired it by groaning.

"I missed you too," she panted.

He laid his hands overtop the stretchy sheer bra cups. Ari jerked when she caught a clear look at his fingers.

"You have claws," she said in surprise. They were dark and hard and curved like his teeth. Ari's nipples tightened painfully under their light clasp, her body releasing another surge of arousal. Adam smiled . . . well, wolfishly would be the best way to describe it.

"I'm really glad you don't mind them. Sometimes, when I'm overexcited, they come out unintentionally."

"Are you overexcited now?"

"Like you fucking wouldn't believe."

Ari trembled, which he seemed to enjoy. "Maybe I should undo my bra hooks myself."

"Maybe I should use my claws to rip your underwear off you."

"Yes, please," Ari said with a grin.

He snarled as he indulged her fantasy. His eyes were glowing, his breathing harsh and uneven. Once her breasts were bare, he covered each in turn with his hard sucking mouth. The pull of his tongue and lips on her excited nipples caused her to writhe in his arms. He lifted her, saving himself from bending, then slammed her into the wall.

"I'm grabbing something from my bag," he rasped.

He didn't release her to open it, just dipped down at the knees. He returned with a single wrapped condom. He handed it to her.

"You found your special shipment," she said breathlessly.

"I did. And I have a few guesses about who the delivery boy might have been. His scent was all over it."

"I'm glad," she said. "I wanted you to know, but I didn't want to betray a confidence."

Adam rested his brow on hers. "You," he said, "are my favorite person in the whole world."

She didn't know why this made the last of her doubt crumble. Maybe because he could have been mad at her for not telling. Maybe because it suggested his brain was involved in loving her.

"I love you too," she burst out. "I missed you so much I was sick with it."

He growled and hugged her and kissed her so deeply he gave her chills. He tore loose reluctantly.

"Put that thing on me now," he said.

She was lucky the rubber was extra large, because the fit was tight to roll down. Ari smoothed it over his shuddering cock with loving attention, inspiring him to curse at her thoroughness. She had a feeling what came next wouldn't be leisurely. Fortunately, she was far too wet to worry.

"Ready?" he asked, his glans nudging anxiously at her entrance.

"Like you fucking wouldn't believe," she said, quoting him.

His eyes flared hot as he breached the outer ring of muscle. He probably wouldn't want to be told, but he purred like a cat for the whole twenty seconds it took to push fully into her.

"Mm," she said, purring a bit herself. "You've no idea how much I missed that."

But maybe he did. He gripped her bottom tight with his clawed fingers, drew one of his bracing breaths, and fucked her against the wall like jackhammer. They came within seconds of each other, in under five minutes. He pulled out long enough to switch condoms, then body-slammed her onto her narrow bed.

"Okay?" he asked.

She wrapped her arms and legs around him. "Do it fast again," she urged.

This was no hardship, apparently. It wasn't until the fourth time that either of them was in the mood to slow down. Adam was in the mood for something else as well.

He pulled her to the edge of the mattress, kneeling on the floor with her thighs clamped around his ears as he went down on her. His tongue did things ordinary human tongues couldn't. His was harder and quicker and just plain hungrier than any man's she'd met. He used that advantage to flick and penetrate her by turns. When he simultaneously sucked her clitoris and rubbed it with his tongue, Ari couldn't hold back her yelps of pleasure, or keep her nails from pricking his broad shoulders. He certainly didn't mind her reaction. As he worked to control the violent thrashing of her hips, his claws had yet to retract.

She guessed he was still overexcited.

"Ari," he rumbled, shifting his upper body over hers. Her bed was low and his knees remained on the floor. Ari caressed his butt with the soles of her feet as he rolled a fresh rubber on.

"You *can* do that with your claws," she exclaimed.

Adam flashed a grin at her. "I can do lots of things with my claws. I just like when you handle me."

Understanding that very well, she smoothed her hands down his chest to his sweating belly, relishing the way his diaphragm went in and out with his hard breathing. That breathing got choppier as her thumb worked the looser latex gently across his tip. "Do you mind wearing these?"

He shook his head. "Don't get me wrong. I want kids, and I want them with you. I also want you to marry me and be my mate forever."

Ari's heart gave a happy excited flutter, one she hadn't quite expected. She'd known he wanted this, but the words were still precious. She made herself ask the question she had to. "What if I don't ever feel ready? About the kid part, I mean."

His eyes were the softest she'd ever seen, and the most compassionate. "I hope that doesn't happen, but if it does, I'll still be happy you're my wife. You're more than my mate. When people's spirits are the other half of each other, werewolves call them twin flames. You're that to me, Ari. No other woman could complete me the way you do."

This was so hokey, she should have teased him. Instead, a tear slipped from the corner of her eye. "I feel the same way," she confessed. "And also that . . . that I didn't just helplessly fall in love. My brain picked you right along with my body and my heart. You are the warmest, most trustworthy, funnest guy to have sex with in the world. If I am your other half, I'm very proud that's true."

"Those are good words," he said solemnly. "Thank you for saying them."

His eyes were shining as he kissed the track the tear had left on her cheek.

"I'm making love to you now," he said.

She didn't need to be coaxed. He scooted them all the way up onto the bed, holding her gaze and stroking back her hair as he pushed in and out so luxuriously she couldn't help but arch with pleasure. Now and then his eyes closed with bliss, but mostly he looked at her.

"I love you," she said.

His next thrust drove in noticeably harder.

"Hah!" she laughed. "You like *I love you* as much as dirty talk."

His chuckle was sex bottled in a sound. He ducked his head to her earlobe. "I know what you like too," he warned.

She liked him—everything he did and everything he was. Their pace picked up as they both grew more impatient. Adam shifted angles and strafed something really good.

"Oh God," Ari gasped.

Adam hit the spot again. The sensation was like a mini-punch of orgasm. "Squeeze your hand between us," he panted. "I want you to rub my gland."

After four orgasms, the thing was swollen up like a hot walnut. Maybe the moon being full made it more active. His interest certainly hadn't flagged since they'd started.

"Yes," he said as she rubbed it, doing her best not to interfere with his thrusts. His head flung back with enjoyment. "Mm. You could do that harder."

When she did, his claws jerked longer against her bottom. Fortunately, they were hard but not sharp.

"Yes," he said, flexing them like he enjoyed the sensation as much as she did. "Yes, oh God—"

He yanked one hand from her bottom and wedged his thumb claw over her clit. She had to bite his shoulder or she'd have screamed with pleasure. Sensing this perhaps, Adam grunted and latched onto her neck. His tongue worked her skin, his suction intense. His pre-climactic thrusts were so forceful she had to fling her second hand up to the headboard.

He wrenched his mouth free before he gave in to his instincts and bit her. "Unh," he said, really close now, driving into her with big slamming motions. "*Unh.*"

His bulbus gland went hot and vibrated. Ari had never seen anyone come like Adam did then. His eyes rolled back and his muscles tightened until they were more steel than flesh. His bared teeth were completely beastly, his veins ropy everywhere. Best of all, his claw clamped on her very favorite spot on her clit.

Despite Adam's orgasmic state, Ari didn't think this was an accident. He'd been tongueing that very spot not too long ago. Waves of ecstasy jolted from the point of pressure, and from his cock, and her nipples, and pretty much every place his body was jammed to hers.

She might have forgotten to muffle her scream that time.

"Shh," he murmured when the incredible assault on her nerves finally spiraled down. "Shh, sweetheart, it's all right."

Luckily, she was only whimpering by then. "Don't pull out yet," she pleaded.

He was heavy enough, and she was out of breath enough, that he had to hold himself off her. When even his strong arms began to tremble, she knew she had to surrender.

"All right," she said. "You can roll off me now and rest."

He couldn't roll very far on her narrow bed. To her delight, he laid his cheek sweetly on her breast. His hand covered her belly possessively, his claws slowly retracting. He didn't fall asleep like a lot of men would have. Maybe he didn't want this to be over. "I think your friend Maxwell might have some mojo," he said.

"Really?" Ari squirmed a bit more toward him. She remembered what Grant had said about the concentration rune Max had designed for her hair. Though Max claimed he just made it up, maybe he was a bit psychic.

"I'm not an expert, but he might be a Level Three. His energy is very . . . buzzy."

"Do you think he'd see the real Resurrection? Could he cross the border?"

"I think he might have enough juice to bring Sarah with him, if they wanted to visit you."

"That would be so awesome!" she exclaimed. "Oh my God, I'd take them straight to Evie's. Do you think they'll let us in? You did set the stage on fire."

Adam smiled at her. "I expect Lord Grygir has explained about that by now. I did think, however, that attending our wedding might make a nice first trip for your friends."

"Shit," Ari said, embarrassed she hadn't thought of that. "Sometimes I am so bad at being a girl."

"You make up for it," Adam teased. "Here and there."

She scooted one of her legs between his long hard ones. "I'll wear a dress," she offered. "In fact, I'll ask Maria to help me pick it out."

"That might be a good decision. I'm not sure what my relatives would think about you wearing your Yankees jacket down the aisle."

Ari shoved the spot on Adam's chest where his heart felt like it had swelled to ten times its normal size. This wasn't how he'd pictured her accepting his proposal, but he enjoyed it all the same.

"I would *not* wear my Yankees jacket. I wouldn't even wear sneakers."

"Not even sneakers!"

Smiling, Ari wriggled closer and closed her eyes. Her apartment bedroom was ridiculously small, but right then—to him—it was heaven.

"Adam?" she said in a sleepy, surprisingly girlish voice.

"Mm," he responded, running one hand down her warm silky back.

"Why didn't you bite me tonight? I could tell you wanted to."

He hadn't bitten her because he wanted her to make up her mind about them with her wits perfectly intact. "Oh," he said. "I thought we'd save that as a treat for our honeymoon."

She snorted, evidently finding that amusing. She was quiet for so long he thought she'd fallen asleep. He stroked her newly dark hair, feeling utterly peaceful and unwilling to give up that pleasure for a little thing like rest.

He had no fears left. Not that she loved him. Not that she'd have any trouble accepting the differences in their natures. Whatever bumps they encountered in the future, he felt confident they'd get over them. He could trust her, he realized, not only in matters of life and death but in the simpler day to day issues. He wouldn't have his parents' marriage, but what he'd have would be wonderful.

To his surprise, considering how long she'd been still, Ari squirmed against him. "Adam?" she asked. "I don't know if this is the right time to bring it up, but before I have a kid, I'd like to adopt a kitten. You know, to see how responsible I can be."

"A kitten."

Her answer was suspiciously innocent. "I've always wanted one. My life never seemed stable enough before."

He glanced to where she'd tucked her head toward his chest. It was hard to tell from his angle, but he thought her lips were pressed together against a laugh. Ari was yanking his canine chain. She didn't know werewolves and cats got on fine—though cats were sometimes annoyingly good at ignoring silent commands. They pretended they couldn't understand even when they did.

A way to tease her popped into his mind, one so mischievous he couldn't resist it.

"All right," Adam said agreeably. "Would you prefer to adopt an ordinary kitten or a were?"

The way her mouth fell open would entertain him for quite some time.

# SIX MONTHS LATER

To Ari's delight, Maxwell and Sarah enjoyed their trip to Resurrection for her wedding so much they decided to move down the street from her and Adam—into a unit in Nate's building. Happily, the couple could afford the nice condo. Maxwell's comic series, *Evelyn's Adventures in Elfland*, proved a hit with local teenagers. They loved its mix of inside and Outside jokes. Ari had heard the original Evie—on whom Evelyn was loosely based—had been miffed at first but got over it. Sarah had a job as well. She was working as a preschool teacher to the neighborhood wolf children.

When she'd heard, Ari had feared the werekids would eat her sweet friend for breakfast—God willing not literally. That had turned out not be the case. Sarah's delicacy brought out even little wolves' protective streaks. The wereboys were forever trying to walk her home, and the girls considered it a fight-worthy honor to fetch her sweaters if she got cold. Sarah confessed she'd never expected to be coddled by four- and five-year-olds. Werekids who'd once been problems now behaved like relative angels. Since Sarah was the first fully human teacher the school had hired, the Board was now wondering if they should recruit more.

Sarah and Max were talking about getting married in the autumn.

Ari wasn't snoozing her days away either. She'd gotten a part-time waitressing position at an Italian restaurant close enough to her and Adam's place that she could walk to it. Adam remained perplexed as to why she liked restaurant work, but Ari was never bored. How could she be when anyone or anything might sit down at her table? No one ever gave her any trouble. All the locals knew she was married to an alpha.

Adam liked the fact that she'd taken and passed her magical certification, reducing the chance that she'd be thrown in the pokey for violating local ordinance. Now that she had her license, twice a week, when she was off shift, she was tutored in medical manipulation by a curmudgeonly elf-practitioner. Ari didn't know that she aspired to go into this as a profession, but she figured honing her gift this way would be useful.

Werewolf kids banged themselves up a lot. They were too rambunctious and too fearless not to. Smiling, Ari rested both her hands on her baby bump.

Warmth and contentment welled up in her. How right being pregnant felt was her biggest surprise of all. She might never make a model parent, but she couldn't doubt she'd be a loving one. She adored their child already.

"Is it kicking?" Sarah asked, scooting around to face her on the park bench.

They were sharing a bag lunch at what they both considered the hilariously named Harry Potter Park, which was next to Sarah's school. Many Resurrection natives were convinced the Boy Who Lived was real.

"Just flutters," Ari answered, pressing Sarah's palm over the place. "You should have seen Adam's face the first time he felt the baby move. He lit up like Christmas, then immediately volunteered to run out for pickles and bacon."

"Pickles and bacon?" Sarah's nose wrinkled.

"I guess that's what werewolf mothers crave. I told him I'd let him know if that started to appeal to me."

"No biting!" Sarah turned to call to a pair of her students. Her class was enjoying the bright spring day by rampaging, more or less peacefully, around the monkey bars and sandpit. *No biting* was, not surprisingly, Sarah's most frequent scold.

"Sorry, Miss Thompson!" piped two little girl voices. "We'll try to remember."

Sarah covered her giggle behind her palm. "It's like magic," she whispered. "Every night I pray my superpower won't go away. Oh, I forgot to tell you. Speaking of superpowers, Ethan changed the first time this morning."

"He's only four," Ari gasped. "I thought werekids didn't shift until they were five. And *yesterday* was the full moon."

She knew this because Adam had gone for a run with his friends, then came home to make love to her really well. Being a dad-to-be seemed to make him even more creative in bed.

"I'm told that's the way it happens sometimes," Sarah said. "Plus Ethan is precocious. You wouldn't believe how cute he was. He tore through his little outfit like a miniature Hulk, and then I had this out-of-control wolf puppy scampering between the desks. The other kids went nuts chasing him around. I had to call his mother to take him home. It made me wish I could have a werepup myself."

Ari elbowed her. "You can babysit mine."

"You won't have to beg me." Sarah smiled at Ari, so happy she was glowing. "I wonder if they'll throw a party for Ethan. Oh God, I wonder if they'll expect us to bring a dish."

"Err," Ari agreed, attuned to Sarah's dread. Then, "Take-out," they both chimed in unison. They kept laughing until they sighed pleasurably.

"This is good," Sarah said. "This is better than I ever dared dreamed my life would be."

Ari's eyes filled with shared tears of happiness, made even sweeter by the crazy hormones zooming inside her. Who'd have thought she'd enjoy getting weepy?

"I know," she said before she got too choked up. "And you and Max being here is totally the cherry on the sundae."

Sarah laughed and wiped Ari's tears away with her thumbs. "Don't let my kids see you crying. All the girls will run over here with Kleenex."

A familiar scent had Ari's hormones zinging in a new direction. She jumped up from the park bench and spun around before she could stop herself. Her very own alpha hero was striding toward her across the grass, grinning a mile wide, still excited to see her after half a year of marriage.

"There's my girl," Adam said, pulling her off her feet in a gentle hug.

Ari buried her nose in her favorite spot on his neck.

"Love you," he whispered before he set her down.

"Love you back," she said. He didn't get tired of hearing that. His eyes glowed a little brighter than the sunlight could account for. "What are you doing here in the middle of the day?"

Adam bent to give their baby bump its kiss. "You and I have been designated to host Ethan's first shift party, because our roof deck is the biggest. And before you ask: no, you don't have to cook."

"I can help shop," she said. "I'm not too bad at that."

Adam took her face between his big warm hands.

"You're perfect," he said huskily.

It wasn't true, but Ari thought she'd go on letting him believe it.

# # #

# ABOUT THE AUTHOR

Emma Holly is the award-winning, *USA Today* bestselling author of more than twenty romantic novels, featuring vampires, demons, fairies and just plain extraordinary ordinary folks. She loves the hot stuff, both to read and to write!

If you'd like to find out what else she's written, please visit her website at: http://www.emmaholly.com. She also runs monthly contests and sends out newsletters. To receive them, go to her contest page.

Her first indie project, *The Prince With No Heart*—a VERY grown up fairytale—is also available.

Thanks so much for reading this book!

CPSIA information can be obtained at www.ICGtesting.com
Printed in the USA
LVOW05s1615170214

374029LV00014B/596/P